TRAVELERS REST

**Center Point
Large Print**

Also by Ann Tatlock and available from
Center Point Large Print:

The Returning

**This Large Print Book carries the
Seal of Approval of N.A.V.H.**

TRAVELERS REST

Ann Tatlock

CENTER POINT LARGE PRINT
THORNDIKE, MAINE

This Center Point Large Print edition is published in the year 2012 by arrangement with Bethany House Publishers, a division of Baker Publishing Group.

L. J. E,
Tatlock

Brief quotations taken from: "O the Deep, Deep Love of Jesus" by S. Trevor Francis; "Spring Night" by Sara Teasdale; "On Hearing a Symphony of Beethoven" by Edna St. Vincent Millay.

The text of this Large Print edition is unabridged.
In other aspects, this book may
vary from the original edition.
Printed in the United States of America
on permanent paper.
Set in 16-point Times New Roman type.

ISBN: 978-1-61173-442-3

Library of Congress Cataloging-in-Publication Data

Tatlock, Ann.
Travelers rest / Ann Tatlock.
pages ; cm.
ISBN 978-1-61173-442-3 (library binding : alk. paper)
1. Large type books. I. Title.
PS3570.A85T73 2012b
813'.54—dc23
2012005408

To
Janine Hughes

There will be a day when
the burdens of this place
Will be no more; we'll see Jesus face to face.
—Jeremy Camp

— 1 —

The man she loved was in one of the rooms of this enormous pale brick building, but she didn't know which one. She would have to stop at a nurses' station and ask. *Please, can you tell me where Seth Ballantine is?* But even when she found him, he wouldn't be the same Seth Ballantine who had kissed her good-bye a little less than a year ago. She knew that, but it didn't matter. She had to see him.

Jane pushed open the front doors of the Asheville Veterans Administration Medical Center complex and stepped into the air-conditioned coolness of the hospital lobby. A rectangular wood railing ran around the center of the room, which was open to an atrium one floor below. Jane stepped to the railing and looked down at the sofas and chairs and the potted plastic plants arranged to give an air of hominess to this decades-old hospital that had catered to the wounded of far too many wars.

The atrium was bright with sunlight that filtered in through the glass-paneled ceiling high overhead. The sunshine seemed determined to infuse a certain cheeriness into the mass of humanity below, the men and women sitting on the sofas and chairs and moving along the periphery of the room, inching forward with canes or walkers or rolling slowly in wheelchairs, some dragging canisters of oxygen behind them. Jane wondered briefly what they had seen, what battles they'd been through that brought them here. She wondered too if any of them heard what she heard now, or whether music had somehow become lost to them. Because somewhere down there in the atrium was a piano, and someone was playing a piece by Debussy.

From where she stood, she couldn't see the piano, but she was grateful to whoever had decided at that very moment to play "Clair de Lune." The music gave her an excuse to pause and listen, and maybe if she listened long enough she could get her heart to stop racing wildly, and she could enter Seth's room looking calm and unafraid.

But she was interrupted when a voice nudged its way through the music and asked, "Can I help you find anything, dear?" Jane turned to find a matronly woman, white haired and plump, smiling amiably at her with unpainted lips. She wore a volunteer badge, and her dimpled hands clutched the shiny stainless steel handle of a coffee cart.

"No, thank you," Jane said, trying to smile. "I'm fine."

"Cup of coffee? We've got decaf. And more than a dozen flavors of tea, if you'd prefer tea."

Jane's eyes scoured the cart, then turned back to the woman. "You don't have any Seagram's Seven, do you?"

The woman's eyebrows arched and her forehead filled with deep furrows. "Why, no! I'm afraid I don't."

Jane shook her head and forced out a laugh. "I was just kidding," she said. "I don't drink." *At least not anymore.* Though heaven knew, she could use something right about now to settle her nerves. "I'm fine, really. But thank you for asking."

"Well, let me know if I can do anything for you." Another smile, though somewhat dubious this time.

"I will. Thank you."

With a small nod the woman gave her cart a shove and moved along. Jane turned back to the music, shutting her eyes to take it in.

How often she had heard this very tune when she was growing up, her grandmother's album spinning circles on the ancient phonograph in the room always referred to as the parlor. Most certainly it was not to be called the living room. They resided, after all, in the Rayburn House, one of the oldest houses—and the largest—in Troy, North Carolina. It was built in 1822 by her great-great-great-grandfather, Jedediah Rayburn, a forward-thinking entrepreneur who had made his fortune in textiles.

With her eyes closed she was a child again,

curled up on the cushion in the window seat, listening to Debussy and staring through the beveled glass at her grandmother's garden in the side yard. Gram was out there now, on her knees, broad-brimmed sun hat hiding her face as she weeded the rows of freshly sprung tulips and budding delphinium. Laney Jackson was in the kitchen; Jane could hear the occasional banging of a pot or pan as Laney prepared dinner. Her father and mother were . . . somewhere . . . but that didn't matter, so long as Gram and Laney were near. With them she was safe and very nearly happy. With them she could move out from under the cloud that hovered permanently over her parents' lives. She didn't know why her mother and father lived in shadow, but she didn't want to linger there with them any longer than she had to. Young as she was, she preferred the company of Gram, who taught her to love music and poetry and art, and Laney, who personified quiet satisfaction as she went about her tasks in the kitchen.

As she listened to the final strains of "Clair de Lune," though, it was the voice of her mother that came back to her most clearly, breaking into the moment like the unwelcome twitch behind the eyes at the onset of a migraine. *"Honestly, Janie, you're such a dreamer. Come back to earth and make yourself useful."* How many times had she heard her mother say that?

But she wasn't dreaming. Not now, nor even when she was a child gazing out the window at the yard. She was looking and listening, latching on to whatever passing beauty she might find, however briefly. A snatch of a symphony, the scent of lilac, the pale shimmer of the summer sun as it lay down at dusk on the green grass—all these were what gave her the courage simply to live.

And, at the moment, courage was what she needed more than anything.

Seth had told her not to come, but here she was. How could he expect her not to come, to just give up as though he'd died in that strange desert called Iraq? He hadn't died. He was still alive. And she still loved him. Nothing changed that.

And so she had defied him, although he didn't know it yet. Seth didn't know she was here, listening to some unseen piano player and working up the nerve to ask him not to give up. Not on himself and not on her.

Jane opened her eyes and moved along the railing until the piano came into view. There it was, tucked up under the entryway where she'd been standing. A grand piano, it was shiny and sleek and somehow out of place in the midst of all the walking wounded, the vets both young and old, many of whom looked weary and dazed and shell-shocked, long months and even years after their final days in battle.

A tall young man was seated at the piano, his

nimble fingers frolicking over the keys. Jane didn't recognize what he was playing now—something much livelier than "Clair de Lune." Something her grandmother wouldn't have liked. *"Too common,"* Gram would have said. *"Something only the tone-deaf would appreciate."* But the musician played it with such vigor and joy, Jane couldn't help but smile. His face was turned away from her, but she could see the back of his blond head, the width of his broad shoulders beneath his suit jacket. Though he was dressed like a businessman, he was no doubt a veteran, like most everyone else here. He had probably served over in Iraq, or maybe Afghanistan, though he had obviously returned home whole and sound. Unlike Seth.

Seth Ballantine, her fiancé. Who lay in one of the rooms of this vast institution, unaware that she was on her way to see him.

Dear God, give me strength, she thought. She was not one to pray, but there it was, a plea from the center of her soul to the God she hoped was listening.

She started down the long corridor, not at all sure she was headed in the right direction. She was about to pass a young man leaning up against the wall, sipping something hot from a Styrofoam cup, when she turned back and said, "Excuse me?"

"Yes?" He wore the maroon uniform of a

hospital orderly, a name tag clipped to the breast pocket. He must know something about this place.

"Can you tell me where the spinal cord unit is?"

He raised a hand and pointed. "Straight ahead to the elevators, then up to the fifth floor."

"Thank you."

She moved through the hall to a trio of elevators, where she pushed the first available Up button. In another moment one pair of stainless steel doors slid open with a whoosh and a ding. She stepped into the elevator and pushed the button for the fifth floor. *I can still turn around and leave. He'll never know I was here.*

The doors closed and the lift ascended. The bell dinged again as the 5 light on the panel went off and the elevator jerked to a stop. The doors sighed open and Jane stepped out. She found herself on an L-shaped floor, with a nurses' station located where the two wings met. A young nurse, about Jane's own age, sat at the desk making notes on a chart.

"Excuse me," Jane said hesitantly.

The nurse looked up and smiled. "Yes?"

"I'm looking for Seth Ballantine."

"Oh yes." She pointed toward one of the wings. "He's in five-sixteen. Last room at the end of the hall on the right."

"Thank you."

She stepped lightly, not wanting to make a

sound, as though she wasn't there. As she walked she looked to the left and to the right, glancing briefly into each room as she passed. They were all singles, one narrow bed in each narrow room. One bedside table. One vinyl chair. One television suspended from the ceiling. And one broken body draped into a wheelchair or tucked between white linens on the bed.

She heard bits and snatches of daytime television; jagged edges of murmured conversations; people coughing; machines beeping, wheezing, clanging. And oddly, as though misplaced, a burst of laughter, two people sharing something amusing; she couldn't imagine what, in a place like this.

Then quiet. A man stepped out of the room where the laughter had been. He was a tall man and commanding somehow, his shoulders back, his chin lifted slightly. His skin was the color of fertile ground, like the richest soil in her grandmother's garden. He wore civilian clothing, pale slacks and a blue button-up shirt. He must be visiting someone, as he couldn't be a patient here, not on this wing where people no longer walked. And walk he did, though hesitantly, as though his knees objected. When he and Jane came parallel to each other, he acknowledged her politely with a smile and a nod. She welcomed the gesture and returned the smile, wishing she could freeze the moment and memorize his gaze. Serene and warm, the eyes of this stranger were the kindest she had ever seen, and she drew a certain strength from them.

He nodded once more and moved on.

In another moment, Jane stood at the threshold of 516. She took one steadying breath and entered the room.

— 2 —

Seth was awake and gazing out the window, unaware that anyone was there. In that brief interval Jane drank in his profile and felt the familiar rush of love. She'd known him almost all her life, and she'd known there was something special about him even when they were still children sitting in the same grade-school class. Their being together seemed inevitable, though it took him years to come to the same conclusion. But she was patient, and over time her waiting was rewarded. He'd asked her to marry him seven months before his National Guard unit was deployed to Iraq.

She quietly stepped closer. "Seth?"

His head rolled on the pillow, turning toward her. When his eyes met hers, his face registered confusion, surprise, delight, and finally anger, restrained but unmistakable.

She moved to his bed and touched the rails. "Hello, Seth."

He turned away. "I told you not to come."

"I know."

"Then why are you here?"

"I couldn't stay away."

He didn't respond.

Now that she was beside him, she could see how thin he looked. His once-full cheeks were sunken, and his jaw more pronounced. His too-large T-shirt accentuated his shrunken frame. Jane's eyes traveled down his chest, over the splayed arms, the motionless fingers cradled on handrests, the lifeless legs extended under the sheet. Arms, hands, legs, feet—useless append-ages now and for the past six months, ever since the sniper's bullet hit him in the neck.

"You didn't answer my letters," she said.

"Yes, I did. I told you not to come. After that, there was nothing else to say."

"Seth—"

"I mean it, Jane. I don't want you here."

She willed herself not to cry. "I don't believe you," she said.

He glanced at her, frowning. "What is it that you want?"

She touched the engagement ring she'd worn for more than a year now. "I want what I've always wanted. I want to be your wife."

He laughed. It wasn't at all like the happy

16

laughter she'd heard coming from the other room a few minutes ago. "Right. Don't you get it? Look at me. I'm paralyzed. I'm a quad. What about that don't you understand?"

"I know all that. Of course I—"

"Listen, the ring is yours. Sell it and do something with the money. Take a trip. Go on a cruise. Forget about me, Jane. I'm not here for you anymore."

She had to lift her head so that the tears didn't roll down her face. If she could just take a moment to look out the window, just a moment to take a few deep breaths, she could get through this. She sniffed, cleared her throat. Finally she said, "I've been doing a lot of reading—you know, about people with spinal cord injuries. People still get married and some even have kids. I mean, lots of people go on and live good productive lives. Some even gain some movement—"

"Save it, Jane. Just stop." He shut his eyes and shook his head. "Just stop."

"I know you're angry right now. That's normal."

"You can spare me the psycho-babble. Nothing's normal. Nothing will ever be normal again. I'd rather have died than ended up like this."

"Don't say that, Seth."

"Why not? Why not say the truth?"

She gave up then trying to hold back the tears. They wouldn't be stopped. They coursed slowly down her cheeks, two salty lines.

17

She heard Seth sigh heavily, and when he spoke again his voice was quiet. "I'm sorry, Jane. God knows, I'm sorry for everything. I always knew I might not come back alive, but I never dreamed I'd come back like this. This isn't what I want for you. I want you to have a real marriage, to be happy—"

"But I *would* be happy. *We* would be happy. I know it."

"No, Jane. Forget it. For your own sake, find someone else to marry and forget about me. I mean it. That's what I want."

As her breath quickened, Jane turned the diamond round and round on her finger. "I don't want to find someone else to marry. I still love you, Seth."

He swallowed. She watched his Adam's apple travel up and down the length of his throat. There was a scar there now, near the hollow of his neck, from the ventilator that had breathed for him while he was still in the hospital in Landstuhl, Germany. He'd been weaned off of it, which meant he had improved. Who knew what other improvements he might make? She was a patient person; she was willing to wait and see.

Very slowly, as though talking to a child, Seth said, "I'm going to close my eyes and rest now. When I open my eyes again, I want you to be gone. Go back to Troy, Jane. Go back and make a life with someone else. I don't want you coming back here."

She gazed at his face, the face she knew so well and had loved so long. She wanted to reach out her hand and touch his cheek, his brow, but she didn't dare. His eyes were closed; she had been dismissed.

"Seth," she said, "just do one thing for me. Tell me you don't love me anymore. Tell me that, and then I'll go away."

His eyelids trembled and his jaw tightened, but he didn't speak.

"I'll be back tomorrow," she said.

She saw the tear that slid down the side of his face. She turned to go without brushing it away.

— 3 —

Pritchard Park was a small triangular oasis situated near the center of downtown Asheville. The park, like the city itself, was no respecter of persons. All were drawn to it at one time or another—the locals, the tourists, the wealthy, the homeless, young Goths, aging hippies, radical intellectuals, raging alcoholics, lovers, the lonely, families, drifters, and dreamers. They all came and sat in the shade of its few scattered trees, settling themselves on the benches or the natural boulders, or on the concrete tiers that dropped down toward the bricked center square that, on Friday nights when the weather was warm, served as a dance floor for those inspired to motion by the synchronized drumming.

Jane sat on the sun-warmed concrete facing the tier where several dozen people sat beating out a rhythm on bongo drums and conga heads. Others tapped out the tempo using wooden claves, while still others added an unobtrusive backup with shakers and cowbells. On and on it went, the rhythm played over and over, with seemingly no beginning and apparently no end. The dance floor was crowded with men, women, and children in a vast array of dress and undress, swaying, jumping, gyrating, and spinning, as though even the fairest of them had roots that ran deep into an ancient tribal culture. One man with dreadlocks down to his waist managed a series of improbable somersaults and back flips, then grabbed a partner and joined her in a dizzying array of staccato-like dance steps. Jane watched in amazement, only vaguely aware that her right foot tapped along with the rhythm. The drumming had a hypnotic pull that lulled the listener in and took her to places unknown, just as the tug of the ocean might carry a swimmer out to sea.

"They say it helps connect them with the universal mind, or some such thing."

Jane turned toward the voice. "Diana! How long have you been here?"

"Just got here. Sorry I'm late." Diana spoke loudly over the drumming and squinted momentarily against the sun as she sat down on the tier beside Jane. "I got caught in a very long and very tedious staff meeting about grants for the biology department next year." She gazed skyward in a gesture of disgust, her brown eyes looking weary behind the rectangular lenses of her dark-framed glasses. Her auburn hair was cropped short in a no-nonsense style, as though outward appearance was a frivolous time waster if one was a tenured professor.

"That's all right," Jane assured her. Glancing at her watch, she added, "Is it seven thirty already? Wow, I lost track of the time. I'm afraid I got kind of swept up in the drumming."

Diana nodded. "That's the point, I think. You're supposed to let it carry you off into the cosmic consciousness." She paused and smiled. "It boggles my scientific mind, but it's fun to watch. They all seem to be enjoying themselves."

Jane looked out over the crowd, then back at her friend. "Where's Carl?"

"Grading term papers."

"On a Friday night?"

"You know Carl. Work, work, work. He won't be able to leave for Europe next week unless he has all his ducks lined up in a row, feathers all fluffed and shiny. But he sends his apologies for skipping out on dinner tonight."

"That's all right," Jane said again. "If I were going to spend the summer in Europe, I'd want to have all my ducks in a row too."

The two friends fell quiet for a moment, but it was a comfortable lapse in conversation for them both. Diana Penland was as close to an older sister as Jane Morrow would ever have. They'd known each other since Jane was a child and Diana a young teen, going back almost twenty years now. Diana's parents, both avid antique collectors, had begun staying at the Rayburn Bed & Breakfast in Troy not long after Nell Rayburn Morrow, Jane's grandmother, had made the first rooms available to the public in the 1980s. They would come down from Asheville for the weekend, or sometimes for as long as a week in the summer, which gave the girls plenty of time to get to know each other. While her parents perused the shops around Troy, Diana preferred to stay at the Rayburn House with young Jane, rummaging through the attic for treasures or playing board games in the parlor.

Diana patted Jane's hand and leaned a little closer. "Was it a bad day?"

"Awful."

"I'm sorry, Jane. What did Seth say when he saw you?"

"He told me to leave and not come back. He said a few other things, but that was the gist of it."

Diana nodded. "So what are you going to do?"

"I'm going back, of course."

Jane waited for her friend to respond, but Diana didn't say anything. With one final climactic thud the drumming stopped. The silence was jarring. A moment passed before the crowd applauded, as though they had to shake themselves free from the rhythm's hypnotic grip. Jane wondered who the lead drummer was and how he or she had signaled everyone to stop. There had to be some method to this music, but she couldn't imagine what it was. A few more minutes went by before a single drum began to sound, digging around for a tempo and finally finding it. The other musicians soon followed suit, and the drum circle was back in full swing.

"Listen, Jane," Diana said at length, "are you very sure you want to marry Seth? I mean, you're twenty-five years old. You have a lot of life ahead of you. No one would blame you, you know, if you backed out of the commitment. Maybe if you were married it would be different, but you aren't married yet."

Jane turned toward her friend, eyebrows raised. "I have no intention of backing out of my commitment. I'm engaged to Seth, and I intend to marry him."

"But, sweetie, that means spending your life taking care of someone who can't do anything for himself. Is that really what you want?"

"What would you have done if it had happened to Carl? Wouldn't you have married him anyway?"

"Well, honestly, I'm not certain I would have. Carl is an artist, a sculptor, a college professor. So much of our life together revolves around academia. We may be in different fields, but our teaching, our work . . . it's central to our lives. If Carl couldn't use his hands to create art and to teach his students, well . . ."

"But he would still be Carl."

"I'm not so sure."

Jane shook her head. "I can't agree with you there, Diana. Seth is still Seth. He's still the man I fell in love with. Nothing changes that."

"But he *has* changed, sweetie. Surely you can see that. Maybe not on the inside, but . . . his body isn't his body anymore."

"No? Then whose body is it?"

Diana sniffed out a chuckle. "Come on. You know what I mean."

"Listen, Diana, you're supposed to be on my side in this, remember?"

"I *am* on your side. I want what's best for you. That's all. I want to make sure you know what your life would be like being married to a quadriplegic. I mean, the day-to-day routine of caring for someone—"

"I've done little else for the past six months other than read about spinal cord injuries. I'm pretty sure I know what's involved."

"Only in theory."

"Maybe. But I'm ready to practice." Jane looked at her friend for a long moment. "Thanks for letting me stay in your house for the summer."

Diana smiled and shook her head, seemingly unaware that Jane was changing the subject. "You don't have to thank me, you know. You're doing me a huge favor. Not only will I know someone is watching the house, but taking care of Roscoe and Juniper too, which is far more important. What would I have done with them otherwise—put them in a kennel for the summer? I'd have sooner stayed home from Europe than put my babies in a kennel."

"I'll take good care of them."

"I know you will. So I should be thanking you for allowing me to go off to Europe and play for three months without worrying."

"Play? I thought you were going to work."

Diana laughed. "It's Carl's fellowship. He'll be the one doing the research. I'm just along for the ride. I intend to have fun and do as much sight-seeing as I can, even if I have to do it alone."

"Maybe you'll end up meeting some other expatriates and you can spend the summer traveling with them."

"Maybe so," Diana said, "though I don't imagine Carl would be too happy about that." She shrugged and looked toward the drumming circle. Jane followed suit, and for several minutes they simply listened and tapped along. Finally Diana said, "What if you do decide to stop seeing Seth? You really won't have any reason to stay in Asheville. Will you want to go back to Troy? Because if you do, I don't know what I'll do with Roscoe and Juniper."

"Don't worry." Jane shook her head. "I'll be staying in Asheville this summer, no matter what. There's nothing for me to do in Troy when school's out, except lesson plans, which I can do just as well here as there. I'll be teaching third grade next year instead of second. Did I tell you?"

"No, I don't think you did." Diana took in a deep breath and let it out. "Listen, honey, if marrying Seth is what you want, I'll support you completely."

Jane smiled and gave her friend a small nod. "Thanks, Diana. Yes, it's what I want. And I still want you to be my maid of honor. Are you in?"

"Of course I'm in."

"Anyway, it's possible Seth will regain some movement, you know. He may even walk again someday. I mean, really, Diana, there's all sorts of research going on. Who knows what kind of advances will be made in spinal injury treatment. Someday I imagine there will even be a cure for paralysis. Maybe in our lifetime."

"I suppose it's always worthwhile to hope."

"Of course it is. You know me—always the

incurable optimist. Accentuate the positive and all that."

Diana laughed. "Well, Miss Accentuate the Positive, are you hungry?"

"Famished."

"There's a lovely Thai restaurant right up the street at the Grove Arcade."

"Sounds good."

"There's even a very fat smiling Buddha at the entrance to welcome you."

"As long as he's happy, it works for me."

The two women pulled themselves away from the drumming circle and started up Haywood Street. There the summer throngs were strolling, passing in and out of shops and bakeries and the old Woolworth's that was now part art gallery, part 1950s-era lunch counter. At the corner of Haywood and Battery Park Avenue, Jane and Diana turned left and started up the slightly inclined street where the restaurants began. From there to Page Street and the Grove Arcade, crowded tables spilled out of cafés and onto the buckled sidewalks. The air was heavy with the scent of food and the colliding voices of a hundred conversations. At length, the pounding of the drums receded, replaced by the ringing of bells. The music came from somewhere overhead, somewhere above the street noise and the busyness of the city, and as they approached the Grove Arcade, Jane became aware that she heard not only the bells, but the words to the hymn being played by the carillon. They bubbled up from memory, coming to her conscious mind in Laney's strong, clear voice.

O the deep, deep love of Jesus,
Vast, unmeasured, boundless, free!

Jane laid a hand on Diana's arm. "Where are the church bells playing?" she asked.

Diana paused to listen. "Oh, that's the old Catholic church at the end of Haywood Street, the Basilica of St. Lawrence. Pretty, isn't it?"

How He watches o'er His loved ones,
Died to call them all His own. . . .

Jane nodded. "Beautiful."

As she gazed down the length of the sidewalk, busy with pedestrians, diners, waiters, and a lone cop patrolling the street, she was surprised that no one else appeared to notice the bells. It seemed everyone should have stopped whatever they were doing to listen for just a moment, though no one did. No one seemed aware at all of the song rolling out of the belfry, though the bells went on stubbornly ringing, their notes drifting down like absolution over the dusk-shrouded city.

— 4 —

Jane was determined to make her way up to the fifth floor, but she wasn't quite ready yet. She needed some time to collect her thoughts and calm her nerves. A little walk might help, a leisurely stroll through the maze of hallways in the VA medical complex. Like yesterday, the halls were busy with the two-way traffic of veterans coming and going to appointments at the various clinics that fronted the hospital proper. Unlike yesterday, no one sat at the piano in the atrium; the lobby was quiet, save for the murmuring hum of voices and the tapping of dozens of footfalls on the linoleum floor.

As Jane walked, her eyes swept over the crowds in search of an empathetic soul. She longed for someone she could pull aside and ask, "What should I do? What's the right thing to do?" Because today she didn't feel nearly as sure of her future with Seth as she had sounded yesterday with Diana.

She had lain awake a long time in the night, thinking about what Seth had said. *"I always knew I might not come back alive, but I never dreamed I'd come back like this."*

Before he left for Iraq, Jane had willed herself

to believe he would come back and they would simply pick up where they'd left off. She didn't think of injury, and she didn't think of death. She envisioned no scenario other than that of Seth completing his tour and coming home. After all, that was the ending that played itself out in real life more than any other ending. She'd seen it a hundred times, on the news, in the papers, on the Internet—returning warriors swept up into the arms of their loved ones who had come to airports and bus stations to welcome them home. That's how it would be for her and Seth.

Only that wasn't how it was at all.

He had come back, but he was different, and maybe that changed everything. Maybe Seth had survived but the dream had been lost. Maybe the best thing she could do for him would be to acknowledge the end of their relationship and say good-bye.

After wandering through a tangle of unfamiliar corridors, Jane pushed open an exit door and stepped into a spacious courtyard. Carefully tended flowers bloomed in a variety of gardens around the grounds, and a brick path led from the door to a large white gazebo at the center of the yard. Jane walked to the empty gazebo and sat down. The June sun was at its height, but the little structure offered up its shade as a refuge. Roses sprang up beside the railings; Jane paused to smell one red blossom. The subtle fragrance, tender and sweet, was comforting.

If I don't marry Seth, Jane thought, *I'll go on living, and it will be all right. After all, I lived for years without him.*

If one could call it living. Jane sniffed. Who was she kidding? It would be more accurate to call it . . . what? Striving? Trying very hard to push against the loneliness, the emptiness, and all the unanswered questions that came with adolescence and young adulthood. Trying very hard to fill the void with all she believed to be good and perhaps even eternal—music, art, poetry, nature, beauty in all its varied forms. Yet for all her effort, she had failed repeatedly. She was, she realized, the woman in Sara Teasdale's poem, the seeker of beauty whose heart was empty.

> Oh, is it not enough to be
> Here with this beauty over me?
> My throat should ache with praise, and I
> Should kneel in joy beneath the sky.
> O, beauty, are you not enough?
> Why am I crying after love?

The poet knew. One can try to be noble, but the heart won't be fooled. It wants what it wants. The heart has a narrow appetite. Only love will satisfy.

"Oh, excuse me. I didn't see you sitting there."

Jane gasped silently, startled by the voice and by the tall dark figure leaning into the gazebo. He

31

was the man she'd seen yesterday, the one who had stepped out of the room filled with laughter, who had passed her in the hall, who had the kindest eyes she'd ever seen.

Jane recovered quickly and, smiling, said, "Please, don't let me bother you." She waved a hand toward the bench running around the interior of the gazebo. "Have a seat if you'd like."

The man nodded, his eyes twinkling. "Thank you." He sat and stretched his long legs out in front of him. He wiggled his feet and sighed. "Sometimes the old dogs get tired. Seventy-four years is a long time to have to carry me around, after all."

Jane chuckled. "I suppose it is." She stared at the worn leather of his Oxfords, amused at the way the laces were knotted together in several places. It did indeed look as though he'd been walking in this very pair of shoes for more than seventy years. "I saw you yesterday. Up on the fifth floor."

"Yes." He lifted his chin in recognition. "You were on your way to see Seth?"

She was momentarily surprised. "Yes, I was. Do you know him?"

"I've met him. Briefly. He doesn't want to talk much. Are you his sister?"

Jane held up her ring shyly. "His fiancée."

The man put one large hand on each of his knees and absently began to knead muscle and bone, as though to subdue an ache. He winced, and Jane noticed for the first time the freckles that lay across his cheekbones and nose like Zorro's mask. His wiry hair was a white hood, a sign of age in stark contrast to his alert and youthful eyes. He licked his lips and opened his mouth a time or two, as if trying to decide how to respond. Finally he simply said, "I see."

When he didn't say anything more, Jane blurted awkwardly, "Seth doesn't have a sister. Just a brother. David. He's something of a wanderer. Right now he's up in Alaska, doing some sort of work on a fishing boat. But he'll be back. He promised to be best man at the wedding."

She was rambling. She didn't know why, except perhaps to keep the man from saying something she didn't want to hear. Something like *I'm sorry.* Or *Are you sure?* Or *How can you expect to marry a man who no longer moves from the neck down?*

But when he spoke, he didn't say any of those things. "Remind me," he said. "Was Seth regular army?"

"No." She shook her head. "National Guard."

"Old Hickory, I suppose?"

"Yes, that's right." Jane smiled at the nickname given to the National Guard's 30th Heavy Brigade Combat Team, of which Seth had been a part.

"They were the first, you know."

"The first?"

"Yes. The first Guard Brigade Combat Team to deploy to war since my own war—Korea. You must be proud of Seth."

"I'm very proud of him, yes. I see him as having played a part in history. You know, Operation Iraqi Freedom and all that. Seth was there."

The old gentleman nodded. "Too few people see it that way. So much anger about the war, people forget to be proud of our troops."

"I don't forget."

"That's good." Quietly, almost tenderly, he said, "But while he was there, Seth took a bullet to the neck."

"Yes. A sniper's bullet hit him."

"It fractured his vertebrae between the C-5 and C-6 levels. Did you know that?"

Jane held his gaze for a long moment before nodding slightly. "Yes. His mother told me he's what they call a C-5."

"Yes, that's right. While he was still at Landstuhl, in Germany," the man went on, "they performed a cervical fusion to stabilize the area of injury. That was almost six months ago now, I believe."

"That's right. He was wounded right before Christmas last year, but—"

"And then from Germany he was sent on to Walter Reed, where he was determined by the doctors to be incomplete."

"Incomplete?"

"Yes. Has anyone told you that?"

"No. No one told me."

"Do you know what incomplete means?"

Jane nodded slowly. She felt a small surge of hope. "It means he might regain some movement below the level of injury, doesn't it?"

The man's eyes narrowed slightly in thought. "He might, yes. But according to the ASIA classification—"

"The ASIA classification?"

"The American Spinal Injury Association."

"Okay."

"He's been classified as a C."

"C?"

"He may regain some voluntary motor function, but it will be minimal."

Jane felt herself frown as she considered the man's words. "Maybe the doctors are wrong," she countered. "Maybe he'll do better than they think."

The man shrugged and offered Jane a smile. "Maybe. Medicine is an art, after all, not an exact science. A prognosis is often little more than a best guess."

Jane smiled in return, a slow quizzical smile. "How do you know all this?" she asked.

"I'm a doctor." The man peered at Jane and laughed lightly. "Don't look so surprised."

"I'm not surprised, I—" She what? She *was* surprised. Not to learn that a black man was a doctor, but that *this* man was. "I thought you were a veteran."

"I'm that too. Like I said, I saw action in Korea."

"But you work here?"

"Oh no. I'm retired. I live here." He nodded over his shoulder. "This part of the facility is the Community Living Center. I took a couple bullets myself in the battle for Yechon. They didn't do much harm, more or less just passed on through. Of course, it hurt like the dickens at the time." He looked down at his hands and chuckled. "But being wounded earned me the right to spend my last days here."

"But how do you know so much about—"

"About Seth? I make it my business to know about all the patients laid up in the hospital here. The staff, they let me keep an eye on things. It gives me something to do, and the doctors and nurses, they don't mind having an extra pair of eyes. It's like any hospital: too many patients, too few staff. I've actually been able to intervene a time or two, catch something that might have otherwise been missed. There's a certain satis-faction in that."

"Yes, I can imagine there is," Jane said.

The man stretched out a hand across the length of the gazebo. "My name's Truman Rockaway, by the way."

Jane took his hand and squeezed it gently. "Jane Morrow. I'm happy to meet you, Dr. Rockaway."

"Truman," he said. "It's easiest all around."

"Well, all right."

"I'm going to keep a special watch over Seth. I'll do what I can." He took a cell phone out of his breast pocket and looked at it, as if he was expecting to be paged at any moment. Satisfied that he had no messages, he tucked it back into his pocket and smiled again at Jane.

"I appreciate you keeping an eye on Seth," she said. "Speaking of which, I guess I'd better go up and see him."

As Jane rose to leave, Truman Rockaway stood also. "Jane?"

"Yes?" She looked up into those eyes.

"Don't worry. You will make the right decision."

He didn't elaborate. He didn't have to. Jane understood. Though how he knew her heart, she couldn't say. Neither could she find the words to respond. She merely nodded, then turned and stepped out of the gazebo into the hot noonday sun.

— 5 —

As soon as the elevator doors slid open, Jane saw the middle-aged couple lingering in the hallway outside Seth's room. She smiled as a feeling of warmth came over her. Sid and Jewel Ballantine, Seth's parents, were more father and mother to her than her own parents had ever been, and when she became engaged to their son, they had lovingly welcomed her into the family.

Because Troy was a small town, the Morrows and the Ballantines had known each other all their lives. Not intimately, but at least by name and by sight. Ballantine's Garage had been a landmark in Troy since the 1940s, when Seth's grandfather opened the gas station and auto repair shop on East Main Street. Sid had worked there from the time he was big enough to pump gas and wash windshields and finally took over ownership when Ballantine Senior retired in 1976. Sid was newly married by then and brought on his wife, Jewel, as primary bookkeeper. They'd been working together for nearly thirty years now at a business that allowed them little time away. In fact, the first time they stayed away from the garage for more than a weekend was in February of that year, when Seth was transferred from Germany to Walter Reed Army Medical Center in Washington, D.C. They stayed a month. Now that Seth was closer—though it was still a good four-hour drive from Troy to Asheville—they were determined to come up every weekend possible to be with their son.

Jane moved toward the couple with open arms. "It's so good to see you here," she said, hugging Jewel first, then Sid.

"I was hoping we'd see you today," Jewel said. "Did you get settled in all right?"

"Just fine. The Penlands have a wonderful old house up on Montford Avenue. Where are you staying?"

"At the Best Western, out on Tunnel Road."

"Is it comfortable?"

"It's great," Sid said. "And between AAA and AARP, we get a pretty good discount."

That was Sid Ballantine for you, always counting pennies. It came from years of having to be frugal, of having to make a dollar stretch like warm taffy so all the many expenses of life were covered.

Jane could hear her grandmother now. *"You're marrying beneath you, Jane."*

"What do you mean by that?"

"Well, just think about it, dear. They've never had any money, you know."

"You mean the Ballantines?"

"Of course I mean the Ballantines."

"Oh, Gram, don't be such a snob. They're good, honest, hardworking people. What more can you ask for?"

"Yes, they're decent people. I'm not saying they're not. But money always helps in a marriage."

"Seth and I will make our own money. That's what most couples do."

"But it's not just that. There's also education, you know."

"What do you mean? Seth went to college."

"Yes, and now he's a carpenter."

"So? You know he intends to start his own business. He earned a degree in business, Gram. Don't you remember?"

Grandmother wrung her hands and sighed. "I just want what's best for you, Jane. I want you to be happy."

"I am happy, Gram. You worry too much about things that don't matter."

Jane looked into Seth's room, found it empty, and turned back to his parents for an explanation.

"They've got him down in physical therapy," Jewel said. "We had about twenty minutes with him before they came and whisked him away."

Jane wondered briefly what Seth might do in physical therapy. What does one do with a body that can't move below the neck? But of course, the muscles had to stay toned, and the limbs couldn't be allowed to atrophy, just in case . . . someday . . .

"We were just about to find the cafeteria and get some lunch," Sid said. "Want to join us?"

Jane shook her head. "I had a late breakfast. But you go on."

"Are you sure, Janie?" Jewel asked. "Do you want some coffee or something?"

"No thanks. I'll wait here for Seth. You're coming back up after lunch, aren't you?"

"Oh yes. We plan to be here most of the afternoon."

Jane smiled. "Then I'll see you when you get back."

Jewel leaned forward and wrapped her arms around Jane again. She was a short, solid woman, the tip of her gray head barely reaching Jane's chin. In spite of her age, her skin was still smooth, her eyes still bright, her unmade-up face as homey and comforting as a Norman Rockwell painting. She took her husband's arm and they turned away. He towered over her as they walked together down the corridor, his beefy shoulders reminiscent of his high school football days, his bald spot proof that those days were long ago.

Her heart ached with love for them. And with sorrow for the burden the three of them bore together.

She was standing at the window looking down at the gardens below when a commotion at the doorway let her know Seth was back.

"Watch it, man! Suzy will have your head if you total another wheelchair!"

"Another one, nothing. It's not my fault what happened to that other chair. I'm the best driver on the floor."

"A-ha! If that is so, we are all in danger."

The bantering came from two male aides, both tall and wiry, with skin like darkest ink and eyes like roasted chestnuts on small white saucers. Their speech was melodious, with rounded vowels and a tinge of the British Isles, though the young men themselves had obviously sprung from Africa.

As they worked on maneuvering the wheel-chair into the room—knocking first into the doorway and then into the side of the bed—Seth's face registered mock horror. "Listen, Hoboken, I'm with Sausalito," he said. "I think your license needs to be revoked."

"Ah no!" the one called Hoboken said. When he smiled a full-tooth smile, his mouth was a crescent moon in the middle of a night sky. "I have never lost a patient yet. I am an excellent driver."

Seth turned his eyes to Jane. "If these two clowns dump me out of this chair," he said, "you're a witness."

The first aide nodded toward the other. "Only he is a clown. I am the straight man. I'm the responsible one."

"Oh sure, Sausalito," Seth said. "Should I pretend I didn't see you making balloons out of rubber gloves yesterday?"

The young man raised one long finger to his lips. "Shh. If Suzy finds out, I don't have a job anymore. All right now, wait right here. I'll bring in the lift."

Seth said, "Yeah, well, I'm not going any-where."

The room fell quiet as the one called Sausalito

left. Finally Seth said, "So you decided to come back."

It took Jane a moment to realize he was talking to her rather than to the remaining aide. "Well, yes," she said quietly, glancing at the aide, then back at Seth. "I told you I would."

They got no further than that when Sausalito reappeared, pulling a metal contraption into the room. "Okay, Mr. Seth, you ready to fly?"

"Do I have a choice?"

"No, unfortunately. We're the boss of you, and you must do whatever we say," Sausalito said with a snicker.

"I thought I was supposed to spend most of my time in a wheelchair rather than the bed."

"That's right. You are."

"Well?"

"Right now we need the chair for someone else. We'll get you out of the bed again later."

"I'd like to file a formal complaint about this."

"You are free to do that, Mr. Seth," Hoboken chimed in, "but you know it will end up where all the other complaints end up. In the . . . what do you say? . . . in the black hole of bureaucracy."

"Very good, Hoboken!" Seth exclaimed. "You're learning our American ways."

The three men laughed as Hoboken and Sausalito went about the task of hooking Seth up to the lift. As they worked, Jane began to understand that Seth was already cradled in a

43

huge sling that would carry him from the chair to the bed. When all the clasps were in place, Sausalito gingerly unhooked Seth's urine bag from the chair and settled it on Seth's stomach. Then he began pumping a lever on the side of the lift. A few swift pumps rendered Seth airborne, dangling like a baby from the beak of a stork.

"Move the chair! Move the chair!" Sausalito demanded.

"I'm moving it. Calm down," Hoboken responded. "Anyway, you may be the boss of Mr. Seth here, but you are not the boss of me."

"Yes, I am. And I always have been, little brother."

In another moment, Seth dangled over the bed as Sausalito once again vigorously pumped the lever, this time lowering the sling.

"They're not really brothers," Seth told Jane. "They're cousins. From Uganda."

"I see."

"No one can pronounce their real names, so everyone just calls them Hoboken and Sausalito."

"And"—Jane looked from one to the other— "which is which?"

"It doesn't matter," Sausalito said. "We will answer to either name."

"But our real names are not so hard," Hoboken added. "They are Hangson Bwambale and Bwanandeke Baluku. Easier than the nicknames we've been given."

44

"That's what you think," Seth said. "By the way, I haven't introduced you to . . ." He paused a moment before going on. " . . . to my friend, Jane Morrow."

The young men acknowledged her with smiles and nods. "So how long have you been in the States?" Jane asked.

"Almost two years," Sausalito replied. He was on one side of the bed now, unlatching the straps, while Hoboken was on the other side doing the same. "We are both students at the university. We work here at the hospital part-time."

When the straps were unlatched, the two young men rolled Seth onto his side, tucked the sling up against his back, rolled Seth onto his other side, then pulled the sling out from under him.

It's like rolling a log, Jane thought. Insentient wood. Dead weight. Anyone could do anything to Seth, and he couldn't stop them.

"What are you studying?" Jane asked, trying hard not to feel unnerved.

Sausalito lifted the bag of urine and hooked it onto the side of the bed. The catheter snaked its way upward from the bag and disappeared underneath Seth's shirt. "We are both in the nursing school," he said. "We have an uncle in Uganda who is a doctor. Right now he works in a hospital in Kampala, the capital, but he wants to open a rural clinic where there has never been one. We will work for him."

45

"That's wonderful."

Seth said, "Hoboken is taking special classes in how to push a wheelchair without killing the patient."

The cousins laughed again, and Jane joined in. Seth was still there, his sense of humor still in place. It made her feel hopeful.

Sausalito began to pull the sheet up to Seth's shoulders and then paused, looking thoughtful. "Mr. Seth, why don't you show Miss Jane what you accomplished in physical therapy today?"

Seth looked up at Sausalito, then looked away. "It's nothing."

"Oh no, Mr. Seth. It's not nothing. It's something very good."

"What is it, Seth?" Jane asked. She took a step closer to the bed.

"Come on," Sausalito prodded. "Show her what you can do."

The luster evaporated from Seth's eyes, and his face turned stony. For a moment Jane wasn't sure whether he was angry or simply concentrating. Then, finally, she saw the movement, the slightest bit of lift to his left shoulder. His arm rose from the bed an inch, maybe two, before falling again.

"Seth! You can raise your arm!" Jane cried.

Both of the cousins smiled proudly. "He did it for the first time today," Hoboken explained. "It's a huge accomplishment. It is for Mr. Seth . . . how do you say? It's a red-letter day!"

46

"Oh, Seth, it's wonderful," Jane said.

Seth looked at her, said nothing, looked away.

After a few more words of encouragement, the two aides left, taking the wheelchair and the lift with them. The room was suddenly very large and very quiet.

Seth looked at Jane, then up at the ceiling. "Well," he said, "I hope you understand now."

Jane placed both hands on the bed railing. "What do you mean?"

"We had wanted a simple life. Nothing is simple now. You can see that, can't you?"

Jane drew in a deep breath and let it out slowly. "I'll learn to do whatever needs to be done. Other people do it all the time."

Seth's head moved from side to side on the pillow. His voice was quiet and calm when he said, "I don't care what other people do. I don't want you spending your life taking care of me."

"But what if that's what I want?"

"Don't be an idiot," he snapped.

The Seth of a moment before was gone. Jane reeled against the sting of his words. "I'm going to pretend as though you didn't say that, Seth."

"I'm sorry. I didn't mean it."

"I know you didn't."

"Listen, do you know anything about the reality of this? And don't think it's going to be just like taking care of an infant, Jane, because it's not. Babies don't get bedsores. Babies don't have catheter tubes embedded in their groins. Babies grow up—"

"Seth, I never said it would be like taking care of a baby—"

"You'd be a full-time nurse. Twenty-four seven. Being a nurse is not the same thing as being a wife—"

"Yes, I realize—"

"So I want you to really think hard about it, what life would be like if we got married."

"I *have* thought hard about it. It's almost all I've thought about for the past six months."

"And how do you think we're going to manage?"

"We'll manage the way other people do who are in the same situation. I'm willing to try if you are."

"It will never be what we'd dreamed of."

"So we change the dream."

"To what, Jane? I'm helpless and I'm useless. I can't do anything."

"You're not useless. And anyway, you might improve. I mean, look, you can raise your arm now."

"So? So maybe someday I'll feed myself with a spoon strapped to my hand. Big deal. I won't be getting my fine motor skills back. They've already told me that. I'm not like Stephen Hawking who can do his brain work from a wheelchair. I'm a carpenter. I work with tools and wood. I work with my *hands,* Jane."

Oh yes, he worked with his hands. How often had she watched him work his magic? To Jane, he was more than a carpenter, he was an artist. He could take ordinary wood and fashion it into objects of beauty. Even before he began a new project, he saw the end, the finished product, the way Michelangelo was said to see the statue in the untouched slab of marble. Seth's talent was a gift. What was he to do if he couldn't use his gift?

As though he could read her thoughts, Seth asked, "So what am I going to do now? How am I going to make a living?"

Jane frowned as she shook her head. "You can get disability. I'll keep teaching. We'll be all right."

A small muscle worked in Seth's jaw. "I can't decide whether you're trying to be a martyr or a saint."

"I'm not trying to be either one. I'm just trying to marry the man I love."

"Yeah? Well, the man you love doesn't exist anymore."

"Oh yes he does. I saw him just a minute ago when those two aides were here, though he seems to have left right along with them."

He didn't take the bait. Instead, shifting topics, he said, "I'll never build you that house now. I was going to buy us a plot of land, build the house from the ground up."

"It's all right, Seth. I don't have to have the house—"

"And what about children? You always wanted children."

After a long moment, Jane said, "If we can't have our own, maybe we can adopt—"

Seth cut her off. "If we had children, I could never pick them up, put my arms around them." Then, in a whisper, "Please don't do that to me."

Jane backed away from the bed. She walked to the window and looked out again. "Listen, I can't figure it out all at once. I can only get through today and that's it. Getting married and having kids, that'll come later. We'll handle those things when we're ready."

She gazed up at the cloudless sky, but the blue escaped her. She didn't see anything except what might have been. At length Seth's voice, a wounded whisper, drifted to her across the room. "Jane?"

"Yes, Seth?"

"I've been thinking a lot since yesterday, since you were here yesterday," he said.

She turned from the window. "About what?"

A pained look settled on his brow. "Do you really still love me?"

"Of course, Seth. I love you."

"Then, will you help me?"

She took a step toward him. "You know I'll help you. I'll do anything."

"Anything?"

She went to him then and, bending down close

to his face, laid a hand on his cheek. "Yes. Just tell me. What do you want me to do?"

He looked up at her beseechingly, his eyes restless on her face. "I don't want to live like this," he said quietly. "If you love me, please help me die."

— 6 —

Church bells were ringing somewhere. Jane could hear them through the open window in the breakfast nook of the kitchen. She wondered whether they might be the bells in the Basilica of St. Lawrence, but she decided that the downtown church was too far away. It must be another church, one closer to the Penlands' house, sending out a hymn on this warm Sunday morning.

Jane took another sip of coffee. She had scarcely slept all night, and what little sleep she could manage was filled with troubled dreams. At 5:00 a.m. she'd finally given up. She'd come to the kitchen to drink coffee and wait for dawn. Three hours later she was still drinking coffee while watching the sunlight play across the grass. The two rat terriers, Roscoe and Juniper, lay curled up at her feet beneath the kitchen table, waiting for breakfast.

Jane wasn't aware of the dogs or of her own

gnawing hunger. Both hands circled the ceramic mug as she gazed intently out the window and back in time. The morning light gave way to a darkened room in the Rayburn house where she sat beside her mother, watching the movie on video that they had already watched over and over. Meredith Belmont in silk and crinoline, the leading man heartbreakingly handsome in the pale gray uniform of the Confederate soldier . . .

"Good morning, Jane."

Jane jumped at the sound of Diana's voice. She turned and saw her friend headed toward the coffeepot. "Oh, you startled me."

"Sorry about that."

"It's all right. Carl still sleeping?"

"Like a baby. You looked like you were deep in thought."

"I guess I was."

Diana poured herself a cup, then sat down beside Jane at the table. Roscoe came to have his ear scratched, and Diana obliged. "Well," she said, "as the old saying goes, penny for your thoughts?"

Jane gave a small, tentative smile. She raised the mug to her lips, took a sip, set it back down on the table. For a moment she considered lying, then decided to tell the truth. "I was just thinking about my mother," she confessed.

Her friend looked puzzled. "What about her?"

"Oh, you know, about the movies."

"Yeah?"

"Well, you remember how she used to sit in our apartment at the house watching those three or four movies over and over, the ones that ended up on videotape?"

Diana nodded. "Yeah, I remember."

"When I was real young, she would sometimes pat the couch and invite me to sit down beside her. You know, watch with her. And when it came to certain parts, she'd point to the television and say, 'Look, Janie. That's your mother. That's me.' "

"Uh-huh." Diana sounded decidedly unimpressed.

"I couldn't understand it. I'd look at that beautiful young face on the screen, and then I'd look at the woman beside me, and . . . well . . . I didn't believe her. I thought she was lying. One day, though, I saw the credits, and there was her name, her maiden name, Meredith Belmont, and I realized the woman in the movie really was my mother. But it still didn't make sense. It was this huge mystery to me. Kind of like . . ." Jane paused and laughed lightly. "Kind of like Jim Nabors, you know? How could someone who talked like Gomer Pyle sing like Jim Nabors?"

Diana guffawed at that. "I know what you mean," she said. "By the time I knew your mom, I'd never have guessed she'd once been a Hollywood beauty."

"You're right. And it wasn't because she was old or because she had let herself go all that much.

She might have still been pretty, if it weren't for the sadness. She was just so sad and weary and, I don't know, worn-out before her time, I guess."

"And I don't think the alcohol helped."

Jane turned her gaze toward the window. She felt her throat tighten. "I'm sure it didn't."

"I've always thought when she bled to death, more booze than blood came out."

They were quiet then, remembering. Roscoe turned circles under the table, then lay back down and closed his eyes. Jane said, "Once, I asked Laney why Mom was so sad. Laney stopped what she was doing, and she sat me down at the kitchen table. 'Jane, honey,' she said, 'I'll tell you why your mother's so sad if you promise not to tell her I said so.' I told her I wouldn't say anything. I just wanted to know what was wrong with Mom. All these years later I still remember how Laney put it. 'It's because no one worships her anymore.'" Jane paused in thought. "She said Mom went and fell off her throne when she couldn't get any more parts in the movies. Then Laney just kind of patted my hand and went back to cooking like I was supposed to be satisfied, but I still didn't get it. I just couldn't understand why Mom was depressed, why she'd sit in our apartment watching herself on television. I wouldn't understand for a long time."

Quietly, Diana asked, "And do you think you understand now?"

"I think so. She had five good years in Hollywood. She lived her dream. She made it into the movies. She could go to the theater and see her own face up there on the screen. For a few years she was adored by her fans, and she got addicted to the attention. I mean, it really did become an addiction, like she had to have it to stay alive, you know?"

Jane looked at Diana, who nodded.

"Then, the roles dried up," Jane went on, "and she couldn't get any more parts. She became a has-been. Finally, I think more out of financial desperation than anything else, she married Dad." Jane frowned thoughtfully. "Dad was in his hippie phase back then, drifting around out west, trying to find himself. I don't know if he ever found himself, but he did find Mom, and not long afterward he brought her back to Troy, a place where no one seemed to recognize her. Or if they did know who she was, they didn't care. She became just another small-town nobody, a role she could never accept. And so began the long downward spiral that killed her when she was only forty-three."

Diana got up from the table and headed back to the coffeepot. Watching the stream of steaming coffee flowing into her cup, she was conveniently turned away from Jane when she said, "Your mother killed herself, Jane. She wasn't killed by circumstances."

Jane still cringed when she thought of her mother slitting her wrists. On that spring day, she lay down in the bathtub and put a pillow under her head, as though she was simply going to sleep. "I know, Diana. When she couldn't live the life she wanted, she chose not to live."

Diana settled the carafe back into the coffee maker. "What I've never understood is why your father didn't try to get her any help."

"Maybe he did. I just don't know. I was their only child, but even so, I was never exactly privy to their private lives. I was always kind of floating around the edges of things, never really sure what was going on."

Diana sighed heavily as she finally turned back to Jane. "All this happened years ago. Why are you thinking about it now?"

Jane shrugged, started to lift the mug to her lips, decided against it. "She was my mother, Diana. I'm not sure I've ever really stopped thinking about her and what happened to her."

"Fair enough." Diana moved back to the table and sat. "But, honey, you've got a different dragon to slay at this point. You hardly need to borrow any sorrows from the past."

"I suppose you're right."

"Your mother"—Diana shook her head—"she made her choices, regardless of what it would do to the people around her. She could have found plenty to live for if she'd pulled herself away from that cursed television set long enough to think about it. She had a pretty good life in Troy, and most of us common people would say she was pretty lucky. She had you, for one thing. She might have tried to be a mother to you. But that was never enough."

"I guess motherhood was hardly as glamorous as Hollywood."

"Yeah, well, welcome to the world of real life."

"She didn't much care for real life."

"She was completely selfish, and that was the bottom line."

"Do you think so, Diana?"

Diana paused and laid a hand over Jane's. "I'm sorry, Jane. I shouldn't have said that."

"No, it's all right. You're only calling it like it is."

"It's just always made me mad, thinking of what she did to you. Sometimes when we were at your place in Troy, I'd want to bring you home with me where you could have halfway decent parents and a sister who loved you. You're my only little sister, you know."

Jane smiled. "Yes, I know. I'm glad I have you."

"Me too." Diana patted Jane's hand and went back to drinking her coffee. "Well, not to change the subject, though I guess I am, since talking about your mother makes me angry . . ." Diana laughed and ran the fingers of both hands through her short, unruly hair. "Are you going to the hospital to see Seth today?"

"I don't think so. I want to give Sid and Jewel the chance to spend some time alone with him this afternoon."

"In that case, do you want to go shopping with me a little later? I can't believe we're leaving in two days and I still don't have everything I need for the trip."

"Sure. Shopping sounds good to me."

Diana stepped to the refrigerator and opened the door. "Let's have spinach omelets for breakfast, and then for lunch, I know this wonderful little café on Lexington . . ."

She went on, but Jane wasn't listening. She had already returned to Troy, where she sat beside her mother on the leather couch watching one of the scenes she had watched a hundred times before. Her mother—young, fresh-faced, achingly beautiful in a nineteenth-century ball gown—was playing the part of Clara Delaney, a Southern belle in love with a Confederate soldier.

"You'll come back to me, won't you, William? When this awful war is over, promise me you'll come back."

"Of course I'll come back to you, Clara. I promise I will."

"If my love were enough to protect you, I'd know you were always safe."

"Then don't stop loving me."

"Never! I'll never stop loving you."

"And you'll be here when I come home."

"Oh yes. I'll be here for you always, waiting, loving you, praying for your safe return."

Music begins to play. Clara and William kiss. Camera pans to sunset.

Meredith Belmont Morrow sighs. Jane Morrow wishes Clara Delaney were her mother.

— 7 —

He was at the piano again, playing something by Chopin. Or Schumann, maybe. Jane wasn't sure, even though she'd heard it played an untold number of times before on Grandmother's phonograph back home. She stood at the railing in the medical center lobby early that Monday afternoon, listening to the music coming up from below. She shut her eyes and breathed deeply. The notes were soothing, something bright in the midst of a rainy day, a day full of shadows inside and out. She needed the music to comfort her and give her strength before she headed upstairs to see Seth.

When the song stopped and another one started, one she recognized and loved, Jane decided to take the elevator down to the atrium to meet the mysterious musician. All she knew about him so far was that he was a blond-haired man in a business suit.

Once in the atrium, she paused just beyond his right shoulder and watched him play. His fingers searched out the keys and seemed to find them effortlessly as he played the familiar tune. When he finished, Jane stepped closer, into his range of sight, and said, " 'Clair de Lune.' "

At the sound of her voice, he looked up with a start. Then he smiled. "Yes. Light of the moon. Or more simply, Moonlight. Lovely, isn't it?"

"Yes, it is."

His eyes were a startling shade of blue, the central feature in a pleasant face. He had a high forehead, a narrow nose, and a generous mouth. His skin hinted at time spent in the summer sun, though the bronzed sheen was undoubtedly heightened by the white of his dress shirt and the pale blue of his tie.

"Are you a professional musician?" Jane asked.

"Me?" He laughed. "No. I thought about it once, way back when. I studied classical piano for years with the idea that I might end up on the stage, but"—he shrugged—"I changed my mind. Now I just play for the joy of it."

"Well, you're very good."

He smiled modestly. "Thanks. By the way, I'm Jon-Paul Pearcy." He extended a hand, and Jane shook it.

"Jane Morrow," she said.

"Pleasure to meet you."

Jane withdrew her hand and laid it on the

smooth, shiny surface of the piano. "I've seen you here before. Do you work here?"

"Here? Goodness no. I'm a partner in my father's law firm. But thankfully Dad lets me out of the cage long enough to have lunch once in a while."

"You're a lawyer?"

"Yes." He smiled. "But if you give me half a chance, you might decide I'm not such a bad person."

Jane smiled in return. "I suppose you hear a lot of lawyer jokes."

"I hear my share."

"But it's the family business?"

"Believe it or not, it is. My father and his brother both went into law and eventually started their own firm. Now my cousin, my brother, and I are all partners in the firm. We all have the same last name, so we might have called it Pearcy, Pearcy, Pearcy, Pearcy, and Pearcy, but we decided that would be a little too redundant. So we simply call it The Pearcy Law Firm, and we let that cover all of us."

Jane laughed aloud and Jon-Paul Pearcy joined her. "It must get a little confusing for the secretary," Jane said, "when someone calls and asks to talk to Mr. Pearcy."

"That it does," Jon-Paul said with a definitive nod. "Especially since both my brother and my cousin are juniors. So we have David Pearcy Sr.

and David Pearcy Jr. and Stephen Pearcy Sr. and Stephen Pearcy Jr."

"My goodness! Your poor secretary must be pulling out her hair!"

Jon-Paul looked serious and waved a finger at Jane. "I think you might have just solved the mystery of why Marion wears so many wigs." He chuckled and played a few lively notes on the piano to punctuate his joke. "But we all have our own area of specialty. Mine is disability law."

"Oh, I see. So you have clients here at the VA?"

"I've had some clients here but—oh, you're wondering what I'm doing here playing the piano."

"Yes, I guess I am."

"Well, it's because of my sister Carolyn. She's a nurse up on four. I try to get out here about once a week or so to have lunch with her in the cafeteria. Sometimes I end up waiting for her to break away from the floor, so I figure I might as well spend the time entertaining the troops."

"I think it's great that you do. And it's really nice that you come out and have lunch with your sister."

"Well, otherwise—the way both our schedules are—I'd never see her, even though we both live right here in Asheville."

Jane smiled at him, but he didn't smile back. He turned his eyes away, seemed to be listening to something. The elevator doors opened, and a young man in maroon-colored scrubs stepped out and marched deliberately to the piano.

"Hey, Jon-Paul," he said as he casually rested both arms atop the instrument.

"Hi, Gus," Jon-Paul greeted him. "What's going on? You on break?"

"Yup." The young orderly nodded and pulled a cigarette out of the breast pocket of his uniform. He stuck it in his mouth but didn't light it. It moved up and down as he spoke. "Carolyn sent me down to tell you she's going to be a little late. She said if you can't wait, she understands, but she hopes you will, since Melissa is joining you for lunch."

"No problem," Jon-Paul said. "Any idea how long?"

"Twenty minutes tops," Gus replied, the cigarette flapping. "Believe me, Jon-Paul, it'll be worth your wait. That Melissa, she's a looker."

"Yeah?"

The orderly let go a long whistle. Then he looked at Jon-Paul and seemed chagrined. "Well, sorry, I didn't mean—"

"No problem, Gus. Hey, thanks for passing along the message."

"Sure thing." He rapped the piano with the knuckles of one hand. "Well, gotta get the smoke in before my break's over. Then it's back to bedpans and mopping floors. I'll tell ya, it'd be nice to have a cushy job like yours. One that would impress the ladies too. Well, take it easy, counselor."

When he left, Jon-Paul turned back to Jane. His cheeks were slightly ruddy. "I love my sister dearly, but she has one irredeemable fault."

"Oh?" Jane said. "What's that?"

"She's always setting me up on blind dates." Jon-Paul paused, frowned, and finally chuckled. "No pun intended."

Jane cocked her head. "All right."

"Well, enough of that. So Jane, what brings you to the VA?"

Jane looked at her hands, stealing a moment to think before answering. How much to say? "My fiancé is here," she said at length. "He was wounded in Iraq."

Jon-Paul leaned closer. "I'm sorry," he said somberly. "Will he . . . do the doctors say he'll be all right?"

"Well"—another glance away, then back—"he was shot in the neck. He's paralyzed. They don't expect him to regain much movement."

"I'm so sorry. Really. If there's ever anything I can do . . ."

His voice trailed off. Jane nodded and attempted a smile. "Thank you. Well, I'd better go visit with Seth. Have a good time at lunch today."

"Yeah, thanks. Say, what time is it anyway?"

Jon-Paul pulled back his sleeve to look at his watch. Except that he didn't look at it. Instead, he pushed a button that released the crystal covering the face. With an index finger, he tenderly touched the hands of the watch beneath.

And with that, Jane understood his joke about the blind date. Jon-Paul Pearcy, player of Moonlight, was blind.

— 8 —

"Did you think about what I asked you to do?"

Jane felt her jaw tighten. Seth hadn't even bothered to say hello when she walked into the room. He had simply glanced up from his wheelchair, then looked away. "Of course I thought about it," she said.

"Well?" he asked quietly.

"Well what? I wasn't considering whether or not I would do it, because I won't. What I can't understand is how you can even ask me. I can't . . ." She was angry now. She stopped herself, not wanting to slip into a tirade, not wanting to say things she would later regret. She slumped down in the one chair in the room and looked at the floor.

After a moment Seth said, "I was hoping you'd see it my way."

"Well, I don't."

"Maybe you'll change your mind."

She took a deep breath. "This isn't like you, Seth. I don't even know who you are anymore."

He almost smiled then. He latched on to her gaze. "Now we're getting somewhere."

"What do you mean?"

"I'm not the Seth you knew, Jane. That's just it. I will never be the same person again."

"Then maybe you can be someone different but just as good."

"It's not possible. There's nothing left."

"*You're* left! *You* are left. The you inside. That's something."

"But I'm trapped. I can't—"

"And you might get better. You've already regained some movement. You might regain more."

"That's not enough."

"It has to be enough."

"What? That maybe someday I can bend an elbow or flex my wrist? It's not enough, Jane. I'll never have my hands back."

"So you want to give up?"

"Yes."

She slapped the chair's armrests with both hands. "How can you do this to me?"

"Jane, I—"

"You're only thinking of yourself! What about your parents? What would it do to them if you . . . if you gave up?"

He shut his eyes, opened them, said quietly,

"You will all go on. I know you will. You'll be all right."

Jane cried out in frustration. "I can't believe you. I can't believe you're talking like this. You've never been a quitter before. Now look at you. You're not the only person who's ever had a spinal cord injury, you know. Other people are injured and then go on to live perfectly happy lives—"

"Stop it, Jane. Just stop. I don't want to hear it. You don't have a clue what it's like. You're not the one in this chair, unable to move, unable to do anything . . ." He didn't finish. He turned his face to the wall.

She stood abruptly, crossed her arms, and moved to the window. For a long while she leaned a shoulder against the glass and looked out at the drizzling rain. "You were always the one who believed in a loving God," she said. "I was always the one who didn't know for sure. What about your loving God now, Seth? Has He stopped being loving because you were wounded? Or have you decided He was never really there after all?"

Minutes passed. Dirty drops of rain slithered wormlike down the glass. Voices drifted in from the hall, and a medicine cart clanked across the linoleum. Somewhere, a nurse's bell rang and rang again. When Seth finally spoke, Jane turned away from the window to look at him.

"When we got off the plane in Germany," he

said, "we were put in buses and taken to Landstuhl, the military hospital. It was raining, like today, only it was cold. The rain was like ice. Everything was gray."

Seth moved his gaze to Jane, as though to see if she was listening. She nodded for him to go on. He looked away, up toward the ceiling, and started again. "I didn't know the other guys on the bus, but everyone was wounded to one extent or another. A couple of guys had had limbs amputated back in Iraq. One guy was blind, I think. At least he had bandages over his eyes. The person next to me had been burned pretty bad. And of course a few of us had been shot. Most of the guys tried to joke about it, saying things like our injuries were our ticket out, our pass to go home, blah blah blah, you know, like something good had happened to us. We were the lucky ones because we were getting out. Still, a couple of the guys were crying. They tried to be quiet about it, but I could hear them. I couldn't talk at all because of the tube in my throat. I could only listen. What I really wanted to do was put my hands over my ears, but of course there was no way I was going to do that. It was like I was trapped in concrete. I was still inside my body, but I couldn't make it move anymore. So I just had to lie there and listen to the jokes and the men crying and the rain beating against the windows."

He swallowed hard. Jane watched as a crimson streak snuck up the side of his neck and fanned out across his cheek. Whether red was the color of anger or sadness, or both, she didn't know. She waited. He blinked a few times while moistening his lips with his tongue.

"When we finally got to the hospital," he went on, "the bus pulled up to the emergency room entrance, and a whole crowd of people came out to meet us. They opened the rear door of the bus and started taking guys out. I was just lying there waiting and watching them work. They worked with this kind of quiet efficiency that I found both comforting and frightening. I mean, I knew I was in good hands, but I didn't want to be there. I didn't want to be part of this incoming paddy wagon of wounded soldiers, you know? I just kept thinking, *Can somebody get me out of this picture? I'm not supposed to be here. I don't belong here. Somebody take me back to where I belong.*

"But like it or not, I was there, and there was absolutely nothing I could do about it. Finally my turn came to be lifted out of the bus. One of the nurses was holding an umbrella over the door, but she couldn't keep out the cold and the rain. I looked up at the faces around me. A priest was there. I could tell by his collar he was a priest. He came up to my stretcher, and he leaned over me and said, 'Seth, you're safe now. You're in

Germany.' And I remember thinking it was too late. There was no use pretending I was safe and that everything was all right. It was far too late for that.

"Then, just as they started to take me away, the priest raised his hand and made the sign of the cross over me. He was wearing the same kind of rubber gloves the medical people were wearing, like not even the priest could touch us with his bare hands or he'd catch our bad luck or something." Seth paused and sniffed out a laugh. "So I watched his hand making the sign of the cross over me, and for the first time in my life I thought, 'Maybe it's all a lie. Maybe everything I ever believed is a lie.' "

Jane was beside his wheelchair now, gazing down at him. She wondered at his sudden calm. His expressionless eyes refused to meet hers but stared dully up at the ceiling. They looked like two round patches of frozen earth. Jane leaned down and pressed her cheek against his. "I'm so sorry, Seth," she whispered. "I'm so sorry for everything that's happened. But I promise you, we're going to be all right. We're going to make it all work somehow."

She pulled back and waited for him to meet her gaze. But he went on staring at the ceiling, as though she weren't there.

— 9 —

On the first floor of the VA Medical Center, just beyond the lobby, was a small canteen called The Bistro. Vending machines lined the back wall. A dozen tables with corresponding chairs were bolted to the floor. The wall between the corridor and the canteen was full of windows so that one couldn't pass The Bistro without being enticed to stop and have a snack.

Jane stopped, but not because she was hungry. She stopped because she saw Truman Rockaway, alone at one of the tables, drinking from a pint carton of chocolate milk.

He raised a hand toward her, beckoning her in. She entered the canteen and sat down across from him. They were the only two people in the room.

"Got milk?" he asked, lifting the cardboard carton.

He smiled. She smiled in return. "I haven't drunk chocolate milk since I was a kid."

"We ought to remedy that. My treat."

"Well . . ."

"I insist. After all, chocolate is a natural antidepressant, you know."

She looked at him, chewed her lower lip. "Is it that apparent?"

"It doesn't have to be apparent. It can be deduced. You're in a hospital visiting your fiancé who is upstairs in the spinal cord unit unable to move from the neck down." He rose and rummaged around in the pocket of his slacks while he walked to one of the machines. He dropped a series of coins into the slot and pushed a button. A carton of milk nose-dived off the shelf behind the glass and landed with a thud in the lip of the machine. Truman retrieved it and set it on the table in front of Jane. "Drink up, young lady," he said.

"Thank you, Truman."

He settled himself back down at the table as she bent back the spout. She took a long drink and nodded. "Tastes good."

"I drink it every day."

"You go straight for the hard stuff to drown your sorrows?"

He laughed. "I guess I do."

They were quiet for a time, lost in their own thoughts, downing their chocolate milk. Finally Jane asked, "Where are you from, Truman?"

"Here and there," he said. "But originally? I'm from Travelers Rest, South Carolina."

"Oh yeah? I used to know someone from there. She was one of our cooks."

"What was her name?"

"Laney Jackson."

Truman thought a moment, shook his head. "It

doesn't sound familiar. But anyway, I haven't been in Travelers Rest for a long time. So Laney, she cooked for your family?"

"Well, kind of. My dad and my grandmother ran a bed-and-breakfast in Troy. They still do. We have our own apartment at the back of the house, with a private kitchen and everything. Anyway, when I was a child, Laney was one of the cooks who took care of the guests. She left Troy years ago, though, and I've lost touch with her."

"Uh-huh." Truman finished his milk, crushed the carton with one hand, and tossed it toward the open trash can. It went in.

"Two points," Jane said.

"I should have played basketball," Truman quipped.

"Yeah, if you'd gone pro, you'd be rich."

"You're right. Instead, I became a doctor, and I can tell you, not all doctors are rich."

"No, I suppose not."

Truman folded his hands on the table and seemed to study them. "Have you seen Seth today?"

Jane nodded. "I just left his room."

"And how was he?"

"Depressed."

"That's normal. Everyone in his situation goes through that. It's part of the healing process."

"I know." Jane drew in a deep breath. "I'm trying to be patient. But he's so different. I've never seen him like this before. It's like he came back from Iraq a totally different person, not just in body but . . . I don't know, in soul too, I guess."

Truman tapped the table with the soft balls of his hands. "Tell me about him, Jane."

"Tell you about Seth?"

"Yes. What was he like before?"

As Jane thought about his question, a smile spread slowly across her face. "He was just about the greatest guy in the world. Oh, I know, probably every woman says that about her fiancé, but I really mean it. He was a great guy. Everyone liked him."

"You met him in Troy?"

"Yes. We grew up together. I've been in love with him since second grade. It took him a little longer—well, about fifteen years longer—but he finally noticed me."

Truman smiled. "I'm glad he did."

"Me too." Jane nodded her head absently for a moment. "It was Christmastime, and Gram and Dad were hosting our annual open house. Dad always grumbles about it, but Gram does it every year anyway. Practically the whole town comes through, just to mingle and drink eggnog and listen to Christmas carols on Gram's old phonograph. I think it's kind of a nostalgic trip back in time for most people, since the house is so old and full of antiques. Anyway, in . . . let's see, it must have been 2002, Seth came to the open

74

house with his parents. For whatever reason, he'd never been in the Rayburn House before. That's the name of our B&B. Fortunately for me, he was taken with the woodwork." She laughed lightly. "Seth's a carpenter. He says he's addicted to wood the way a hillbilly's addicted to moonshine."

Truman laughed out loud, a deep throaty laugh. It made Jane smile.

"Anyway," she went on, "I gave him the grand tour of the house, attic to basement. He pointed out things I'd never even noticed before or maybe had stopped seeing a long time ago. You know, the shape of the balusters on the staircase, the handcrafted trim between the walls and the ceiling, the little rosettes carved into the wood-work above one of the fireplaces. I guess you could say he ended up giving me a tour of my own home. Well, afterward we sat by the fire in the parlor for a long time, talking about everything from spiral nails to cordless saws to what we planned to do with our lives. As they say, the rest is history."

Truman nodded; his eyes shone. "It sounds like a nice story."

"It was. It was like a fairy tale. But then two Christmases later, Seth was in Iraq and"—she shrugged—"now we're here."

"I see." Truman nodded and gazed back down at his hands. "You've entered a chapter you didn't expect."

Jane slowly shook her head. "I didn't expect this at all. We would have been married this summer if he hadn't been wounded."

"And now?"

"Now?" Jane sighed. "I just don't know."

"What does Seth say?"

"Mostly, he says he wants me to go away." She tried to laugh, but her laughter fell flat. For a moment she wondered why she was spilling her thoughts to a stranger. Yet, oddly, she felt perfectly comfortable in the company of Truman Rockaway. Maybe he was just one of those people who'd never known a stranger in his life. She looked at him, locking onto his gaze. "What should I do, Truman?"

"Give him time," came the reply. "He'll come around."

"You mean, you're not going to tell me to just forget about him?"

"No. Why should I tell you that?"

"Everyone else is, it seems. Even his own mother. After she spent a month with him at Walter Reed, she came back and said to me, 'If you no longer feel you can marry Seth, I understand.'"

Truman frowned and leaned toward her over the table. "Do you still want to marry him, Jane?"

"Of course."

"And why is that?"

"Because I love him."

"Then that's good enough for me." He leaned back and seemed to relax. "And it should be good enough for everyone else."

"But it isn't. Not even for Seth."

"Well, now, like I said, Seth will come around. He's suffered a huge loss, you know. There's a whole lot of grieving ahead of him, and that's something he can't get around. He has to go through it. But once he's through it, he'll begin to see things more clearly."

"Do you really think so?"

"Yes, I do. I've seen it happen plenty of times. You wouldn't believe what some people survive, only to go on and lead productive lives. Happy lives too, for the most part."

"But some people don't. I mean, some people never adjust."

"A few, maybe. But they're in the minority. The will to live can't be underestimated, Jane."

"That's what I'm counting on, I guess. Seth was always so—I don't know—full of life, happy, upbeat. It made me happy to be with him. We laughed a lot together."

"It'll be like that again."

Jane felt suddenly nervous. "Right now, Truman, he doesn't even want to live, much less laugh. I mean, he really doesn't want to live."

"Like I said, that's normal. Give him time."

"But—" Jane stopped and took a deep breath.

"Truman, he said if I loved him, I would help him die."

Truman's eyes, placid only a moment ago, now flashed anger. He leaned over the table again and laid both large hands on Jane's slim shoulders. "Now you listen to me, Jane. Are you listening?"

Jane nodded. She was rendered mute by his sudden surge of emotion.

"We never let anyone die. Never. Do you hear me?"

Another nod.

He squeezed her shoulders lightly. "Tell me you won't help him die. Promise me that."

She drew in her breath and let it out slowly. "Of course I won't."

"But do you promise?"

"Yes, I promise. I could never . . ."

She couldn't finish. For a moment they sat staring into each other's eyes, unable to look away. Finally he loosened his grip. His hands fell to his sides.

"I've got to go. Got to finish my rounds." He stood, stared off toward the hall.

"All right."

He took a few steps toward the door, then turned back. "Jane, I—"

"Yes?"

He started to say something, stopped, then said, "I'll see you later."

"All right."

She watched him walk away, her eyes moving with him as he shuffled past the row of windows and out of sight. She looked down at the half-empty pint of chocolate milk on the table. When she lifted it to her lips, her stomach turned. She threw it away and headed home.

— 10 —

Overhead, the stars flickered like far-off fire-storms while a half-moon squatted among them, pale and serene. Jane lay on a reclining lawn chair in the Penlands' backyard, one arm tucked beneath her head and one cradling Roscoe, who was curled up beside her. The other dog, Juniper, was stretched out on the grass beside the chair.

She had lost track of time—it might be mid-night, perhaps a little later. She knew she should go inside and go to bed, but she couldn't pull herself away from the radiant display in the sky.

"Well, Roscoe," she said, scratching the terrier behind one ear, "it's beautiful, but it makes you feel kind of small, doesn't it?"

Roscoe yawned and shifted position on the chair. His ears perked up a moment, and he seemed alert to some unseen danger, but deciding there was nothing there, he lowered his head to his paws, took a deep breath, and went back to sleep.

"Okay, so maybe you're too busy being content to worry about your place in the universe, huh?" Jane smiled briefly. "I think it's because you don't ask for much. Some food, a warm place to sleep, a little love, and you're good. Maybe that's the secret of a satisfied life."

Then again, Jane reflected, that was all she wanted for herself. Her dreams were simple. She wanted nothing beyond the basics—marriage, home, family, a little money in the bank. She was not like her mother, who wanted the world and despaired because she couldn't have it. *"Sometimes,"* Grandmother had said of Meredith Morrow, *"a driving ambition can steer you right into the grave."*

Apparently Meredith Morrow had wanted to continue her quest for fame through her only daughter. Jane was nine years old the year her mother took her to Raleigh to audition for a television commercial. Jane had wanted to do well for her mother's sake, had tried to push past the timidity and fear that had left her voice squeaking and her lips trembling, but she had failed miserably. Not only did she have no acting talent, but she couldn't remember a few simple lines. She'd been dismissed summarily with a callous wave of a hand and a voice hollering, *"Next!"*

Mother and daughter had trudged through a haze of shame on the way back to the car. Before

Meredith put the key in the ignition, she paused dramatically and said, *"Well, young lady, you just blew your chance to be somebody."* After that, the two of them rode home in agonizing silence. Meredith had been a star, or at least a starlet of some acclaim. Her daughter, on the other hand, would be a commoner, consigned to a life among the nobodies of the world.

Jane had stared out the window, not because she wanted to watch the scenery go by but because she wanted to hide her tears from her mother. She felt as though she ought to apologize for who she was. She felt even more strongly the urge to tell her mother she hated her for who *she* was. She wanted to scream that never in a million years would she want to be like Meredith Morrow, a sad old lady who drank too much and made everyone around her miserable.

But she didn't say anything.

Jane remembered that day as she lay there looking up at the night sky. From a distance of sixteen years, she could see the whole episode in sharp focus, could feel every ounce of pain and embarrassment and anger. Now she could see too, though, that maybe she and her mother finally had one thing in common: Their life dreams had been tampered with and left seemingly derailed.

But she didn't want to think about her mother or lost dreams or broken hearts. Not now, not with the whole Milky Way glittering overhead, a bejeweled crown on the brow of the earth. If she lay quietly enough and listened hard enough, she might hear the music of the spheres, the legendary songs sung by the stars themselves.

After a moment, surprisingly, she heard something. The words rose up like a mist in her mind, then hardened into song.

My Lord, what a morning
When the stars begin to fall . . .

The voice belonged to Laney, not to the cosmos. It was years ago; Laney was in the kitchen singing while kneading her homemade bread.

"Why will the stars begin to fall, Laney?" Jane had asked.

"Because, child, we won't need them anymore."

"We won't?"

"No. Won't need the moon either. Not even the sun. God himself will be our light."

She was always singing Negro spirituals and gospel songs. Songs about deep rivers and sweet chariots and freedom trains and bright mansions above. Young Jane would stand by the kitchen island, watching Laney's dark slender hands at work, listening to her sing, wondering what it was all about. *"Laney, why do all the songs sound so sad?"*

"The slaves—they had sad lives, Janie. Sad lives. But you know what? When you think about

it, you realize, they weren't singing so much about their sorrow as they were singing about their hope." Laney paused in her kneading and looked up smiling. *"Their bright and shining hope. That's what they sang about."*

That was what Jane most needed now. Hope. Bright and shining. And seemingly as elusive and unreachable as the stars.

"Come on, Roscoe," Jane said, nudging the dog. She pulled herself up from the lawn chair and stretched. "You too, Juniper. Let's go in. Time to get some sleep."

She walked across the dark lawn with Roscoe and Juniper prancing at her heels. As she thought about sleeping and waking up and going back to the hospital once again, she sensed an unwelcome heaviness inside. Even before she reached the house, she knew she was feeling something that she'd never before felt in relation to Seth.

In her heart was a tight and unmistakable knot of dread.

— 11 —

Seth wasn't in his room, but one of the aides was there putting fresh linens on the bed. He snapped open a clean white sheet and let it drift down over the fitted sheet already hugging the mattress.

He must have noticed Jane out of the corner of his eye, because he paused in the midst of smoothing out the wrinkles with his thin dark hands. He looked up at her and smiled. "Hello, Miss Jane. You looking for Mr. Seth?"

"Yes, um, let's see. You're Sausalito, right?"

He shook his head and laughed quietly. "No, I'm Hangson Bwambale. Or as they say it in English, Hoboken. My cousin is Sausalito."

"Oh. I'm sorry."

"No, no. It doesn't matter. As we say, we answer to either name."

"Well, you're good sports, then. People should at least try to learn your real names."

Hoboken chuckled again and shrugged. "It doesn't matter."

"So you don't mind being called Hoboken?"

"Not at all. One day I will visit this great city in New Jersey that I'm named after." He finished tucking in the sheet and reached for a pillowcase from a pile of linens on the chair.

"Hmm," Jane said, leaning one shoulder against the doorframe of Seth's room. "You might be disappointed. I've never been to Hoboken, but it's not known as one of our country's great vacation spots."

"But it's close to New York City, right? I hear that's the greatest city in the world. I'll visit there too, right after I see Hoboken."

Jane nodded. "That might make the trip worthwhile, then."

"Of course the trip would be worthwhile, Miss Jane. I hope to see many places in America before I return to Uganda. This is a most amazing country, you know. In the short time I've been here, I've grown to love it almost as much as my own."

"Really?"

"Really." He smiled. "You know the song you have, 'God Bless America'?"

"Yes?"

"Well, God—He has blessed America, even though many people here don't know it or don't believe it."

Jane thought a moment. "I suppose we take so much for granted."

Hoboken tucked a pillow under his chin and worked the pillowcase over it. "Yes. Sometimes . . . what do you say? It's hard to see the forest for the trees. But these people"—he dropped the pillow on the bed and waved a hand—"they know. That's why I am happy to work here. The men and women I help take care of, they were willing to fight to help defend the blessings."

Jane pushed herself away from the doorframe and took one step into the room. "That's a nice way to put it, Hoboken. I'm going to remember that. So many people think this war is senseless and that our troops are being wounded and killed for no reason. If they're right, that makes Seth's injury so much harder to accept."

Hoboken looked kindly at Jane as he shook his head. "I've never known of any war that made sense, Miss Jane. To me, they all begin for a reason that is senseless. Greed. Power. Just plain hate. You know? All these things are evil." He paused as he laid a thin woven blanket across the foot of the bed. "I know many Americans thought the war in Vietnam was senseless too, and when the soldiers came home, they were scorned for a war they didn't start. That is . . . what do you say? That is barking up the wrong tree."

"Barking up the wrong tree?" echoed Jane.

"Yes. Soldiers don't start the war. They only do what they are told to do by their country, even if it means a great sacrifice for them. That's why I admire them—the people I work for here. I am proud of all my patients."

"You're a wise man, Hoboken."

He shook his head. "Not so wise, I'm afraid. Just a simple man who hopes he has the same kind of courage if I ever need it. Some people might feel sorry for Mr. Seth, but not me." He shook his head again. "I am proud of him."

"Thank you," Jane said. "I'm proud of him too."

Hoboken picked up the remaining linens on the chair and moved around the bed. "And I know you came to see him," he said, laughing lightly, "not to listen to me. So without further ado"—a flash of white teeth—"I will tell you that Mr. Seth is out on the porch."

"Out on the porch?" Jane echoed.

"Yes, there's a screened-in porch at the end of the other hall. Go back to the nurses' station and turn left. You'll find it."

"Okay. Thanks, Hoboken."

"You're welcome, Miss Jane."

The porch ran the length of the building and provided an airy alternative to the sterile confines of the ward. Wicker chairs and ceiling fans gave it a homey appearance, making it a popular haven for patients, nurses, and aides. Even now, a number of men in wheelchairs were parked there, chatting among themselves and with the aides who were assigned to accompany them. Jane's gaze traveled from face to face, a winged hope looking for a place to land. As soon as she saw Seth, the dread she'd felt last night began to lift, replaced by the familiar ache of joy.

She went to him and kissed his forehead. Seth gave her a passive glance in return. "I see you've come back for more."

"I wanted to know how you're doing today."

"Ready to run a marathon, as you can see."

Jane winced as she glanced at the aide in the wicker chair beside him. She was young and pretty, hardly more than a teenager, fresh and full of life. She seemed a strange contradiction, sitting there among all the broken soldiers.

"Here, take this chair," she said to Jane, jumping up and waving a hand.

"Are you sure?" Jane asked.

The aide nodded. "So long as someone's with him, it's all right. I'll wait over there till you finish visiting."

With that, she moved away, leaving Jane and Seth alone in the middle of the crowded porch. "Nice girl," Jane said.

Seth didn't respond.

Jane sat down and, sighing, looked off toward the hospital grounds. She was well aware of Seth's body beside her, heavy and inert, stretched out in the huge padded wheelchair, his head cradled in a headrest, his arms and hands lying flat on the armrests.

She hated that chair. She hated that he was in it. She hated the sniper's bullet that had stolen his body and their dreams. She wanted the life they had before, wanted it desperately.

Jane sighed again, and even as she did, she heard Laney's voice: *Well, child, as Mamma always said, life's gearshift's got no reverse, so you have to just keep moving forward.*

She turned to Seth and took a deep breath. "You know, Seth," she said, "everyone on this floor has a spinal cord injury. You're not the only one."

"So?" He avoided her gaze.

"Do you ever talk to anyone else, just to see how they're coping? I mean, it might help to talk to other people who are going through the same thing."

Seth was quiet a moment before saying, "Sure, I talk to the guys. How can I avoid it? But what you don't understand is that it's different for everyone."

"But there must be some common ground—"

"Most of the guys on the floor—their injuries are lower. They might have lost the use of their legs, but at least they still have their arms." Seth paused again, another long moment. His face sank a shade deeper into pain as he added, "And their hands."

Jane nodded. One look around the porch showed many of the men able to wheel their own chairs, talk on cell phones, scratch their own noses. None of which Seth was able to do.

"If I had my hands," Seth went on, "I could keep on working. It wouldn't be impossible for me to at least do some carpentry work."

She couldn't disagree. "I know, Seth." She laid a hand over one of his. It was large and warm and unresponsive.

"I can't feel that, you know," Seth said.

Jane nodded. She willed herself not to cry.

Seth finally turned his face toward her and locked on to her gaze. "Nights are the best, Jane," he whispered.

"What do you mean?"

"The dreams," he said. He looked up at the ceiling and swallowed hard. "When I'm asleep, I'm whole again. I mean, I know I've been shot, just like in Iraq, but it doesn't matter. In my dreams I can still walk. I can sit down and stand back up. My arms and legs do whatever I want them to do, and . . . I don't know, I'm me again. I'm who I was before."

He glanced at Jane. She nodded for him to go on.

"In most of my dreams, I'm working again. I'm using the saw or the drill or the wood plane, and it's all so real, I can feel the texture of the wood, and I can smell the sawdust."

Jane remembered briefly how she used to kid him, how she used to say he loved the scent of sawdust more than any perfume she might wear. He laughed and said it wasn't so, but she threatened to carry wood shavings in her pockets if he didn't comment on her choice of fragrance once in a while. "So," she said now, "you can smell the sawdust?"

"Yeah." He nodded. "I can actually smell it, and I can tell whether the wood I'm working with is pine or cedar or walnut. But then I wake up . . ."

His voice trailed off. He blinked several times.

"You wake up," Jane said, "and it must seem like real life is a nightmare."

He nodded again. A small vein throbbed at his temple. "Sometimes, Jane, I dream I'm hugging you. And the thing that's the most real is you put your cheek against mine, and I can feel your skin and how soft it is." He moved his gaze to her

90

again. "Will you put your cheek next to mine? I want to feel you again."

Jane pulled her chair closer and leaned toward him. She pressed her cheek against one of his, while cupping his other cheek in the palm of her hand. Their tears met and mingled on the pallet of their warm flesh.

"I want to live, Jane," Seth whispered. "I do want to live. But not like this."

— 12 —

She went to the gazebo in the hopes that Truman Rockaway might be there. He wasn't, not at first. But he showed up shortly afterward, as though he knew she needed his company.

He nodded as he sat down on the bench across from her. For a moment they sat in silence. Truman's elbows rested on his thighs and his hands were folded, as though in prayer. Then he spoke. "You've just come from seeing Seth."

"Yes." She couldn't look at him. If she did, she would cry.

Truman drew himself up and put a hand over each knee. He took a deep breath. "I'd like to tell you a story, if I may."

"Sure," Jane said quietly. "Go ahead."

Truman rubbed his knees a moment and

91

frowned in thought. Then he said, "It might explain . . . well . . . my behavior yesterday in the canteen."

"All right. I'm listening."

He cleared his throat. "It was 1946," he began. "I was fifteen years old and the eldest of seven children. At that time my father was a bale breaker at one of the textile mills there in the Upcountry, and my mother was a maid in the house of the mill owner, a Mr. Evans. Now, my mother and father were both intelligent people, but being black in the South . . . well, they simply had no opportunity. Jim Crow was in full swing back then. Jim Crow was the law, designed to keep us Negro folk in our place.

"Our place was one of poverty, of course. We didn't have much, other than each other, and my mother's books. The little house we lived in just outside of Travelers Rest—it had no running water, no electricity, no heat other than the wood-stove. But we had books. Plenty of those. See, Mrs. Evans—she saw my mother had an interest in reading and in learning. Since Mrs. Evans had been a teacher at one time, she knew the importance of a good education. For whatever reason, she decided she was going to see to it that Mamma's children had a chance at learning. She was pretty forward thinking for a white woman, as most white folks thought blacks weren't capable of learning much. But Mrs. Evans—she gave Mamma all kinds of books, told her to bring them home and read them to us, everything from literature to philosophy to science."

"Truman," Jane interrupted, "didn't you go to school?"

"Oh yes." Truman nodded. "We went to the school for Negro children. But tell you the truth, we learned more at home from those books Mrs. Evans sent us. Not that the teachers at the school weren't good. They were. They were fine teachers and fine people. But we just didn't have the resources that the white school had.

"So as I say, my family—we had each other, and we had a pile of books. I guess that's about my best memory of those days, sitting around in the evenings, listening to Mamma and Daddy read to us by the light of the kerosene lamp. We'd memorize passages of Shakespeare and all kinds of poems and even chapters of the Bible. We'd make a contest out of it, see who could memorize the most and recite it without making any mis-takes." Truman paused and laughed lightly. "Being the oldest, I always thought I had to be the best, but my brothers and sisters, they gave me a run for my money. I had to work hard to outdo any of them. I spent hours by myself, reading and memorizing and reciting and—"

He stopped himself and looked up. "I'm getting sidetracked, Jane. This isn't what I meant to tell you."

Jane offered him an encouraging smile. "That's all right. I like the picture of all of you gathered together like that. I don't imagine that kind of thing happens very much today."

"No, I suppose not. Times have changed since then, some ways for the better, some ways not. But here's what I wanted to tell you," Truman said. "That autumn of 1946, the youngest of us, my brother Daniel, was two years old. He was a little fellow. He'd been born somewhat prematurely, but otherwise he was all right. And he was a happy boy. He had a way of lighting up the room when he smiled, and he smiled a lot.

"Well, one night when we were eating supper, something hit him. One minute he was fine and the next he was shaking with fever and complaining of an ache in his jaw. We didn't have any real medicines at home back then, just some herbs my grandmother collected and made teas out of. She had a tea for whatever ailed you, whether it was toothache or migraine or a sprained ankle. That's how it was for us, and it was the old women mostly who kept the traditions alive, picking leaves and making poultices out of this or that. You had pneumonia, your grandmother would take a rag and cook some meal on it and put turpentine in that and then wrap your chest up with it and wait for you to get better."

"Did it work?" Jane asked.

"Sometimes," Truman said with a shrug. "Sometimes not. There's no medical reason for some of these things to work, other than the power of suggestion."

Jane hesitated, both wanting and not wanting to know. Finally, she asked, "What about Daniel? What happened to him?"

Truman nodded curtly, looked down at his hands. They were clenched together in his lap now. "We tried everything."

"What about a doctor?"

"That's what I'm getting at, Jane. Two days of herbal tea and poultices, and he was only getting worse. The skin on the side of his face was red and tight, and his fever was raging. He was really only semiconscious the morning Mamma took him to the doctor. We didn't have a car. I had to push him to the doctor's office in a wheelbarrow. We laid him in blankets, and he whimpered as I pushed him along the dirt road toward town.

"We had no black doctor to take him to, of course. There was only the white doctor. There were two waiting rooms, one for whites, the other for blacks. Only after all the whites had been attended to would the doctor see any of the black folks who'd come in. That is, he'd see them if there was time. If it was late in the day and time for his supper, he'd send the Negro folk home and tell them to come back in the morning."

"Is that what happened, Truman?"

"Yes. He wouldn't see Daniel, though my

mother begged him. 'Just take a minute, sir. Please, just give us a minute of your time, Dr. Coleman, sir.' But he refused. He sent us away, along with the other black folks in the office that day. He said we could try the county hospital if we wanted to. Well, instead of going to the hospital directly, we walked three miles to Mrs. Evans's house near the mill village. Mamma thought Mrs. Evans might be able to help."

"And did she?"

"She took one look at Daniel, and she piled all of us into her car and drove us to the county hospital herself. We turned some heads that day, the four of us coming into the emergency room, three Negroes and a white woman demanding we be seen. She was a brave woman, that Mrs. Evans." Truman almost smiled. "One of the earliest pioneers in civil rights in the Upcountry. Not many would have stormed the ER, demanding that a little Negro boy be seen."

Jane leaned forward on the bench. She gazed at Truman intently. "So was he seen? Did a doctor see him?"

"Eventually. We were there about two hours when a doctor came out to the waiting room and looked at him. That was all he did. Didn't even touch him, just looked down at him lying there in Mamma's lap and said, 'Take him home and keep him hydrated. He should be better in twenty-four hours.'

"Well, he turned to go, and Mrs. Evans jumped up from her chair and grabbed his arm and said, 'Is that all?' He looked angry and said, 'What more do you want?' Mrs. Evans said, 'I want tests done. I want to know what's wrong with this baby.' And the doctor said, 'Who are you anyway, that you come in here telling us what to do?' Well, that Mrs. Evans, she straightened herself up real tall and said, 'I'm Mrs. Ernest Evans. My husband owns the mill where half this town is employed.' We were all hoping that might impress the doctor, but it didn't. 'Well, that doesn't make you or Mr. Evans a doctor, now does it?' he said. 'I don't need to do any tests to know this boy has a common fever and all he needs is rest and fluids. Now if you'll excuse me, I have sick people to attend to.' 'Sick *white* people, I suppose,' Mrs. Evans said, but by the time she got the words out, the doctor was already gone.

"Mrs. Evans drove us home. She gave us a bottle of aspirin that she had in her pocketbook, and she told Mamma she didn't have to come to work until Daniel was better. She said she'd come back the next day to see how Daniel was doing.

"Mamma, Daddy, and I took turns holding Daniel all night. We held him and prayed. Oh, how we prayed, asking God to take the fever away, to make our little Daniel better. We sent the other children to bed, but the three of us stayed awake, rocking Daniel, keeping watch, praying.

We knew he needed water, and we tried to give him something to drink, but we couldn't get him to wake up. He had slipped into something of a coma. We couldn't even give him any of the aspirin Mrs. Evans had left with us.

"The kerosene lamp burned all night. I was holding Daniel, rocking him, when he died at daybreak. He died in my arms, and I felt him go. I pulled his body to me, and I begged him to come back, but he was gone. Mamma and Daddy had both been trying to get a little rest, but soon as they heard me crying, they came and saw that Daniel was dead. You never heard such wailing, Jane. You never heard such heartbreak." When Truman looked up at Jane, he had tears in his eyes.

"Oh, Truman," Jane said, "I'm so sorry. I can't begin to imagine. Do you think, if he was sick today—do you think he might have lived?"

"He would have lived then, Jane, if he'd been properly diagnosed and treated."

"What do you mean?"

"I mean, looking back, my guess is that Daniel had cellulitis. It's a simple bacterial infection that today is treated with any number of antibiotics, but even back then, it might have been treated with penicillin or even quinine or sulfa. If it isn't treated, the infection can spread and become septic. That alone can kill you. I don't know for sure, but in Daniel's case, since the infection was on his face, it might have spread to his brain and developed into meningitis. I'm not sure he showed all the symptoms of meningitis, but I don't know, I wasn't a doctor then. I was just a kid myself. A kid who had to watch his brother die for no good reason other than that he was black."

Jane waited a moment before asking, "Is that why you became a doctor?"

Truman gazed beyond her shoulder as he answered. "When Daniel died, that started me thinking maybe I could become a doctor so I could be there for the black folks, so they could see a doctor when they needed one. When I went to Korea and lived day in and day out with the wounded and the dying—that's when I really became serious about medicine. After I was discharged, I went to Fisk University on the GI Bill, and eventually I attended Meharry Medical College, both in Nashville." He put his elbows on his knees and leaned forward. "But my point is this, Jane. We don't let people die, not so long as there's still hope. No matter how you look at it, it's just plain wrong."

Jane thought a moment. "We don't let children die, of course. Not children who could go on and live normal lives."

"And what's a normal life? Life in any form is precious."

"Truman, I know you're talking about Seth. But for someone like him, someone who can't do anything for himself—wouldn't it be more merciful just to let him go?"

Truman looked at Jane a long time before saying, "What do you think, Jane?"

"Honestly, I don't know what to think." She shook her head. "He says he wants to live, but not the way he is now. I mean, he's a carpenter who can't use his hands. That part of his life is over for good. That part of him is dead. Maybe it would be better, more merciful . . ."

When she didn't finish, Truman said, "Who's to say what mercy is? Maybe mercy kept him alive instead of allowing him to die."

"Oh, I know, I know." Jane put her head back and sighed. "I should be happy he's alive. *He* should be happy he's alive. But maybe mercy, whatever that is, should have kept him from being shot in the first place. I tried to pray for Seth, I really did. I asked God to protect him. They always talk about God being merciful, and yet it seems no matter what you ask for, He always lets the hardest things happen."

"He *is* merciful, Jane, *and* He lets the hardest things happen, which in itself might be a mercy. Who are we to say?"

Jane didn't respond. Truman stood. "I'm going to go finish my rounds now. I'll stop by Seth's room, see how he's doing."

Jane nodded.

"You'll be all right?" he asked.

She looked at him then, directly in the eye. "You say we don't let people die so long as there's hope. Where is Seth's hope now, Truman?"

Truman, looking thoughtful, nodded once. "That's exactly the right question, Jane," he said. "But only Seth himself can tell you the answer."

He laid a strong hand on Jane's shoulder, then left to make his rounds.

— 13 —

Roscoe and Juniper, tails wagging, met Jane at the door. Otherwise the house was quiet. Diana and Carl had caught the seven o'clock flight to Heathrow that morning and would be in Europe the rest of the summer. Jane was on her own now, free to make herself at home in the big rambling house on Montford Avenue.

Jane shivered. The house was filled with books, Carl's paintings and sculptures, antique furniture collected by Diana and her parents, and yet it seemed overwhelmingly empty. She wasn't afraid to be alone, but she deeply feared loneliness. It was a sinkhole, sure to trap her if she wasn't careful.

She dropped her pocketbook on the kitchen table and looked around the room. Where to go? What to do? She moved from the kitchen to the dining room to the den at the back of the house, where she sat down in the overstuffed chair by the empty fireplace. The room was small and cozy, with a fieldstone hearth, large braided rug, built-in bookcases jammed with aging volumes. She called for the dogs, who came running. She patted her lap and they both jumped up, licking her chin briefly before curling into a nap.

"Well, at least I have you guys," Jane said, stroking their fur. Both dogs sighed contentedly.

Jane leaned her head back and shut her eyes. What an amazing thing contentment was! She remembered the day she felt all was right with her world, the day her dreams and her life lined up with each other and fell into place. It was the day Seth proposed, not quite a year ago.

"I'll pick you up at nine tomorrow morning," he'd said the night before. "And be sure to wear your walking shoes."

"But where are we going?"

He shook his head and gave her a crooked smile. "You'll see."

At nine o'clock on that July morning, he pulled into the circular drive of the Rayburn House and honked the horn.

"When will you be back?" Gram asked.

"I don't know," Jane said with a laugh. "I don't even know where we're going."

And so they had driven, on and on, taking

Route 40 more than a hundred miles toward Asheville, but cutting off onto 64 and heading south toward Ruth and west again toward Lake Lure before finally arriving in the little tourist town of Chimney Rock. The town was a narrow strip of restaurants and souvenir shops nestled in a gorge with an expanse of mountains on either side. The Rocky Broad River cut a natural divide between the town and Chimney Rock Park, a vast stretch of mountain trails and waterfalls, the pinnacle of which was the 315-foot monolith for which the park was named.

Seth drove through the entrance to the park and over the bridge to the parking lot. When he opened the door for Jane, he pointed to the rocky spire and said, "That's our destination."

Jane put her head back full tilt and shielded her eyes from the sun. She had long known about Chimney Rock, of course, but she'd never been there. More than two thousand feet up, on top of the jut of rock that, in fact, looked like a chimney sprouting up out of the mountain, an enormous American flag rippled in the wind. "We're going up there?" she asked.

"Come on," he said, taking her hand and twining her fingers with his.

To get there, they walked through a lighted tunnel cut into the mountain and entered the elevator that would take them to the Sky Lounge at the base of the spire.

"I've heard this elevator goes up the height of twenty-six stories," Seth said casually.

"Really?" Jane said, chewing her lip. "Did I ever tell you I'm scared of heights?"

Seth only smiled. The elevator doors opened, and they walked through the Sky Lounge out into the open air and the wind. The sun was high in the sky, reaching toward noon. Jane squeezed Seth's hand more tightly as they walked the trail to the base of the metal stairway leading up to the top of the rock.

Jane put her hand on the railing and froze.

"Don't be afraid," Seth said. "I'm right beside you."

She looked up into his eyes and, after a moment and a few deep breaths, gave a small nod. "I'm ready."

Up they climbed, step after dizzying step, the wind strong at their backs, the sun warm on their heads. "Don't look down at the stairs," Seth said. "Keep your head up."

Seth was right. The stairway was open, and down was very far down indeed. Sweat moistened Jane's palms, but she lifted her chin and concentrated on the top, the flag, the open cloudless sky.

And then they were at the top where the Blue Ridge Mountains stretched out toward a horizon that was miles upon miles away. The view was an immeasurable span of green, broken to the southeast by the shining blue of Lake Lure. Jane had the sense that she was soaring without wings, that she was viewing what for centuries had belonged only to the birds and the angels.

She and Seth stood silently for several minutes, their arms about each other but their faces turned outward. Jane wanted to say something about the beauty of it all, but there were no words to describe it, not a single one that would do it justice. Surely there was no more glorious place in all the world.

When someone finally spoke, it was Seth. "You may be wondering why I called this meeting," he said.

She looked up at him and laughed. He didn't join her. He seemed suddenly nervous.

"Well," he went on, "it's just that I wanted to be on top of the world with you . . . or kind of, anyway, when I asked you to be my wife."

She was momentarily stunned. "What?" she asked.

"My wife, Jane. I'm asking you to marry me."

Her eyes widened. "You are?"

He released his hand from her waist and dug around in his shirt pocket. "I hope it fits," he said.

She took the ring and tried it on. The diamond flashed in the sun.

"Does it fit?"

"Yes. Perfectly."

"Will you be my wife, then?"

She wanted to say yes, but she couldn't speak. She was laughing and crying at the same time while Seth kissed her forehead and brushed away her tears with his thumbs.

Jane smiled even now as she thought about it. On that day, July 12, 2003, she was completely satisfied. She was satisfied not only in what was but in what was to come. Because even the future was tucked into the moment; she could see it all so clearly, their children, their home, their happiness. She could see it just as though it were all right there with her on the heights of Chimney Rock.

But the satisfaction was brief, and now everything was different. Seth had gone off to war, and together the two of them had tumbled down the mountain.

Jane nudged the dogs off her lap and rose from the chair. Across the room, the Penlands' liquor cabinet beckoned. Jane walked to the cabinet and looked through the glass doors at the bottles lined up inside. She remembered how, when her mother died, she had sworn never to do what her mother had done in the final years of her life. She would never dull her heartache with drink. When she grew older, though, she had failed. Those years at college especially, when she had let the drink burn her throat and soothe her heart. Her friends all thought they were simply having fun.

Jane knew otherwise. She wasn't looking for fun; she was looking for peace.

She hadn't had a drink since the day Seth proposed. She'd made no conscious decision about it; she simply had no need for it anymore. It was easy to leave behind. After all, in Seth she had every-thing she wanted. The hollow place in her heart had been filled.

Jane lifted her hand to the cabinet and hesitated a moment. At one time the stuff inside had worked very well to ease the pain. And heaven knew she was in a world of pain right now.

She turned the knob, opened the cabinet door, and after reading the labels on the bottles, she reached for one.

— 14 —

Jon-Paul Pearcy was at the piano, singing a duet with a one-armed sailor who had a voice as smooth as gravel and a smile as big as the moon. They had drawn an audience and were hamming it up as they harmonized on "Some Enchanted Evening" from the Rodgers and Hammerstein musical *South Pacific*.

Jane hung back and watched. She had no choice; to reach the piano she'd have to elbow her way through the crowd. She could only suppose that those at the VA today hadn't expected to be serenaded, so when the song started they had flocked to the piano, only too glad to have the reprieve from the medical routine of their lives.

With the sailor crooning loudly just inches from his ear, Jon-Paul looked as though he was straining to stay on key. He must have faltered, because he broke out in laughter even as he sang. The sailor waved his one hand in the air, inviting the crowd to join in on the last line. In that moment the lobby became stage to a motley and unlikely choir, with nearly everyone lifting whatever voice they had in the grand finale: "Nev . . . er . . . let . . . her . . . GO!"

The room erupted in cheers, applause, and piercing wolf whistles. Even Jane couldn't help smiling. The sailor stood and bowed, enjoying the admiration. He leaned over and said a few words to Jon-Paul, slapped him on the back, and meandered off on the arm of a pretty nurse. With that, the spectators dispersed, heading off to appointments in the clinics, to visit loved ones in the hospital, or perhaps to head back to their rooms in the community center where Truman lived.

Jane stayed, hesitating only a moment before stepping to the piano. Jon-Paul was chatting with an elderly man, but when the man moved on, Jane stepped in.

"Hello, Jon-Paul."

The young man turned toward the sound of her voice, frowning slightly. Only then did Jane remember he couldn't see her.

"It's Jane Morrow. I met you the other day."

"Oh yes." Jon-Paul brightened in recognition. "Jane. How are you?"

How was she? She had awakened that morning with a headache, a queasy stomach, and a rock-solid disgust that she had drunk enough rum and Coke to get that way.

"I'm fine," she said. "And you?"

"I'm doing great. What's up? You been visiting with . . . um . . ."

"Seth. Not yet. I'm on my way to see him but . . . I wonder, do you mind if I ask you a question?"

"Ask away."

"It may be none of my business."

"If it isn't, I'll tell you so." He smiled.

She took a breath and said quietly, "I was wondering whether you were born blind."

He cocked his head at that, and two lines formed between his brows. "Actually, no," he said. "I lost my sight gradually, beginning when I was a teenager."

"I see." Then, alarmed, she added, "Oh! I mean . . . I guess that's not the right expression to use."

Jon-Paul laughed agreeably. "It's all right. I use the expression myself, even though I don't see. Or at least, I don't see very well. I do still have some vision, mostly peripheral. But . . ." He paused a moment, as though trying to discern Jane's reason for asking. "Look," he said, "would you like to go talk somewhere?"

"Well, I don't want to keep you. You probably need to get back to work."

He shrugged. "I'm my own boss, so far as that goes."

"All right, then. There's a canteen where we could sit. Maybe you've seen it? Oh! I mean—"

Jon-Paul waved a hand and stood. He picked up his folded cane from the piano bench, but he didn't open it. Instead he slipped a hand into the crook of Jane's arm. "Lead the way," he said.

Jane fed the vending machine enough change for a couple of sodas—a Coca-Cola for her and a Dr. Pepper for him. She carried them, an icy-cold aluminum can in each hand, to the table where the tall young man in the suit and tie sat waiting. She placed the soda in front of him and wondered whether she should pull the tab, but before she could decide, he had popped it himself and was taking a long drink.

"Guess I was thirsty," he said absently. "Must have been that duet."

Jane laughed lightly as she stared at his eyes. They were clear and bright and such a stunning shade of blue she couldn't believe they didn't work as well as her own. He was in fact looking at her; she felt the illusion of eye contact even knowing he couldn't see her face. She marveled to think a person might have an entire conversation with Jon-Paul Pearcy without realizing he was blind.

"I hope you don't mind my asking," she said. "About your blindness, I mean."

"Not at all." He took another long swallow and settled the can back on the table. "I have a pretty good idea why you'd like to know, since you're engaged to a man who's also suffered a loss."

"Yes."

"So what would you like to know?"

"Can you just tell me the story of how you went blind?"

Jon-Paul nodded. "You probably won't believe me if I tell you I once had perfect vision." He paused, as though he expected her to say something.

She tried to travel with him back to that time in his life, but it was difficult to imagine. "You didn't even wear glasses?" she asked.

"Nope. Didn't need them. I was fine. That's why it came as such a shock when I started losing my sight. It was completely unexpected. And because it came on so gradually, I wouldn't let myself believe it was happening for a couple of years. I tried to convince myself that what I was seeing was normal."

"What were you seeing? What was it like?"

"It started with small things back in high school. At first it was simply that I couldn't see the blackboard in school as well. And then I started holding my textbooks closer to my face. And I had to lean closer to the sheet music when I was learning a new piece on the piano. I hid it from my parents, though. I never complained, and no one knew, so I was never taken to get my eyes checked. I was acting like a normal kid, and I just wanted to *be* a normal kid. I had my driver's license, I played sports, I dated the cheerleaders." He paused and laughed, but it petered off to a sad smile. "And then I went to college. By then I'd decided the life of a classical musician wasn't for me. I went to Duke to study Premed, believe it or not. Dad, of course, wanted me to join him in the family business, but I didn't want to be a lawyer. I guess I was a bit of a maverick. I wanted to be different, do my own thing. Besides, I was always fascinated by the way the human body works. Not just the remarkable way it works when it's healthy, but the way it was created to heal. You know, broken bones mend. The immune system suppresses disease. White blood cells battle infection. The possibility of healing seemed a great tribute to the Creator, that He would grace our bodies with a means of restoration. I always found that intriguing. I wanted to contribute to that healing process by picking up where the human body left off, helping when a body needed help in coming back around to health."

He stopped and took a sip of Dr. Pepper. "I suppose it sounds a little crazy."

Jane shook her head. "Not at all. I never thought about it that way. I guess I've always taken the body's ability to heal for granted."

"Most of us do, I think," Jon-Paul said. "We don't know how blessed we are to be given multiple chances to go on living."

They were quiet a moment. Jane waited. At length she said, "So then what happened?"

"Oh." Jon-Paul raised his brows momentarily as Jane nudged him back to his story. "So I went to college, and during my freshman year, things got worse. By the end of the first semester, I couldn't see the blackboard at all. I finally admitted to myself something was wrong. I guess it was handy I was right there at Duke, because my parents arranged for me to be seen at the Duke Eye Center. The doctor there put me through a battery of tests, and when he was done, he told me I had Stargardt's Disease. I didn't even know what it was. I'd never heard of it. My parents asked him what the plan of action was, and he said there wasn't one. I was going blind, and there was nothing anyone could do about it."

Jane sat in stunned silence a moment, trying to imagine how he must have felt. Finally she whispered, "How awful."

"Yeah," Jon-Paul said. "It was pretty awful. His

announcement signaled the end of life as I knew it. Ironically, the body is able to heal itself in so many ways, but not with this disease. So there I was, eighteen years old, just kind of watching my sight slip away and wondering where I was going to end up when it was gone."

She had to stop herself from reaching out to take his hand. Words tumbled through her mind as she searched for the right ones to say. Not *I'm sorry*, but something else. Something reassuring. "And yet," she ventured, "you've done so well. You must have come to accept it."

He frowned in thought. "I wouldn't say I've ever come to accept it, but I'm coping with it. I still get frustrated. Some days I even feel the same sense of loss I felt when I first heard the name Stargardt's. I miss things like being independent and driving myself around. I miss reading a book that I'm holding in my hands. I miss looking out over the mountains in the fall when the leaves are changing. There's so much I miss even now, but at the same time I have to believe that there's a purpose for all of this." He paused again, took another long sip from the can of Dr. Pepper. "I believe I told you I specialize in disability law, so I have a lot of dealings with disabled folks. Also, I do volunteer work on behalf of the blind. So I think I've done some good for others who are disabled or who have gone through a loss of some kind. I hope so, anyway."

Jane took a deep breath. "I'm sure you have."

Jon-Paul gave a small nod. "So now, about your fiancé. You say he was shot?"

"Yes. In the neck. It left him a quadriplegic."

"I see. And now he thinks his life is over."

"Well, yes. And I guess in some ways it is. I mean, the life we'd planned . . . well, see, he's a carpenter. Or *was* a carpenter. His whole career revolved around working with his hands. Now . . ." Jane's voice trailed off as she gave a shrug.

"Not much hope of that at this point, I suppose."

"No. None. You were able to go into a different field. I'm sure it wasn't easy to make the change, especially since your interest was medicine. And yet you did make the change, and you've been successful. But for Seth, the options seem so limited. I don't know what he'll do with his life now."

Jon-Paul didn't respond. He appeared deep in thought.

Jane said, "Do you think Seth can come to terms with what happened to him?"

"Well, I'll tell you, Jane, it's never easy, but it's always possible. What I've seen in my experience is this: After the initial shock and grief, people start taking inventory of what they have left, and they begin to concentrate on what they *can* do rather than what they *can't.* It seems to be part of our ability to heal. Sometimes the healing isn't

115

in body but in spirit and mind. And that's just as important, if not more so."

When Jane didn't respond, Jon-Paul asked, "Listen, what else does Seth enjoy? I mean, beside carpentry. What are his interests?"

"His interests? Well, he loved the outdoors. He liked to hike and camp and fish. He really enjoyed fly-fishing." She looked at Jon-Paul, who nodded just as though he could see her gaze. "He liked to watch NASCAR racing with his dad. They'd sit around for hours watching those cars go around and around on the TV screen, and I mean, they were excited about it. I used to kid him. I told him I knew I was going to end up a racing widow just like his mom, and he said yeah, I'd just have to get used to it."

Jane laughed lightly. Jon-Paul smiled. "Anything else?"

"He was great at chess. He was captain of the chess team back in high school when the team went on to the state championship. They won too."

"Chess, huh?" Jon-Paul lifted a hand to his chin. "Believe it or not, I was pretty good at chess myself once."

"Oh, and he liked kids. He was really good with kids. He was always involved with them in one way or another—volunteering at the Y, working at summer camps, things like that. There was a program for troubled youth at the

116

community center, and Seth volunteered to teach woodworking there. It seemed to go over really well. I mean, they all liked him. In fact, I never met a kid who didn't love him." Jane's eyes welled up, making her self-conscious until she remembered Jon-Paul couldn't see her tears. Her voice dropped a notch when she said, "We were going to have a bunch of kids ourselves, you know."

Jon-Paul didn't answer. Instead, he did what she had wanted to do for him earlier. Somehow, perhaps out of what remained of his peripheral vision, he found her hand on the table and covered it with his own. He squeezed gently. Only after several long minutes did he let go.

When Jane finally reached the fifth floor, Seth was napping. He looked serene and satisfied in sleep. His features were relaxed, his face untroubled, just as before the war. She could almost believe he would awaken and get up out of the bed. She remembered then what he had said, that when he was sleeping, he was whole again.

She turned away from his bedside and walked back down the hall.

— 15 —

When she arrived at the hospital the following afternoon, Seth was awake. He wasn't alone. Sausalito was in the chair beside the bed, a laptop computer balanced on his knees as he pecked away slowly at the keyboard. "And when you come . . ." Sausalito muttered as he typed.

Jane stepped into the room and, smiling, asked curiously, "What are you guys doing?"

Seth rolled his eyes toward her. "I'm dictating my last will and testament to Sausalito."

The aide laughed as he looked up from the computer. "Don't believe him, Miss Jane. He's sending an e-mail to his folks."

"Is that your computer, Seth?"

"Yeah. Mom and Dad brought it last weekend. Guess you haven't seen it."

Jane shook her head. "Nice. Good idea. It'll make it easier to stay in touch with them."

"It'd be even easier if I could use the thing myself. I have to bother Sausalito here to come in and play secretary."

The young Ugandan laughed again. Jane liked the way his whole face opened up with delight. "That's all right, Mr. Seth," he said. "I'd rather be typing your e-mail than emptying bedpans. Now, tell me again what you wanted your mother to bring."

"The Nikes. They're in the hall closet."

"Okay. Please bring the—rats!"

"Bring the rats?" Seth echoed.

"Where'd it go?" Sausalito's hands flew up from the keyboard as he stared at the screen in disbelief. "It's gone! The computer sent the e-mail, and I wasn't finished!"

Seth sighed heavily, but Jane was relieved to see that he was trying to suppress a smile. "Sausalito, my man, what kind of secretary are you? You're fired. Get Hoboken in here. He can do a better job."

Sausalito shook his head. "He's not working today. You're stuck with me. You will have to dock my pay."

"I'll do that. And I'm taking away your Christmas bonus too."

"All right, Mr. Seth, but you are a cruel task-master. I ought to quit."

"You ought to, but you won't."

"That's right. I'm too dedicated."

"No. You just know no one else will hire you."

Sausalito threw his head back and howled in amusement. "Oh, Mr. Seth, you are right! No one else would be so stupid . . . I mean, so kind as to hire me as his secretary. I had better throw in my lot with you rather than try to find riches elsewhere."

Seth nodded. The smile he'd been trying to

suppress broke through. "Okay, then, shall we try this again?"

Sausalito was already staring intently at the screen. "Hi Mom and Dad . . ."

"No, no, they got that part. Just pick up where you left off."

Sausalito, without moving his head, lifted his eyes to look at Seth. "I will tell them your clumsy secretary hit Send by mistake, and then we will go on from there."

"Very good, Saus. I'm ready when you are."

As Sausalito typed, Jane leaned over the bed rail and kissed Seth on the forehead. When she drew back, she felt a surge of joy to see Seth smiling at her.

"I didn't see you yesterday," he said quietly.

Jane nodded. "I came by, but you were asleep."

"Why didn't you wake me?"

"I don't know. I thought maybe you needed the rest."

"Next time wake me up."

"Well, sure, but I—"

"I've kind of gotten used to seeing you. The day doesn't seem right when you don't come around."

Jane reached out and touched his forehead, then curled her palm against his cheek. "I promise to wake you up next time."

Seth nodded and leaned his head into the warmth of her hand.

"Mr. Seth?" Sausalito interrupted.

"Yeah, Saus?"

"I'm ready for your dictation."

"All right. Read back to me what you have there."

Sausalito cleared his throat. " 'My clumsy secretary hit Send by mistake. A thousand pardons—' "

"Wait, Saus, I wouldn't say a thousand pardons."

"You're not. I'm the one saying a thousand pardons."

"But this isn't your e-mail. You're just the scribe here. Scratch 'a thousand pardons.' "

Sausalito sighed, highlighted the words, and hit the Delete key. "All right, Mr. Seth. A thousand pardons for the thousand pardons. It has been deleted. Now, to go on. 'Please bring the Nikes. They're in the hall closet.' " He looked up expectantly. "What do you want to say next, Mr. Seth?"

"Let's see." Seth thought a moment, staring up at the ceiling.

When a full minute had passed, Sausalito leaned forward. "Mr. Seth?"

"I'm . . ." Seth didn't finish.

"Seth?" Jane leaned over the railing. "Seth, what's the matter?"

Seth's eyes widened with fear. He moved his head from side to side. "I don't know. All of a sudden my heart started pounding in my chest. I can feel it. And my head—"

"What's wrong?"

"My head hurts and . . ."

Jane laid a hand on his forehead again. It was slick with perspiration. She looked at Sausalito. "What's happening?" she asked.

The young Ugandan lifted the laptop to the hospital table and stood. His jaw went slack as his eyes swept over Seth's face and down his inert body. "I don't know, Miss Jane," he said, his voice trembling. "I don't know."

"My head . . ." Seth moaned. "My head."

Sausalito reached for the call button and pushed it. A light flashed on over the door, but he didn't wait. "I'm going to get help," he said as he rushed from the room.

"Jane," Seth whispered. "What's happening to me?"

"I don't know. Sausalito's gone to get help." Her own heart hammered in her chest as she absently laid her hand over his. His fingers were cold, like meat packed in ice. She recoiled, clutching the railing instead as she willed herself not to panic.

Where was Sausalito? Where was the nurse, the doctor? Several agonizing seconds passed. When she didn't hear the expected footfalls in the hall, she hurried to the door. At the same time a familiar figure exited a room two doors down.

"Truman!"

"Jane." He raised a hand. "How are you?"

"Truman, please hurry. There's something wrong with Seth."

Frowning, he quickened his pace. "What is it?"

"I don't know. Just all of a sudden he said his head hurts and his heart is pounding."

Before Jane finished speaking, they were by Seth's bed. Seth moaned as his head rocked from side to side. Truman touched his forehead, then fingered his wrist to feel for his pulse. "It looks like dysreflexia," he muttered. He reached for the bed control and raised the head of the bed.

"What?" Jane asked.

Truman didn't answer. He winced as he eased himself down into a squatting position by the bed. He was obviously looking for something.

"Truman, please. What is it?" Her words were edged with panic.

But still Truman ignored her as he unhooked Seth's catheter bag and lifted it up toward the light. "Just as I thought."

"Please, Truman . . ."

"His urine isn't draining properly. His bladder is overdistended. He's—"

Truman was interrupted when Sausalito rushed into the room, shadowed by a nurse.

"Dr. Rockaway?" the nurse said, surprise in her voice.

"It's possible dysreflexia. We're probably looking at a mucus plug somewhere in the tubing." Grunting, Truman stood. "What's his BP?"

The nurse unwound the stethoscope from her neck and pulled the blood pressure cuff out of its steel holder on the wall. She quickly positioned the cuff around Seth's upper arm and started pumping. Jane and Truman waited anxiously as she listened through the stethoscope. When she'd got the reading, she let go of the pump, and the remaining air quickly sighed out of the cuff. "One-sixty over one hundred."

"Just as I thought," Truman said. "Who's on call?"

"Dr. Harrington."

"Call him." As the nurse reached for the phone, Truman turned to Sausalito in the doorway. "Get Jane out of the room," he ordered. "Go on. Both of you."

Jane looked frantically from Truman to Seth and back again. "But, Truman—"

"Go on, Jane. You're just in the way here." He had pushed back the linens on the bed and was examining the site where the catheter tubing entered Seth's groin through a small incision. He glanced up at Jane, his brow furrowed. "He'll be all right. Wait for me in the hall."

Sausalito moved to Jane's side and cupped her elbow with one large hand. "Don't worry, Miss Jane," he said gently, guiding her out of the room. "Dr. Truman will take care of everything."

Jane wanted to bury her face in the young Ugandan's shoulder and cry out her fear. But before she could so much as speak, the nurse appeared in the doorway and barked at Sausalito,

124

"Go to the supply closet and get a new catheter. Quickly."

Sausalito disappeared and Jane was alone. In another moment, a young doctor she didn't recognize rushed by her and into the room. She could hear him speaking to Truman, but she couldn't understand the words.

Please, God, she thought, *let Seth be all right.*

The voices inside sounded serious but calm. Sausalito came down the hall with a coil of tubing in a plastic wrapper. He nodded as he reached her. "Don't worry, Miss Jane," he said again. "Everything will soon be all right."

He disappeared into the room. Jane stared at the floor, not wanting to make eye contact with anyone passing by in the hall. She squeezed her hands together. *Please, God . . .*

She waited. Several tension-filled minutes ticked by. Jane felt light-headed with fear and her stomach turned. Finally Truman stepped out into the hall and laid a reassuring hand on her shoulder. "He'll be all right, Jane. Dr. Harrington's got everything under control."

She let out a breath she didn't even know she was holding. "Thank God," she said.

"Yes. He's been given something for pain, and he's resting more comfortably now. They'll be monitoring him closely for the next few hours, just to make sure."

"What exactly happened in there, Truman?"

Truman lifted his hand from her shoulder and wiped at the beads of perspiration that had sprouted along his brow. "There was a mucus plug in the tubing that wouldn't allow his bladder to empty. Basically, when something like that happens, the body rebels in an effort to let you know something's not right."

"You mean, your body pulls a major stunt over something so minor?"

Truman smiled patiently. "Well, to you and me, it's a minor deal. When our bladder's full, we know it and we do something about it. But it's not that way for Seth. He doesn't know when his bladder's full, so the catheter is supposed to be taking care of all that for him. Since it was plugged, it wasn't working. We just now emptied about 1000 cc's of urine out of Seth's bladder. Normally, we'd be looking for a bathroom at 350 cc's."

Jane studied Truman's face for a moment. "So that made his blood pressure skyrocket?"

"Yes. It's a condition called autonomic dysreflexia."

"But did it happen because the catheter tubing is going directly into his groin?"

"Oh no." Truman shook his head. "Nothing like that."

"Well, why is it? Going into his groin, I mean. I didn't know he had an incision like that."

"It's just a different kind of catheter. It's used

126

for long-term situations, when the tubing won't be removed after a day or two. Less chance of infection that way. Though obviously there's still the possibility of mucus plugs. At any rate, there are many causes of dysreflexia, not just a problem with the catheter. The larger problem is that many doctors don't recognize the signs when it happens."

"But you did."

Truman nodded. "I've seen it a few times in my career."

Jane moved her head slowly from side to side. "What if you hadn't been there? What if no one had reached him in time? Could he have . . ."

She didn't finish her sentence.

Truman wiped at his brow again. "I could use a drink," he said, sighing wearily. "Can I buy you some chocolate milk?"

— 16 —

For several long minutes as they sipped chocolate milk from pint-sized cartons, neither of them spoke. They seemed first to need time to come down from the panic, to travel from the frenzied episode on the fifth floor to the quiet, sweet normalcy of the canteen.

Jane breathed deeply, savoring the sense of

relief. Then she said, "If his blood pressure had kept going up, couldn't he have had a stroke?"

Truman nodded. "Almost certainly he'd have had a stroke."

"An episode like that could kill him."

"Yes."

Jane thought about that a moment. "Thank you for saving his life, Truman," she said quietly.

Truman took another swig of milk and settled the carton on the table. "Dr. Harrington saved his life. I don't practice medicine here."

"Oh. Okay." Jane nodded her understanding. "But I'm glad you were there."

"I am too."

Another silence followed. Then, "Truman?"

"Yes?"

"I've done a lot of reading about spinal cord injuries, but I had no idea anything like this could happen. I mean, one minute he was fine, even joking with Sausalito, and the next . . ."

"It's insidious, Jane. The body suddenly revolts without warning."

Jane finished her milk and closed up the lip of the carton. "It makes me realize how vulnerable he is. And about how ignorant I am when it comes to his condition. What else don't I know? What else could happen to him at any time?"

Truman frowned and looked down at his hands, as though he didn't want to answer. "Lots can happen that you'll have to be prepared for."

"Like another episode of this . . . whatever you called it?"

"Dysreflexia. Yes. That and blot clots, pneumonia, bedsores that turn septic. And on and on. Virtually every system in his body has been left compromised by the injury and the resulting paralysis."

"So you're saying he could die at any time."

"Well . . ." Their eyes met briefly, but they both looked away. "Chances are that Seth will live a long time. Just in the past few decades we've gotten very good at keeping people like him alive."

"People like him?"

"People with spinal cord injuries at or above C-5. Still, the higher the injury, the lower the life expectancy."

Silence again. Then, "What does that mean in terms of years, Truman?"

"If you're asking me how old Seth will be when he dies, I can't answer that. If I could, I'd be God."

Jane tried to smile.

Truman went on, "But it's possible he'll live into old age."

"And it's possible he'll die tomorrow."

"Any one of us could die tomorrow, Jane."

Jane breathed deeply, let it out. "I suddenly realize the uncertainty of life, and I don't like it very much."

"None of us does, but we have no choice. This is the story we find ourselves in, and we have to see it through."

"I suppose you're right." She shrugged. "That reminds me of what Laney used to say—"

She was interrupted when a young woman with a small boy in tow moved quickly across the canteen and stopped in front of one of the vending machines. "Make it fast, Jeffrey, we've got a bus to catch," she said, digging around in her wallet for some change.

The little boy pressed one plump finger against the glass. "I want . . . I want . . . I want . . ." His finger moved from pretzels to peanuts to candy bars.

"Sometime in this century, please, Jeffrey," the mother said with barely restrained patience.

"Umm . . . ."

"Come on, kiddo, choose. Or I'll choose for you."

"These!"

The woman dropped the coins in the slot, pushed the appropriate button, and claimed the bag of chips. "Here you are. Now let's go."

She grabbed the boy's hand, passed by Jane, unsmiling, and rolled her eyes.

She doesn't know what she has, Jane thought. Jane would give anything to have a little boy or girl to buy potato chips for, even if it meant waiting for a later bus.

"What were you saying, Jane?" Truman asked.

"What?" She looked back across the table at Truman. "Oh, I don't know. Nothing, I guess."

"You're deep in thought, though."

Jane nodded. "I can't help thinking that I have a wedding dress hanging up in my closet at home. I've chosen the invitations. I've got four friends lined up as bridesmaids, just waiting for me to decide on a color scheme so they can order their dresses. And . . ."

"And?" Truman prodded.

She held up her hand and touched her forefinger to her thumb. "I was this close to my dream coming true."

Truman leaned forward over the table. "Who's to say it won't still come true?"

"I think—" She stopped and sighed heavily. "Maybe I should just accept the fact that it isn't going to happen. I mean, I suppose there are worse things than never getting married."

"Oh yes, I'm sure. But listen, Jane, you're so young. You're far too young to say you'll never be married. If you don't marry Seth—and who knows but maybe you will—but if you don't, there will be someone else. I know it's hard to imagine that now, but I believe I'm right. Most people marry, after all."

"Did you, Truman?"

Truman laughed lightly. "Well now, I guess I'm the exception to my own rule. No, I never married."

"But why not?"

"I almost did once. But—" He looked down at his hands and shrugged.

"Tell me about her, Truman."

"It was a long time ago."

"What was her name?"

Truman looked up, looked resigned. "Magdalene," he said. "Her name was Magdalene Hearne. Everyone called her Maggie."

"Pretty name."

"Pretty girl. She was beautiful and sweet. Smart too. As they used to say, she was quite a catch."

"So what happened?"

Truman frowned, sticking out his lower lip so that the fleshy inner pink was visible. He took a deep breath. "Someday I'll tell you, Jane. But not today."

Jane nodded. "All right. But soon, okay?"

Truman stood and threw away the milk cartons. "Well, back to rounds," he said.

"I thought you didn't work here."

Truman put a finger to his lips and winked as he moved toward the door.

— 17 —

On Friday evening Jane returned to Pritchard Park to listen to the drums. By the time she arrived, the event was in full swing, with at least three dozen drummers beating out a syncopated rhythm. The tiny park itself was crowded, even more so than the week before, the dance floor a rolling wave of human flesh.

Jane found an open spot on one of the concrete tiers and sat down. She had come straight from the VA hospital, where Seth lay in a foul mood, unwilling to do much other than complain. She'd been there most of the afternoon and had intended to stay through the supper hour, but she'd finally had enough. She didn't want to stay and listen to Seth grumble. Neither did she want to go home. She didn't want to go back to the loneliness of the Penlands' house and the pull of the liquor cabinet. She knew its warmth, and she knew its cold destruction, how one led so subtly and relentlessly to the other. She knew what was at the bottom of the bottle, because her mother had repeatedly fallen into it. Head first, no safety net, until the day she simply stopped coming up for air.

Peter Morrow had found her. Jane's father, who would one day tell her all, had found his wife dead in the tub, her head resting on a pillow, her arms crossed snuggly over her chest as though she were hugging herself good-bye. She wore her favorite nightgown, the white silk, now stained a bloody black from the gashes in her wrists. Her skin was pasty, the expression on her face one of bewilderment, as though she were trying to understand what she had done. On the floor of the bathroom lay an empty bottle of valium and an almost empty bottle of bourbon. Meredith had killed herself in the Rayburn House on a Tuesday in April while Grandmother and Laney were serving the guests their lunch. She had taken her life right there under all of their noses, as though she were thumbing her nose at them and at the world at large for having forgotten her.

Laney was sent to the school to fetch twelve-year-old Jane and bring her home. Her father was too distraught and her grandmother too preoccupied with damage control to deal with Jane herself. What would become of the Rayburn House now that Meredith Morrow had committed suicide right there in one of its rooms? Would people continue to frequent the bed-and-breakfast, or would they recoil in horror, leaving the family's main source of income to dry up?

Jane still remembered the school principal, a pale little man with a receding chin, coming to the classroom, calling her out. Laney was with him, looking uncommonly stern as she reached for

Jane's hand. As they moved through the otherwise empty hall, Jane felt sick with fear. "What's the matter? Am I in trouble for something?" She squeezed Laney's hand to emphasize her terror.

Laney didn't answer right away. The principal left them with a curt nod at the school's main exit. Laney pushed down on the steel bar and opened the door. Outside in the school yard she led Jane to a bench beneath a trio of pink dogwood trees that had only just burst into bloom. Together they sat under the aching beauty of a thousand pink blossoms as Jane waited for Laney to speak. Finally, voice trembling, Laney said, "Jane, honey, your mamma's gone."

Jane didn't understand at first. All she knew was that she wasn't in trouble, and that was good. A sigh of relief swept through her as she asked, "Where'd she go?" Where would her mother go on an early spring day such as this, with winter newly past and all the promise of unfolding color ahead?

Laney's large black eyes throbbed with tears. She frowned and pursed her lips, struggling to speak. That's when, for Jane, the fragile relief caved into fear once more. "When's she coming back, Laney?"

The tears spilled over and slid down the smooth dark cheeks as Jane watched their journey curiously. "Honey," Laney said, "your mamma's not coming back. Not ever."

Jane sat in stunned silence as realization dawned on her. She tilted her head back and looked up in wonder at the delicate pink petals pasted against a milky blue sky. How could there be such a thing as death in a world that offered so much beauty? How could it be that her mother was dead and would never be coming back?

She thought that she should cry, but there were no tears. Not yet, anyway. Just confusion. Jane turned back to Laney and asked, "What happened? Was there an accident?"

Laney shook her head. She gathered Jane in her arms and held her tight. Then, pulling back, she said, "I have to get you home now."

By the time they arrived, the ambulance had come and gone. Most of the guests had retreated to their rooms or left the house in deference to the tragedy unfolding under its roof. Gram was in the kitchen, talking with two policemen and a man Jane recognized as the family lawyer.

Jane pulled her hand from Laney's and ran to her parents' bedroom. Her father was there, sitting in profile on the edge of the bed, cradling something against his chest. He was weeping quietly and mumbling words Jane couldn't hear. In another moment the weeping turned to rage as he threw the empty bottle of bourbon against the bedroom wall. The last remnant of Meredith that he'd cradled to his heart now shattered into a dozen shards of glass.

"Daddy?"

Peter Morrow turned toward his daughter's voice. Jane drew back at the bitter anguish sketched into the contours of his face. *I shouldn't be here,* she thought. But to her surprise, he opened his arms. She hung back for several awkward seconds before running into them. The moment tasted bittersweet. Mamma was dead, but for the first time, Jane believed that her father might actually love her.

"Oh, excuse me. Sorry. Clumsy of me."

Jane brushed a peanut out of her hair and looked up at her accidental assailant. "That's all right. No problem. It's pretty crowded here."

The young man holding the bag of peanuts looked around the park. "Yeah. Great turnout, huh? I've never seen this place so crowded. Have you?"

Jane shook her head and shrugged. "I've only been here once before—"

"What's that?" The young man squatted down to hear better over the drums.

"I said, I've only been here once before. I don't actually live here in Asheville. I'm just visiting for the summer."

"Oh yeah? Well, mind if I sit here? It looks like the boulders are all taken."

Jane laughed and nodded at the concrete ledge beside her. "Go ahead. It's open."

The young man sat. For the next few minutes Jane was uncomfortably aware of his body close to hers, so close that in the gentle push and shove of the crowd their elbows occasionally touched. He was tall, with firm sun-browned legs sticking out from a pair of denim shorts and ending in a pair of tattered leather Docksiders. He wore a T-shirt with the letters UNCA emblazoned across the front. Jane wondered whether he might be a student at the university there in Asheville. He ate from a bag of peanuts, his right arm traveling methodically up and down between the bag and his mouth. He had a pleasant face, intelligent eyes behind a pair of unobtrusive glasses, and a head of wild brown curls that obviously refused to be tamed. He exuded a quiet strength, a strength that he himself seemed unaware of or perhaps disinterested in, as he absorbed the activity around him with the same enthusiasm with which he inhaled the nuts.

He looked at her once and smiled, then looked away again. She had come to the park so she wouldn't have to be alone. But she didn't want this either, this reminder of what it was *not* to be alone. This reminder of men in the world whose bodies were strong and young and healthy. Whose bodies worked and whose limbs moved at will and without thought, as though it were something to be taken for granted rather than something to be embraced with gratitude.

At the next break in the drumming, Jane decided, *I'll leave.*

But before that break came, the young man turned to her and asked, "So you enjoying your stay in Asheville?"

"What? Oh yes. Very much." Jane offered what she hoped might pass for a genuine smile. "It's such an eclectic little town."

"That's a good way to put it. Where you from?"

"Troy. You probably never heard of it."

"Nope. That in North Carolina?"

"Yeah. About a hundred and fifty miles east of here. There's not much there but, well . . ." Jane shrugged. "It's home."

"I'm from Atlanta myself. I prefer Asheville, though."

Jane nodded. The rhythmic drumming went on. There should be a break soon, Jane thought, and then she would cut her way through the crowd and head home.

The man beside her wadded up the now empty bag and stood. Jane felt a mixture of disappointment and relief. She pasted on another smile and looked up at him with the intention of saying *Good-bye. Nice to meet you.* But before she could get the words out, he nodded toward the dancers and said, "I'm going down. Want to come?"

She looked from him to the dancers and back again. "You mean, go down there and dance?"

"Sure," he said. "But listen, I'm going to go throw this away. I'll be right back."

He leapt off the tier and headed for a garbage can. Jane sat momentarily paralyzed by indecision. She wanted to dance with him, and she didn't. She felt self-conscious, yet at the same time she didn't care what this crowd of strangers thought. And then there was Seth.

Jane looked at her engagement ring, fingered the diamond. The young man must not have noticed it.

She was in love with Seth, engaged to be married to him. But she was here and Seth was somewhere else, and maybe for a few minutes she could just have fun, just enjoy life again.

She slipped the ring off and tucked it into the pocket of her Capri pants. Then the man was there, standing in front of her, holding out his hand. She hesitated only a moment, and then she took it.

— 18 —

Sent: Saturday, June 18, 2005 11:28 AM
From: Jane Morrow <jane1980@morrow.com>
To: Diana Penland <monkeytrial@unc.edu>
Subject: Hello from Asheville

Hey Diana,

How's London? The house is quiet without you, but Roscoe, Juniper, and I are enjoying one another's company and are doing well. Okay, fairly well, except that last night I ended up giving my cell phone number to some guy I met in Pritchard Park. I can't believe I did it. I went to listen to the drumming and ended up on the dance floor with this guy named Ted Taggert. What's worse is that after we danced for nearly an hour—which was an absolute blast, by the way—he asked me to have dinner with him, and I said yes. We ended up eating at the Grove Arcade, and we didn't pay the bill (Dutch treat, I insisted) until we noticed the kitchen closing up and the light being turned off.

Don't think I'm happy about this, Diana, because I'm not. I'm in love with Seth, and I don't intend to break my commitment to him.

I'm wondering, though, whether you happen to know Ted, or whether you know of him, since he works at the U. It's a large campus, I realize, and you're in different departments, but maybe you've come across him. He's an assistant professor in environmental studies. His PhD is in something having to do with fish and with stream ecosystems, and though he spent an hour over dinner telling me about his studies and his work, I didn't retain enough of it to begin to tell you anything at all. I only know that when he isn't teaching or poking around in stream beds, he's playing guitar with a three-piece band started by one of the other professors. They've actually released a CD! They call themselves the Tree-hugging Trio.

He likes to talk so, thankfully, I didn't have to tell him much about myself. All he knows is that I'm from Troy and I'm in town house-sitting. I couldn't bring myself to tell him about Seth, and I'm kicking myself now for that. I believe that's called telling a lie by not telling the whole truth.

But I guess when it comes right down to it, I wanted a night away, a night of not thinking about my life. When the opportunity showed up, I took it. For a few hours I remembered how it felt to be young and alive. But I should have stopped there and not given Ted the impression

I would see him again. Now I've opened up for myself a pretty can of worms. I feel awful for not having told him about Seth to begin with. And to think I did this behind Seth's back. Last night it was fun; this morning it leaves me feeling sick.

Okay, so help me out with this problem, will you? Tell me what to do, how to get out of it politely if Ted calls. Maybe my old pre-Seth luck will hold out and he won't call. That would make it easiest all around.

Love,

Jane

Sent: Saturday, June 18, 2005 6:18 PM
From: Diana Penland <monkeytrial@unc.edu>
To: Jane Morrow <jane1980@morrow.com>
Subject: RE: Hello from Asheville

Jane,

So what's the problem? I don't consider meeting a nice, intelligent young man a problem. Instead, I'd call that crazy good luck. So you gave him your phone number. Of course you did. You'd have been an idiot not to. Yes, there's Seth. I realize that. But listen, don't be a martyr. Don't sacrifice yourself on the altar of commitment. If you and Seth were already married, that would be different. But you're not. You are still free to pursue another direction with your life. To answer your question, I don't know Ted. But he sounds like someone I would like to know, and someone you ought to know. So when he calls, by all means, see him, talk with him, get to know him. Give him—and yourself—a chance.

Listen, I'm not at all saying you should dump Seth. And I'm certainly not saying you should dump him because he's disabled, though let's be honest here, it does change the situation, and it changes it into something you didn't sign up for when you agreed to marry him. But if you still want to marry him, all right, it's up to you.

What I think you should understand is this: You wouldn't have given Ted your phone number if you hadn't wanted to, right? If you hadn't been attracted to him, you could have easily skipped on the dinner invitation. You know, "Thanks but no thanks. And by the way, I'm engaged." But you went and you had a good time, and maybe that's the first clue that you're ready to move on.

Hey, I may be a woman of science, but I also happen to be an incorrigible romantic. We only have one chance to get it right. Well, ·okay, there's always divorce, but why not try to get it right on the first go-round? Saves a lot of time, money, and heartache when you do. And listen, Jane, no guilt. You wanted to feel young and alive because you are young and alive. And you deserve to be happy, just as we all do.

Must dash. Carl and I are getting ready for dinner with some of his co-workers. London is fabulous; more about that later.

For now, I'm thinking of you and sending love.

Diana

— 19 —

"This your room, Truman?"

Truman looked up from the newspaper in his lap and smiled at Jane, who stood in the open doorway. "This is it. Come on in. Were you looking for me or just happening by?"

"I was looking for you."

"Well, you found me." He waved toward the unoccupied vinyl chair that matched his own. "Have a seat."

Jane sat down and looked briefly around the room. His was one of the private rooms consisting of a single bed, a chest of drawers, two chairs, a TV, and a couple of standard-issue prints on the walls, cheap-motel style landscapes. Few things in the room spoke of Truman Rockaway and his life, other than a couple of medical books on the dresser and a framed photograph of a young woman wearing pearls.

Jane studied the photo curiously, wondering whether it might be Maggie. "Is that . . . ?"

"My mother," Truman said. "When she was young."

"Ah." Jane nodded. "She was very pretty."

"Yes, she was. I don't have many photos of her. It was Mrs. Evans who paid for the sitting for her, a birthday gift, I believe it was. She even let Mamma borrow the necklace for the picture."

"Very nice."

Truman smiled. "Have you been visiting with Seth?" he asked.

"Briefly. His parents are here this weekend."

"And you don't like them?"

"Oh no, don't get me wrong. I love them. We get along great."

"Well?"

Jane shrugged. "I try to give them space. You know, time together. Besides . . ."

"Besides what?"

"It's hard sometimes. Being with them, I mean. Jewel used to look at me with love and pride. Now she looks at me with pity. When Seth is released from here in a couple of months, they'll be taking him home to Troy. So today they were talking about the changes they're making to the house. You know, making it wheelchair accessible and all. Jewel is going to retire to take care of Seth full-time."

"And?"

"Well, it's as though I'm not in the picture anymore. Like we never had a wedding planned. I'm beginning to lose hope, Truman."

"Hope is one thing we must never lose, Jane."

"I suppose. Unless in fact the situation truly is hopeless." She gave a small, sad laugh.

"I don't think your situation with Seth is hopeless."

"My best friend Diana thinks I ought to just move on. Seth's parents seem to think the same thing. And come on, let's face it, Seth wants me to find someone else. He told me so."

Truman folded the paper and rubbed his chin. "I believe we had this conversation before, didn't we, Jane?"

Jane looked away. "I guess we did. Obviously, I'm going around in circles. I can't seem to find the place to settle. I don't know what to do."

"What do you want to do?"

What did she want to do? She thought of the previous night, of dancing to a phalanx of drummers in the middle of Pritchard Park with a man named Ted Taggert. She had given herself

147

over to the rhythm, to the hypnotic pull of the drums, and she had felt . . . well, she had felt what she hadn't felt in a long time. Happy. Carefree. She had laughed! The drumming drew her in, deeper and deeper, until she was not simply listening to the music, she *was* the music. She was one with the drums, with the sea of dancers, with Ted, and who knew but maybe she was even one with God, if God was a sense of well-being and joy.

And then this morning, it was gone. When she awoke, the joy had been replaced by a bitter confusion wrapped around a huge empty chasm in the pit of her stomach.

She didn't answer Truman's question. Instead, she said, "When you make your rounds, Truman, you do stop and see Seth, don't you?"

Truman nodded. "As with everyone, I stop by his room for a few minutes, ask him how he's doing, see if I can do anything for him."

"So how does he seem to you?"

Truman took a moment to think. "He's willing to say more than two words to me now. That's a step in the right direction."

Jane took a deep breath. "Well, maybe if he keeps moving in that direction, everything will be all right."

"I hope so," Truman said. "I pray so."

Jane looked at him, held his gaze. "Truman?"

"Yes, Jane?"

"Do you believe in God?"

"Of course."

"But, I mean, one who has anything to do with us? Do you think He answers if we pray?"

Truman looked toward the window and back again. "Yes."

"You hesitate."

"No."

"But you did."

He shook his head. "No. I've been a praying man all my life. I've seen many answers to prayer. Why, Jane? What are you praying about?"

"Truman, I don't even know how to pray. I don't know how I'm supposed to go about doing it."

"You don't know how to talk to God?"

"Talk to God? We never even talked *about* God when I was growing up. My family didn't go to church, though they'd allow Laney to take me with her from time to time. I went, but I wasn't very interested. I liked the hymns, but as soon as the sermon started, my mind checked out." Jane stopped and laughed, shook her head. "You know, my most vivid memory of church is actually getting mad at Laney because she wouldn't let me take communion. She said I wasn't ready, and it made me feel left out, like I wasn't good enough, while everyone else around us was."

"Hmm." Truman rubbed his chin thoughtfully. "Didn't Laney tell you what communion was all about?"

"Sure, she told me. Not that it mattered to me at the time."

"It ought to matter—"

"Yes." Jane interrupted with a nod of her head. "I want to understand. Especially since Seth has always gone to church, and once we're mar—"

She stopped, couldn't finish the word. She looked hard at Truman, who was waiting patiently. "But that's the thing, isn't it?"

"Marrying Seth?" With a lift of his brows, Truman nodded.

"I don't know what to do. If I thought it would make any difference, I'd ask God to tell me whether I should stay with Seth or just give up."

"Well, why don't you just go ahead and ask Him?"

"I'm afraid He won't answer."

"He will. Maybe you've never heard what they say about prayer. Sometimes God says yes, sometimes He says no. Sometimes He says wait. He'll surely answer if he can."

"What do you mean, if He can? Are there some prayers He can't answer?"

Truman looked back toward the window. He was nodding, but more in thought than in answer to her question. When he looked back, he said, "I was just about to take a walk when you came by. There's a path that runs the perimeter of the grounds. Do you want to join me?"

— 20 —

The day was warm, but not unbearably so. The heat was tempered by a mild breeze that blew off the mountains and down across the grounds of the VA complex. Jane, in a pale blue sundress, liked the feel of the sun on her bare shoulders and the fresh air on her face. It was good to be outside, out of the confines of the hospital with its populace of broken bodies and aging vets.

She glanced over at Truman walking beside her, tapping the ground with a cane. He carried one when he walked outside, he'd explained, so he didn't lose his footing on the woodchips that covered the path. Too, he finally admitted to the arthritis in his knees that sometimes made walking difficult.

He wore a long-sleeved shirt with tarnished cuff links and slacks held up with suspenders. Beads of sweat broke out beneath the beak of his base-ball cap and slid down the side of his face. He looked ahead intently as he walked, and Jane knew he had something he intended to say. She waited, not wanting to interrupt his train of thought.

Finally her patience was rewarded. "You asked about Maggie," he said, "and what happened."

"Yes. But you don't have to tell me."

"I know. But I want to. In a way, it's the continuation of my story about my brother Daniel."

Jane frowned, wondering how that could be. Surely by the time Truman was engaged, Daniel had been dead for years. She lifted a hand to her forehead to shade her eyes as she gazed at the distant mountains. "All right," she said.

They took another few steps before Truman spoke again. "I grew up with Maggie," he began. "We knew each other from grade school on, like you and Seth, though she was a couple years younger than I was." He offered her a sideways glance. " 'Course when you're a kid, a couple years is a lifetime, so I never paid her much attention. In fact, I don't guess I ever really gave her the time of day till after I graduated medical school and went back to Travelers Rest. That was in 1960. I went back home to open that practice I'd long dreamed about, and I brought back someone from Meharry to work alongside me. His name was Cyrus Dooley. He was a fine doctor and a good man. I considered him not just a business partner but a friend.

"Well, not long after we started our practice, I saw Maggie at one of the socials held down at the Negro VFW hall. By then, of course, she was all grown up and pretty as a picture." He paused a moment and his eyes brightened, as though she stood there even now, smiling coyly in her new party dress, her white-gloved hands toying nervously with the bow at the small of her back. "You can be sure I finally took notice. I asked her to dance, and that was it. Before the night was over, we were in love, and I knew I was going to ask her to marry me."

"Did you propose that night?"

"Oh no. I knew I had to wait, exercise a little patience. I waited a week, and that was all I could stand." He glanced over at Jane again and sniffed out a small laugh. "I asked her to marry me, and she said yes, with one stipulation. We had to have a yearlong engagement so we could be sure we were doing the right thing."

"And you went along with it?"

"I went along with it. Otherwise, she'd hold the I-told-you-so card if we ended up getting ornery with each other a few years into the marriage."

Jane chuckled. "Well, I think she was wise."

"That she was," Truman agreed with a nod. "Besides, it gave me some time to save up so we could afford the down payment on a house. Cyrus and I roomed together in the small quarters above our office. It was hardly the place to bring your bride and start your married life. No, I was going to carry my bride over the threshold of a house and make a real home. So Maggie and I got engaged in the fall of '60, and she began planning our wedding for the following year. But the next summer, the summer of 1961, something happened."

He paused, as though reluctant to go on. His face took on a pained expression as he saw what was ahead in the telling.

Jane waited several long seconds before prodding gently, "What happened, Truman?"

He moistened his lips with his tongue and took a deep breath. "It was a Sunday, and the office was closed. That afternoon after church, Maggie and I packed a picnic lunch and took it to our favorite spot by the Saluda River. Pretty little river, not far from Travelers Rest. We'd go there often when the weather was nice. Sometimes we'd go with Cyrus and one of his girlfriends, but mostly we'd go by ourselves.

"So there we were, eating bologna sandwiches on the banks of the river when we heard a commotion coming from somewhere close by. Men shouting, a dog barking, and a minute later, a gunshot. Just one, but it seemed to echo all up and down the river. I started to get up, and Maggie grabbed my wrist. 'Is it a lynching?' she asked. I told her it probably was, and I had to go see. She argued that it was too dangerous, but I told her maybe I could save him, whoever he was. 'They'll kill you too,' she said, but I had to take that chance. Before I could take two steps, I heard a car start up and drive away, and I knew some poor colored man had been left for dead by the river. I ran toward where we'd heard the commotion, and Maggie followed. It wasn't far. Quarter of a mile, maybe less. We found him moaning in the weeds on the riverbank. Only he wasn't a black man. He was white. And I knew who he was."

Truman paused and looked at Jane. "Jane," he said, "he was the son of Dr. Coleman. He was the son of the doctor who turned my baby brother away fifteen years before. He lay there bleeding out of a chest wound, but at that point he was still conscious. I kneeled beside him, but I didn't touch him. He looked at me with pleading eyes. He didn't know who I was or what had happened all those years ago. Maggie kneeled too and she said, 'It's all right, mister. This man is Dr. Rockaway. He's going to help you.' Well, he reached up and grabbed my shirt and held on. 'Help me,' he said. Just like that. 'Help me.' Funny how in that moment he didn't care whether I was white or black. He may not have even believed a colored man like me could be a doctor. All he knew was he didn't want to die, and at that moment I was his only hope.

"Well, I looked at him long and hard, but I wasn't really seeing him. All I could think about was Daniel. I was seeing the agony Daniel went through in the days before he died. And I was angry. So angry I was blind with it. We'd gone to this man's father when Daniel was sick, and we'd been turned away. Dr. Coleman had let my baby brother die. I grabbed the man's wrist and pulled his hand away from my shirt.

"Then I stood up. Maggie asked me where I was going, and I said, 'Maggie, come on, we're getting out of here.' She said, 'What do you mean, Truman? You can't just leave and let this man bleed to death.' 'I can't help him,' I said. 'Anyone finds us near him, they'll think we shot him ourselves, and they'll kill us.' At that point I looked down at my hand. The man's blood was all over it and all over the front of my shirt. I stepped to the river and washed my hands. Maggie came up behind me and said, 'Truman, you can't do this. You're going to let him die because he's white, aren't you?' I turned to her and said, 'Maggie, I can't save him. He won't survive till we could get him to the hospital. It's too late.' She protested, saying we could at least try. She said it was wrong not to try.

"It was wrong and I knew it. But I chose to leave him there to die. It was payback for what his daddy had done to Daniel and to my family. And to me."

"So what happened after he died?"

"Well, that's the thing, see. He didn't die. I underestimated his will to live and overestimated the severity of his wound. I felt sure he'd be dead within a few minutes, but after we left he dragged himself a hundred feet or so to the road where someone in a passing car found him. They made it to the hospital in time. Tommy Lee Coleman lived. And from that moment on, I was a marked man. Tommy Lee had seen me and could identify me. I had to flee or risk being killed."

"So you fled?" Jane asked.

Truman nodded. "I turned the practice over to Cyrus and disappeared into upstate New York. Some distant relatives took me in until I could get myself established. Even then, I didn't stay long. For years I was on the move, swinging back and forth between the East Coast and the Midwest. Just in case."

"And Maggie?"

"Before I left Travelers Rest, I asked her to come with me, but she said no. She said she needed some time to think. She needed to forgive me, she said, for leaving a man to die. She'd seen a part of me she didn't like. It was a part of me she wasn't sure she could live with. I told her I'd give her as much time as she needed to forgive me, and when she was ready, I'd send for her and we'd be married."

Truman stopped, sighing heavily.

Jane said, "You never sent for her?"

He shook his head. "I got to thinking of what I was asking of her. To come with me, I'd be asking her to leave her family, her home, everything she ever knew, just so she could be with a man who was on the run for who-knew-how-long. But the more important reason was, of course, that she'd lost faith in me, not so much as a doctor but as a man. She said there can't be a marriage where the trust has been tampered with. I wanted to hear her say she forgave me, but she never did. For a while, she knew how to contact me through my relatives in New York, should she change her mind. But I didn't hear from her. About a year or so after I left Travelers Rest, she married Cyrus Dooley."

Jane frowned as she thought about that. Finally she said, "I'm sorry, Truman. It seems almost unfair. You know, like the punishment doesn't fit the crime."

He shook his head and narrowed his eyes. "Maggie was right. You don't simply let someone die. Especially when you're in a position to save him. I was a doctor, but I did nothing. I left Tommy Lee to die because of who he was. The son of a white man I hated."

"That's why you feel so strongly about not going along with Seth's death wish?"

"Yes."

"I understand."

"One more thing. Even after she married Cyrus, I went on praying for years that I might hear Maggie say she'd forgiven me for what I'd done. But now it's a prayer that God can't answer."

"Why not?"

"Because Maggie's dead. She died two years ago. I've seen plenty of strange things in my day, but far as I know, words of forgiveness have never fallen from the lips of someone who's dead."

— 21 —

Neither do the words *I'm sorry,* Jane thought. Those who were dead could never rise up and tell you they were sorry. If they *were* sorry, which she wasn't sure her mother was.

It was Sunday morning, a quiet unhurried morning on Montford Avenue. Jane, still in her cotton robe, carried a cup of coffee into the den. She stopped at the stereo player and put in a CD of Brahms, then curled up in the overstuffed chair by the fireplace. Roscoe and Juniper followed, settling themselves on the floor at her feet.

Jane sipped the coffee, then put her head back against the cushioned chair and shut her eyes. Oh, how in making one solitary decision a person affected so many lives. Her mother, who decided not to live. Dr. Coleman, who decided not to heal. Maggie, who decided not to forgive.

Bad enough that a person had to bear the consequences of her own choices, but when the blow came from another, and when that person didn't know or didn't care . . .

"You're going to have to find it in yourself to forgive your mamma," Laney had said. Jane remembered that now. Almost six months had passed since Meredith Morrow's funeral. In that time, Jane had turned thirteen, she had started eighth grade, and she had become alarmingly aware of her new role in Troy: She was the daughter of the town suicide. She saw the stares at school, noted the whispers, heard the rumors about how the Rayburn House was now haunted. A couple of boys claimed to have seen the ghost of a woman in an upstairs window. At the thought of it, even Jane shivered. She didn't really believe in ghosts, but then again . . .

"Why should I forgive her, Laney?" she'd asked. They were sitting on the front porch on a warm Friday evening in late October, waiting for Laney's husband to pick her up. Laney's mother and father were visiting for the weekend, and the elder couple was taking the younger out to dinner.

"She left you in a world of hurt, child," Laney said, "and it'll kill you if you let it."

Jane didn't want to talk about that. She looked out over the yard at the last vestiges of Grandmother's summer garden, at the trees tinged with autumn, at the lengthening shadows on the lawn. It was the kind of evening that had called her to dance pirouettes in the grass when she was a child. But those days were gone. "They say our house is haunted now," she said.

"So I heard." Laney swatted at a gnat circling her head. "No such thing as ghosts."

Jane took a long sip of the sweet tea Laney had

poured for her. Then she said, "But if there was, and if Mom came back, would she tell me she was sorry?"

Laney shook her head. "Child, if your mother came back, even as a ghost, she'd sit herself down on the couch and go on watching herself on television. Nothing would change."

"Then why should I forgive her?" Jane asked again.

"Because that's what the Lord Jesus did when He was up on the cross. His body was broken, and His life was slipping away, and still He said, 'Father, forgive them, for they know not what they do.' "

Another sip of tea gave her a moment to think. "You know, Laney, I've never understood why they killed Jesus."

"It wasn't a killing, Janie. It was a sacrifice. Only them that put Him on the cross didn't know it. That's why Jesus said they didn't know what they were doing."

"It was a sacrifice?"

"That's right. The only one that ever mattered. The only one that ever made peace between us and God."

Jane didn't understand. She wasn't sure she wanted to. She just wanted to be like all the other kids—kids whose mothers were alive and normal, volunteering for the PTA, and making suppers for their families at night.

"If Mom loved me," Jane said, "she wouldn't have done it."

Laney turned toward her and fixed her gaze firmly on Jane. "Now listen, child, there's one thing you've got to understand. What your mamma did had nothing to do with you. I believe she loved you, but she just didn't know how to live. Some people are like that. They strive and they strive and they never can figure out how to live. That was your mamma. She just couldn't find any peace."

"But, Laney?"

"Yes, honey?"

"Could you ever leave Eugene and Sarah and Frankie?"

Laney smiled at the mention of her children. "Of course not," she responded quietly. "I'd keep them all with me forever, if I could."

"See then?"

"I know what you're trying to say, honey, but it still doesn't mean your mother didn't love you. Someday you'll know she did, and I hope someday you'll forgive her."

Jane settled the empty glass on the wicker table beside her chair. "Everybody looks at me funny now. Even Claire and Hayley, my very best friends. It's kind of like there's something strange about me now, or like I'm bad luck or something."

"What do your friends say to you?"

"Nothing. I mean, it's not that they say anything

bad, it's just . . . things are different. It's as though when I'm with them it isn't me they're seeing, it's Mom. Mom and what she did."

"Well, people are funny about death, Janie, especially when a person brings it on herself. In a way, the town is still in shock. You got to give people time. They'll come around and things will get back to normal."

"I don't know. I wish . . ." Jane's voice trailed off.

"What, honey?" Laney asked. "What do you wish?"

"I wish I had a family just like yours."

Another small smile. "That's nice of you to say, Janie."

"Really. I mean it. Mr. Jackson's so nice to you, and you have three good kids."

"I guess I am blessed, aren't I? But you know what? Someday you *can* have a family just like mine. Only instead of being the daughter, you'll be the mother. You can have three good kids too, or as many as you want, and you can let them know you love them."

"I'd never leave them."

"I know that, honey. You'll be a good mother."

Jane nodded. That was her dream. She was going to make sure it came true. Her children would know beyond doubt that she loved them. She would be there for them every moment, listening, caring, helping. She would be every-

163

thing to them that her own mother had never been to her. And perhaps most important, she would never tell them they were destined to be nobodies. Never would she cut them that deeply.

She looked over at Laney. "So where are you going to have dinner tonight?"

"Clapper said he made reservations at the Carriage House."

Jane smiled, as she always did when she heard Mr. Jackson's name. He'd been christened Roderick, but everyone had always called him Clapper. To Jane, it sounded like such a happy name. "That's the fanciest place in town."

"That's right, and my folks are paying." Laney laughed as she looked out over the quiet street. "You know, I think Daddy's going to spend the whole evening trying to talk Clapper into moving back down to Greenville."

"I thought you all were from Travelers Rest."

Laney nodded. "That's where I grew up, mostly. Eventually the folks moved to Greenville, though, because it was a better place for Daddy to make a living."

"So now he wants you to move back down there, to be close to them?"

"Yeah. Clapper's from down that way too, you know. It'd be nice to be back with family, though there's a lot about Troy I'll miss if we do go." She paused and looked out over the street again. "I wonder what's keeping them, anyway."

164

"Maybe your baby-sitter was late."

"Clapper was supposed to drop the kids off at Rachel's for the night."

"Your sister-in-law?"

"Yes. She's keeping them till tomorrow so we can visit with Mamma and Daddy tonight."

Even as she spoke, a dark brown Chevy Impala turned onto Rayburn Avenue and pulled into the circular drive. Clapper, at the wheel, put the car in park but left the motor running. He opened the driver's side door, stepped out, and called over the roof, "Come on, baby, we've got six o'clock reservations, and it's pushing six now."

"I know, Clapper. But don't blame me," Laney hollered back. "I've been sitting out here waiting on you for the past fifteen minutes."

The front passenger window slid down, and an elderly gentleman with a friendly smile leaned forward. "You can blame your mother, Laney. She couldn't decide on which dress to wear. The usual dilemma, you know."

He winked and nodded his head toward the woman sitting in the back seat. Small and dignified, she wore a dark blue dress and a matching hat. Around her neck was a triple string of pearls. Her dark wavy hair was pulled over her ears and into a knot at the nape of her neck. She curled her deep red lips into a sheepish smile and shrugged. Then she lifted a hand to Laney and waved.

"Oh, Mamma." Laney feigned a sigh. "You know you look good in anything." She turned to her husband then. "Clapper, haven't you got a hello for Jane here?"

Clapper Jackson seemed to notice her for the first time. "Beg your pardon, Jane," he said. "How you doing?"

Jane waved at him, too shy to respond in words. Laney stood and kissed Jane's forehead, then ran around the car to sit beside her mother.

Jane remembered how she felt when they pulled away. She felt hopeful. As though maybe someday she really could be a part of a family like that.

Now here she was, all these years later, with a cup of coffee turned cold in her hand, a stereo that had gone silent, and a dream that had been knocked off course when a sniper caught Seth in the crosshairs of his weapon and made the split-second decision to pull the trigger.

— 22 —

"Did you send that blind guy in here to talk with me?" Seth's voice was quiet and without rancor. He sounded more curious than anything.

Still, Jane frowned at the question. "Blind guy?"

Jewel Ballantine answered. "You know, dear,

the nice young man who's a lawyer. He said he's met you."

"Oh, yeah. Jon-Paul. He was here?" Jane asked.

"He came in yesterday afternoon," Seth said, "not long after you left."

Jane shook her head and shrugged. "Well, I didn't send him. What did he want?"

"I wouldn't say he wanted anything," Jewel said, "other than just to say hello."

"He seemed to know some of the other men on the floor," Sid added. "Maybe he just stops up here to visit once in a while."

"Oh. Well, he has a sister who's a nurse on one of the other floors," Jane said. "And he's dating one of the nurses. I can't remember their names, but anyway, he comes sometimes to have lunch with them, and when he does, he plays the piano down in the atrium. He's really good."

"I remember hearing someone playing the piano down there once," Jewel said. "Maybe that was him. Do you remember that, Sid?"

Sid shrugged.

"Probably lots of people play that piano, Jewel," Jane said. "It's there for whoever feels like playing."

"Don't get any ideas, Mom," Seth said.

Jewel waved a hand. "Don't worry. I won't embarrass you, son."

"You know," Sid said, "your mother's a good piano player. Think of all the years she's played in church. She's always sounded good to me."

"That's because you're tone deaf, Dad."

"Seth!" Jane scolded. "What a thing to say!"

Seth winked at his mother. "Mom knows I'm just giving her a hard time. Listen, speaking of church, did you get to the service in the chapel this morning?"

"Oh my, yes," Jewel said. "It was a very nice service. The pastor could use a haircut, though—"

"Ah, Jewel," Sid interjected, "you always think everybody needs a haircut—"

"But he was a nice young man," Jewel said, ignoring her husband, "and he gave a good sermon. Had a good turnout too. The chapel was full."

"Listen, son," Sid said, "half the people there were in wheelchairs, so it's really not an excuse to stay away. Maybe next week you'll come with us?"

"Yeah, maybe." Seth nodded. He turned his head toward the door and frowned. "Hey, Jane, is that Truman out there?"

Jane listened a moment. "I don't know. Do you want me to see?"

"Yeah. And if he's out there, tell him to come here for a minute."

Jane stepped to the door and looked out. Truman was in the hall talking with a nurse. He lifted a hand when he saw Jane. In another moment the nurse nodded and left. "Hello, Jane," Truman said. "What's up?"

"Do you have a minute?"

"Sure." He moved down the hall toward Seth's room.

"Seth wants to see you."

Truman raised his eyebrows, and Jane shrugged in response. One after the other, they stepped into Seth's room.

"Hey, Doc Rockaway," Seth greeted him from the bed. "I want you to meet the folks. Mom, Dad, this is the doctor I was telling you about, the one who knew what to do when I had that episode last Thursday."

Sid rose from his seat and extended a hand. "We're grateful to you, Doctor. I'm Sid Ballantine, Seth's father. And this is my wife, Jewel."

Truman shook hands with each one. "Very nice to meet you both."

"Thank God, you were here, Dr. Rockaway," Jewel said. "I hate to think . . ." Her words trailed off as she looked at Seth and back to Truman.

"He's the best doctor in the hospital," Seth said, "and he doesn't even get paid for what he does."

Truman laughed. "Well, I'm glad you think so highly of me, Seth, but I don't do much. I just kind of keep my eye on things, help out as I can."

"I wouldn't call saving Seth's life nothing much, Doctor," Sid said.

"Yes, I wish we could bring you along when we take Seth home," Jewel added. "I'd feel a whole lot less nervous with someone like you around."

Truman waved a hand and gave a reassuring nod. "Don't worry, Mrs. Ballantine. You'll be fine. The hospital will educate you in everything you need to know for having Seth at home."

The four of them, all still standing, lingered for an awkward moment by Seth's bed. Finally Sid broke the silence by saying, "I hear you saw action in Korea."

"That's right. I was with the 24th Infantry Regiment."

"I did two tours in 'Nam myself. Right before the Tet Offensive, I was out on patrol when a buddy of mine stepped on a landmine. That was our ticket out. He went home in a body bag while I went home on a C-141 jet transport."

While the two old soldiers talked, Jane slipped around the bed and leaned over Seth. "I knew your Dad was in Vietnam, but you never told me he was wounded."

Seth's eyes were apologetic. "I guess I never thought much about it. I mean, by the time I came around, it was ancient history."

"Yeah, well, I remember it very well," Jewel said. "It seemed like the end of the world to me."

"What happened, Jewel?"

"He had to have several surgeries to remove all the shrapnel, even after he got back to the States. After one surgery he developed a blood clot, and after another he picked up an infection that just about killed him. We weren't even

170

engaged yet, just dating, but already I was starting to feel like a widow."

"I never knew."

Jewel shrugged. "He lived. And I guess it *is* ancient history now."

Jane looked at Sid, who was talking animatedly with Truman, and then back at Seth again. "So your dad got a Purple Heart like you did."

"Yeah, except, I think that's backwards. I got a Purple Heart like Dad did. Only Dad . . ."

When he didn't go on, Jewel asked, "Only Dad what, son?"

"Only Dad got better. I never will."

Sid must have been listening with one ear, because he turned to Seth then and said, "Don't say that, Seth. Attitude is everything. Remember?"

"Yeah, Dad, but—"

"Things won't be exactly like they were before, but they'll be better than they are now. That's what we've got to keep hoping for."

"That's right, Seth," Jane jumped in. "It's funny, but I've been thinking about Laney a lot lately, and how she used to say, 'Life's gearshift—' "

"Well, here you are, Doc!"

All eyes turned toward the door where a tall man leaned heavily against a walker.

"Oh, hey Jimmy," Truman said. "Are you waiting on me?"

"Larry dealt the cards a good fifteen minutes ago."

"Sorry about that. I got sidetracked."

The man named Jimmy looked around the room and smiled apologetically. "Sorry to interrupt, folks. We got a little worried when the doc didn't show up on time. I just wanted to make sure he was all right."

"Ah now, Jimmy, you know I'm always all right. I'm too stubborn to not be all right."

"Well, you come on down whenever you're ready."

"I'm ready now." He turned to Sid and held out a hand. "Pleasure. Hope to see you again."

Sid pumped his hand. "We're here every weekend."

"Mrs. Ballantine"—Truman smiled at Jewel—"you take care."

"You too, Doctor. And thanks again for helping out with Seth."

"Glad to help. Jane, I'll see you later."

"Bye, Truman. No cheating at the card game."

"A gentleman never cheats. 'Course, there might be those who'd say I'm not a gentleman." He was chuckling to himself as he left the room.

"Interesting fellow," Sid said. "I'm glad we got to meet him."

"I really would like to take him home with us," Jewel said.

"Not much chance of that happening, Mom." Seth looked up at her and smiled. "They need him around here too much to let him go."

"I suppose . . ." Jewel said with a sigh.

"Don't worry, Jewel," Jane said. "I'll be around to help you too, you know, once you get Seth home."

Jewel nodded, but she was frowning at the same time, as though she didn't quite believe it. After a moment, she perked up and said, "What were you saying about Laney, dear?"

"Oh." Jane cocked her head. "I was just thinking of how she always used to say that life's gearshift's got no reverse, so all we can do is keep moving forward."

"Well, she got that right," Jewel said. "I think I remember her. She was married to Clapper Jackson, wasn't she?"

"Yes. She worked for Gram for several years."

"That's right. I do remember. She made a cranberry delight that your grandmother served during the Christmas open house every year."

"Yeah. I'm surprised you remember."

"She was the sweetest woman. Had a smile that could light up New York. You remember her, Sid?"

Sid shrugged. "Vaguely. I do remember the cranberry delight."

"I don't remember her," Seth said. "Why are we talking about her?"

"I don't know," Jewel said. "Jane mentioned her. Whatever happened to her, Jane?"

Jane thought a moment. "Seems like she and Clapper moved back down to South Carolina. I can't remember exactly when she left. I guess I was around.. . . I don't know . . . maybe thirteen or so when they moved away. I stayed in touch with her for a little while, but I wasn't very good at writing letters, so we eventually fell out of touch."

"Well, that's what happens," Jewel said philosophically. "People move in and out of our lives. People you're close to one day are gone the next. Very few stay for the whole show."

"I guess that's true," Jane said quietly.

"Now, Jewel, don't go maudlin on us," Sid chided.

"I'm not, Sid. Just stating the facts."

"The important ones stay. That's what matters."

"Not necessarily, dear. Sometimes it's the important ones that go. That's the problem right there. We spend half our lives losing the people we love."

Sid waved a hand. "Never mind. My stomach's growling. How about we go down to the cafeteria and bring us back a snack."

"Well, all right. Jane, honey, would you like to come along? Or can we bring you back something?"

"No thanks. I'm not hungry. I'll stay here with Seth."

When the older couple left, Jane sat down in the chair beside Seth's bed. Seth looked at her, looked away. Neither had anything to say to the other. The room was quiet.

Sent: Sunday, June 19, 2005 5:46 PM
From: Diana Penland <monkeytrial@unc.edu>
To: Jane Morrow <jane1980@morrow.com>
Subject: Catch me up

So what's going on with Ted? Did he call you this weekend? Don't keep me in the dark.

Sent: Sunday, June 19, 2005 7:04 PM
From: Jane Morrow <jane1980@morrow.com>
To: Diana Penland <monkeytrial@unc.edu>
Subject: RE: Catch me up

Nothing is going on with Ted. He hasn't called. I can't say I'm sorry, as it would only complicate matters, and heaven knows my life is far too complicated now as it is. What was I thinking when I gave him my number? Obviously, I wasn't thinking; that's the problem.

Your two rascals are doing fine, though Roscoe snapped at a bee yesterday and was promptly stung on the nose. He retreated to the house, whimpering and defeated. I tried to play nurse by holding an ice cube on his nose, but he didn't much care for that either. He's all better today, though, and happily snapping at bees again, so apparently he didn't learn his lesson. Juniper is much smarter and ignores the bees, preferring to spend her time sniffing at molehills.

The pups are perfect companions for me this summer. Their joy at seeing me when I come home is just the diversion I need after spending time with Seth. Speaking of whom, I see some improvement in his spirits, but not much. Whenever he's lost in thought, I fear what he might be thinking.

Gram called yesterday to see how everything's going. Since I haven't yet broken it off with Seth, I'm pretty sure things aren't going in the direction she had hoped. I know she wants what's best for me, but I'm the only one who can decide that.

It's not an easy decision. If I believed in crystal balls, I might consult one. I look at the night sky and wonder if our future is written in the stars. Tea leaves, Tarot cards, palm readers . . . is there someone who can see my future and tell me what to do?

Well, never mind. I've decided I'm not going to ask anyone's opinion. If my life were a democracy and the decision was up for a vote, the final tally would be however many to one. I'd be the only one voting for me to stay with Seth. Everyone else would vote against. Well, maybe Truman would vote for. Have I told you about Truman? He lives at the VA community home, and he used to be a doctor. Nice guy. We've become friends.

I know how you would vote, of course, Diana, and when I try to look at everything objectively, I do see how crazy it looks for me to stay. From the outside looking in, I can almost see the reasons for giving up. But I just can't do it. Not yet.

I'm giving myself a headache thinking of all this. Suffice it to say, Ted is a non-event. I continue to stand by Seth. I think I've settled into a waiting mode with the hope that time will tell me what to do.

So what about you and Carl? What's happening in Europe?

Sent: Monday, June 20, 2005 12:26 AM
From: Diana Penland <monkeytrial@unc.edu>
To: Jane Morrow <jane1980@morrow.com>
Subject: RE: Catch me up

I can't say I'm not disappointed about Ted. Though who knows but maybe he'll still get in touch. It's been only a couple of days, after all.

You know I always liked Seth. You know that, right? So my vote for you to move on does not come easily. I know this has all been devastating to you, and you have no idea how much I wish Seth had never been wounded. You two should have been able to move forward with your lives uninterrupted. But it isn't up to me. It isn't up to anyone, I suppose. Fate has the upper hand, and as far as we mortals go, I'm not sure we have a hand at all.

I have been traveling throughout England while Carl slaves away, though he claims to be enjoying himself. I've taken in the sites at Salisbury, Bath, Dover, and a delightful little town called Hemsby. I never thought I'd do this, but because so many friends and students are wanting to know about the trip, I've started a blog. That way I don't have to write out the same stories dozens of times over. If you want all the grand details, here's the link: cruisingwithcarl. blogspot.com. In two more days we move on to Florence. Heavenly!

Tell Roscoe to behave himself. No more tangling with bees. Don't forget both dogs have an appointment to get their nails trimmed at the vet's on the 27th. Just put it on the credit card I left there for expenses.

All for now, Jane. It's been a long day and my eyelids are drooping.

Sending love.

Diana

— 24 —

On Monday afternoon, as soon as Jane entered the lobby of the medical center, she heard music rising up from the atrium. She hoped it was Jon-Paul at the piano, and when she stepped to the railing and peered over, she wasn't disappointed.

Taking the elevator down, she moved across the room and waited for Jon-Paul to finish. Even before the last note had faded completely, she asked, "Will you play Moonlight for me?"

Jon-Paul lifted his head and smiled. "I thought that was supposed to be Misty."

"Misty?"

"Yes. You know, the old movie, *Play Misty for Me*."

Jane thought a moment then chuckled. "Oh yeah, I remember now. Clint Eastwood, right?"

"That's it. But you want Moonlight. 'Clair de Lune.' "

"Yes."

He patted the piano bench. "Join me, and I'll play it for you."

Jane sat beside him and watched in wonder as he lifted his fingers to the keys and began to play. When she was a child her grandmother had insisted she take piano lessons, which she had, but the noise she banged out on the keyboard left her teacher sputtering invectives and her mother pleading for quiet. Even Gram had to acknowledge Jane's lack of talent and, after little more than a year, Gram released the teacher and everyone else from further anguish by allowing Jane to quit. Music deserved talent, Gram said, and for that reason even Gram herself refused to play, saying it would be almost a sacrilege to subject the great masterpieces to anything less than perfection. Still, Gram and Jane both appreciated music well played, with Gram often quoting the words of the poet who, upon hearing a symphony of Beethoven, wrote, "This moment is the best the world can give; / The tranquil blossom on the tortured stem."

Now as she sat beside Jon-Paul, listening to the comforting tones rise up, Jane's life circled down to this one tranquil moment. She understood exactly what Edna St. Vincent Millay had known when she cried out for the music not to cease; she didn't want to come back to the world again. She wanted to stay here, right here, where it was safe and calm. No painful years behind, no lonely years ahead. Only serenity in the shape of notes. Had the music gone on forever, she would have happily stayed and listened.

But only too soon, the song was finished. Jon-Paul's hands found each other and, fingers laced, settled in his lap.

Briefly, neither spoke. Then Jane said quietly, "Thank you for that."

He nodded as though he understood what he had given her. "You're welcome," he replied.

She lifted her gaze from the keyboard and, with a sigh, looked around the room. After that small reprieve, she had to come back, to rejoin the world of old soldiers, of the sick and the wounded, of the shell-shocked and the brokenhearted. Back to Seth and to all the uncertainties that defined her life. She felt suddenly weary and realized for once the strength it took simply to wait.

Jon-Paul cleared his throat and fidgeted, making Jane aware of the awkwardness of their sitting in silence side by side, shoulders touching. *I should get up now,* she thought, but before she could begin to rise, Jon-Paul unlatched the crystal on his watch and felt the face. "Listen," he said, "have you had lunch? They make a pretty mean burrito in the cafeteria here, you know."

Jane frowned as he snapped the crystal shut and pulled his sleeve down over the watch. "Aren't you having lunch with your sister and . . . the nurse?" she asked.

"The nurse?"

"Was it Melissa?"

"Oh yeah." He gave a small nod. "Melissa. No, not today."

"Then why are you here? I mean, at the hospital?"

"Well, I . . . I don't know, to tell you the truth. I suppose I wanted some time away from the office. Coming here and playing the piano seemed like the thing to do. So what do you say? Would you like to have lunch?"

"Um, I . . ."

Jon-Paul's smile faded as he looked pensive. "Perhaps I'm stepping out of bounds. I didn't mean—"

"No, no. It's all right. Actually, I'm famished. But let's not go to the cafeteria. There's a place called the Eden Grille over by the mall. Have you been there?"

"Once or twice. As I recall, it was pretty good."

"All right, then. My car's in the lot. I'll drive."

The hostess led them to a booth and laid a couple of menus on the table. Jon-Paul took off his suit coat and tossed it on the bench, then slid in beside it. He loosened his tie, slipped a finger and thumb into his shirt pocket, and pulled out a rectangular magnifying glass. Tapping the menu with his fingertips, he said to Jane, "Would you mind showing me where the burgers are listed?"

"Sure. Let me find them." She glanced over her menu, then pointed to the bottom corner of Jon-Paul's. "Here they are. Looks like they've got quite a variety."

Jon-Paul held the magnifier up to his right eye, followed by the menu. With that, he disappeared behind the laminated pages for what seemed to Jane a long time. She turned to the soup and salad section as she waited for him to reappear. Finally he settled both the menu and the magnifier on the table.

"You know," he said, "once I was in a restaurant like this, and I was reading the menu when I heard a little girl in the booth behind me say, 'Mommy, why is that man kissing the menu?' " Jon-Paul laughed heartily at the memory. "The really funny thing is I'm so used to reading this way, it took me a minute to realize she was talking about me. I can only imagine how strange I must have looked to that little girl!"

Jane laughed politely at Jon-Paul's description of the awkward moment. Though he spoke about it lightly, she wondered how such encounters really made him feel. "What did her mother say?" she asked.

"I honestly don't remember." Jon-Paul shrugged. "She probably told the girl not to make fun of the blind guy. So often people don't know what to say or do. You know?"

Jane did know. Sometimes she had no idea what

to say to Seth, or to Jon-Paul, or to anyone else who was somehow different. "I didn't know you could read with a magnifying glass," she said.

"Oh yes. I have enough vision left for that. At least so far."

"So far? Do you expect your vision to get worse?"

"Yes, eventually. Probably in another three to five years, when I hit my midthirties. I don't expect ever to be completely blind, but undoubtedly my sight will get a little worse before it bottoms out. That's generally how it goes for people with Stargardt's."

"And yet, I think it's great that you can read with the magnifier."

"Yeah, I'm glad I can, but it's really not that unusual. Most of us who are blind don't live in total darkness. It's a common misconception to think we do. Most of us are legally rather than completely blind, which means we do have some sight."

Jane thought about that, realizing she was among those who had always assumed the blind couldn't see anything at all. When it came to the world of the disabled, she had much to learn and many assumptions to lose.

"But of course," Jon-Paul went on, "at home and at the office I have more sophisticated help than just this little magnifying glass. At both places I have a closed circuit television system that greatly magnifies whatever I place under the camera. I use it to read letters and write checks, that kind of thing. Then on my computer I have a program called Zoom Text which makes it possible for me to read e-mail and other documents. I actually do a fair amount of reading on the job. But I don't try to read books. At least not for pleasure. I listen to books on tape or, more often now, books on CD."

Jane put both arms on the table and leaned closer. "You know, Jon-Paul," she said, "I'm ashamed to say I've never once thought about what it might be like to be blind. I just can't imagine trying to do everyday things without being able to see what you're doing."

"Why should you think about it if you don't have to? That's just human nature." He paused and smiled. "Anyway, when it comes to being with a blind person, you've got one thing right."

"Oh? What's that?"

"At least you're not shouting at me, as though my ears don't work just because my eyes don't. You'd be surprised at how many people turn up the volume when they find out I'm blind. It doesn't make much sense, but I guess that's just human nature too."

A waitress appeared at the table, her order pad at the ready. "Have you decided?" she asked.

After placing their orders and surrendering the menus, Jane said, "I understand you stopped by Seth's room on Saturday."

185

"Yeah, I did. I wanted to meet him. I hope you don't mind."

"No, I'm glad you did. But I'm wondering what you talked about."

"Oh, nothing much, really. I introduced myself, told him I'd met you, asked him how he was doing. We didn't talk long. I know some of the other guys on the floor, so I stopped by to see them too."

"Do you think you'll go back?"

"I plan to. I asked Seth if I could, and he said yes."

"Really?"

"Yes, really. Is that so surprising?"

"No. Well, yes, in a way. He's been so down I'm just surprised he's willing to talk to anyone. I'm glad he is."

"Well, we have things in common."

Jane nodded absently, then remembered Jon-Paul couldn't see her gesture. "I guess you do," she said. "I'm grateful to you, Jon-Paul. It's good for Seth to talk to someone who's been able to . . . well, as you say, to cope."

Jon-Paul breathed deeply. "Fortunately, Jane, Seth is surrounded by people who have learned how to cope, or are learning how. He's not alone. At some point he'll come to understand that. What *you* have to understand is that it can be a long process. Seth's loss is still new. I've been dealing with blindness for a dozen years now. You'll need to be patient."

"I know. And I'm trying to be. I'm willing to wait. At least I think I am."

Jon-Paul looked directly at her. He seemed to be studying her just as though he could see her face. Finally he said, "You're very unusual, Jane. Not everyone would be willing to stay committed to someone who's become disabled."

Jane cocked her head and frowned in thought. "I don't think I'm all that unusual, really," she demurred. "Lots of disabled people have husbands or wives or significant others who aren't disabled themselves, don't you think? Look at you. Haven't you started dating Melissa?"

"Hmm, well, case in point. Melissa and I had lunch one time in the hospital cafeteria along with my sister, Carolyn. She was a nice enough girl, but I knew we weren't going anywhere as soon as we reached the cashier and Carolyn had to punch in my PIN for my debit card. After that, the conversation we'd been trying to strike up simply crashed and burned."

"Because of your sight?"

Jon-Paul nodded. "She was too uncomfortable."

"She's a nurse. She should be used to anything."

"Well, having a patient who's blind is one thing. Having a date who's blind is something totally different. For some people, having a spouse who's blind is unthinkable."

"Well, I'm sorry. I'm sorry for *her*. She hardly gave you a fair chance."

"Exactly how I feel about it." Jon-Paul laughed. "But at least I was finally able to convince Carolyn to stop playing matchmaker for me. If I ever find a wife, it'll be my own doing."

"I hope you do, Jon-Paul. Find a wife, that is."

He smiled. "I guess it'd be nice. But if I don't, I'll consider it a shame but not a tragedy. Lots of people don't get married, sighted or blind. Lots of people who get married get divorced. Marriage is hardly the end of one's troubles. Nor, very often, the end of one's loneliness."

Again, Jane took a moment to think. With Jon-Paul, she had both the need and the freedom to do that. "And yet we so desperately want it to be," she said at length. "The end of our loneliness, I mean. We want to fall in love and live happily ever after."

"Yes. Well, I suppose if we didn't think we'd live happily ever after, none of us would ever get married. I have a brother who says it's all just a clever ploy by nature to keep the human race going." Jon-Paul shook his head and chuckled. "I guess he should know. He's married with three kids."

Their waitress returned carrying their orders on a tray. She placed Jane's salad on the table, followed by Jon-Paul's hamburger.

"Can I get you anything else?" the server asked.

Jane looked at her salad and back up at the waitress. "I'm fine, thanks."

"Can I have some ketchup?" Jon-Paul said.

Jane watched the way a line formed between the girl's brows. "The bottle's right there beside the salt shaker."

Jon-Paul looked to his left, then back at the waitress. "So it is," he said. "Then I guess we're fine."

When the waitress left, Jane reached for the bottle of ketchup and placed it beside Jon-Paul's plate. "I wasn't sure whether or not you could see it."

"Thanks," he said with a nod. He lifted the top of the bun off the burger and upended the ketchup bottle. Before replacing the bun, he asked of Jane, "Is it sufficiently drenched?"

She looked at his plate. "I can't even see the meat anymore."

"Perfect." He popped the lid back on the burger and closed up the ketchup bottle. "Listen, speaking of seeing things," he went on, "would you mind showing me your driver's license?"

Jane looked up from the slice of cucumber on the end of her fork. "What for?"

"I want to know what you look like."

Jane laughed. "The picture on my driver's license bears no resemblance to me whatsoever. In fact, it's awful. So no, I won't show it to you."

"Well, do you have another picture then?"

Jane settled the fork in the salad bowl and dug around in her pocketbook. In another moment, she pulled a picture out of a slot in her wallet. "This is my engagement picture with Seth. It's the one we had printed in the paper."

She pushed it across the table toward Jon-Paul. After wiping his hands on a napkin, he studied the photo with his magnifier. "I thought so," he said.

"What?"

"You have curly hair."

"Yes."

"Is it still this long?"

"It's down to my shoulders."

Jon-Paul looked up at her. "You've got it pulled back at the moment?"

"Yes. It's loose in the picture, but it's pulled back into a large barrette right now."

"But there are some loose curls around your face."

"Yes. You can see that?"

"Only vaguely. And it's dark brown."

"Yes."

He went back to the photo. "And your eyes?"

"What about them?"

"What color are they?"

"Kind of hazel."

"Kind of?"

"They seem to waver between green and brown."

Jon-Paul smiled. "Can't make up their mind, is that it?"

"I guess so."

"You don't wear glasses?"

"No."

"Is your eyesight twenty/twenty?"

"So far."

"Count yourself blessed."

After a moment Jane said, "I do."

Jon-Paul gazed at the photo intently, moving the magnifier ever so slightly over the two faces captured there. "You make a fine-looking couple, Jane."

"I always thought so."

"You both look happy."

"We were."

Jon-Paul seemed to glance at her, then away. Was he wondering, even as she was, why she didn't say, *We are?* But he didn't ask. When he spoke, he merely said, "I'm glad to see Seth's face too. Now I can picture him when I talk to him."

"Something sighted people take for granted, of course."

"We take everything for granted, until we don't have it anymore."

Jane pursed her lips as she nodded. "You're right about that."

Jon-Paul slid the photo back across the table. "Thanks," he said. "I'm glad to put a face to a voice."

Jane picked up the photo and gently ran her thumb over the image of Seth's face. They had been happy then, both of them. Back during that brief time when they could take even happiness for granted.

She tucked the photo into her pocketbook, picked up her fork and, staring at the untouched plate of greens, wondered where her appetite had gone.

— 25 —

By the time Jane got home that evening, she was nursing a headache. The few moments spent listening to Jon-Paul play "Clair de Lune" seemed like days ago instead of hours. After their lunch at the Eden Grille, she had spent an interminable amount of time in Seth's room, listening to him rant about everything from the tasteless hospital food to the lack of progress he was making in physical therapy.

"I hate that sip-and-puff chair," he had said.

"But why?"

"Because I feel like a fool. First of all, I'm puffing into a tube to get the thing to go, and I feel ridiculous. And then it doesn't go where I want it to go. I'm tired of bumping into the walls."

"But you'll get the hang of it, Seth. It'll just take some time."

"I don't want to get the hang of it, Jane. Don't you get it? I want to walk." His jaw tightened as his eyes grew moist.

Jane drew in a ragged breath. "I understand," she said.

"No, you don't. You can't."

"I'm trying, Seth."

"You walk in here, and you walk back out again. You don't have a clue what I'd give to do that."

Jane knew that if his tears spilled over, he wouldn't be able to wipe them away. He would hate that. He would be left feeling all the more helpless.

"Okay, Seth," she said, "you won't walk again, but you've got to keep moving forward. You've got to find out what you *can* do and then learn how to do those things."

"Why?"

"Because I want you to. If you can't do it for yourself, can't you do it for me?"

He didn't answer. His tears seemed to have dried up, distilled by the heat of anger. He turned his face away.

"Listen, Seth, I read about a guy with injuries like yours. I don't remember how he ended up a quadriplegic, but after he went through rehab he went back to school and earned a degree in business and—"

"I don't care, Jane. I don't care what other people have done." His face was crimson, his voice strained. "All right, I won't walk again. Okay, I could accept that if I could just use my hands. But I can't. I never will."

"But your injury is incomplete, Seth. We don't know how much movement you'll regain."

"Whatever it is, it won't be enough. I won't be able to do the things I wanted to do. I'll never pick up another tool. I'll never build anything again."

Their conversation, circular and fruitless, had left her frazzled and worn out. She dropped her pocketbook on the kitchen table and stepped out back with the dogs to let them romp in the fenced-in yard. Smiling as she watched the tail-wagging Roscoe and Juniper frolic and sniff the grass for a time, she lowered herself into one of the lawn chairs on the deck. And then she lowered her face to her hands and wept.

It's too much. Too much.

She saw the afternoon cloned and multiplied until it stretched out to a lifetime of failure, frustration, anger. This could be it, from now until death parted them. Was it what she wanted?

She lifted her head and breathed deeply. The memory of Pritchard Park flashed through her mind. Four nights ago she was dancing with Ted, and she had laughed. Once, it had been that way with Seth. They too had danced. They had walked and swum and cross-country skied and bicycled along mountain trails. They had strolled through the streets of Troy, and they had climbed to the top of Chimney Rock where he had asked her to be his wife.

They would never do those things again. And yet, he was still Seth.

I'm so tired I can't think straight.

She wiped both cheeks with the palms of her hands and dug her cell phone out of her jeans pocket.

What do you want?

She wanted exactly what Seth wanted. She wanted her old life back, the one that had been so full of promise. But she could never have it back.

Then?

She didn't know.

"Life's gearshift's got no reverse . . ."

But what did moving forward mean? And where was she going?

She flipped open the phone and punched in a familiar number.

"Rayburn House. Peter Morrow speaking."

"Dad?"

"Jane? What's up?"

Jane wiped a stray tear, took another deep breath. "Nothing, really. Just thought I'd call and see how things are at home."

"Everything's fine. Busy—which is good. We've actually got a full house at the moment. Your grandmother's overseeing dinner right now."

"Oh. Well, that's good, then." Her father had never remarried. He had drifted in and out of relationships in the dozen years since Meredith Morrow's death, but he had never committed.

"So how are things in Asheville? How's Seth?"

"He's doing pretty well. They've got him learning how to use a sip-and-puff wheelchair. He moves it by blowing into a tube."

"No kidding. So he'll be able to get around by himself?"

"Eventually, yeah."

"Good deal." Peter Morrow had married the wrong person to begin with and had consequently lived a sad and lonely life. He had never said as much to Jane, but she knew he wanted something different for her. When Seth was wounded, father and daughter had cried together for the second time in their lives. His empathy for her offered a rare glimpse into her father's wounded heart.

"He's struggling, though. I mean, it's hard."

A moment passed before he said, "I can only imagine."

"But of course it's a big adjustment. People do adjust, though. I met a guy here named Jon-Paul. He went blind as a teenager, but he's told me how he learned to cope with it all."

"Oh?"

She was rambling. She didn't know what she was trying to say, didn't even know why she had called.

"Yeah. I'm meeting lots of interesting people here, Dad."

"Oh yeah? Hey, that's good."

She wanted to ask him what she should do, but she had already asked him once. When Seth was at Walter Reed, telling her not to come.

"What should I do, Dad?"

"I can't tell you what to do, Jane. But I'll support you in whatever you decide."

If she asked again, he'd undoubtedly just say the same thing again. Of course he couldn't tell her what to do. Only she could decide.

"You should see the Penlands' house, Dad," she went on. "It's really beautiful. I can't believe I've got it all to myself this summer."

"Uh-huh." He paused, then, "Listen, Jane, I should tell you, the caterer called. They want to know whether they should refund your deposit."

"Oh?" The caterer she had hired for the wedding reception. "Um, yeah, I guess so. Tell them, though, that . . . tell them we'll be rescheduling and we'll get back in touch with them then."

"All right." Silence. Then, "You know, honey, if it gets to be too much there, you can always come home, whenever you want. Your room's waiting for you."

She'd had her own apartment in Troy before the engagement. Afterward, she had moved back to the Rayburn House to save money for the wedding.

"Okay. Thanks, Dad."

"I mean, even if you just need a few days away. A little bit of a break, you know. It might be a long summer."

"All right. But I'm taking care of the dogs for Diana, you know. I'm not sure what I'd do . . ."

"Oh yes. Well, bring them along with you, if you need to come home."

Come home. The idea was appealing and depressing at the same time.

"So is there anything else new with you and Gram?"

Her father let go a brief laugh. "No, it's pretty much the same-old, same-old around here."

Jane nodded. "Okay, well—"

"Listen, do you want to talk to your grandmother? I can have her pick up the extension in the kitchen."

"No, that's all right."

"Are you sure?"

"Yeah. We talked a long time on Saturday. And I know she gets frazzled at dinnertime, so I'll catch her later."

"All right."

Silence again. Then, "Well, I'll let you go, Dad."

"Okay, honey. Take care of yourself."

"I will. And . . . Dad?"

"Yeah, Janie?"

She didn't know where it came from, but the

question was poised on her lips, begging to be asked. *Do you think Mom ever loved me?*

"What is it, Janie?" her father asked again.

She shook it off. It was too late for all that now. "Tell Gram not to work too hard."

He laughed again. "You know those words will only fall on deaf ears."

She pretended to chuckle. "Yeah, I guess. Well, bye, Dad."

Closing the phone, she looked out over the yard. Juniper was stretched out in a ray of lingering sunlight while Roscoe pawed at the grass by the hedge. A few of the tulips Diana had planted were still in bloom in the small garden, while trails of moonflower vines hugged the fence. The summer evening was infused with a loveliness that suggested serenity and rest.

O beauty . . .

Jane shut her eyes, breathed deeply.

. . . are you not enough?

Jane wanted it to be enough, but she knew the truth only too well. Blossoms fell, vines withered, people didn't stay. What then would satisfy the ache? Was there a love anywhere in this vast creation that didn't disappoint? Surely there was a place to lay one's heart where it wouldn't be broken.

"Oh, God." Jane put her head back, spoke aloud. "I'm so tired. Please hear my prayer and tell me what to do."

— 26 —

Jane paused in the doorway of Seth's room, brought up short by the unexpected sight. Seth grinned up from the bed. Sausalito sat in a folding chair on one side of Seth's bed while Hoboken sat on the other side, both with open laptops balanced on their knees. Jon-Paul stood at the window, as though looking out, both hands at the small of his back.

"Am I late for the party?" Jane asked.

Jon-Paul turned toward her voice and smiled. "Yes, you are, in fact. We're having a LAN party. Come on in and join us."

"A land party?" Jane stepped to the vinyl chair and sat down, crossing her legs. "What's a land party?"

"Oh, Jane," Seth said with a mock sigh, "you're hopelessly technically challenged."

"Yes, and you've always known that. So what's a land party?"

Hoboken looked up from his laptop. "That's L-A-N," he explained. "It stands for local area network, Miss Jane."

Jane stared at Hoboken a moment. "That tells me exactly nothing," she said.

Hoboken laughed. "It's simple, really. When

people say they're having a LAN party, they all come together with their computers and hook up with each other to play a game online. Right now, Seth and Jon-Paul are playing chess."

"Playing chess?"

"Yes. I'm moving for Jon-Paul and Saus is moving for Seth."

"You are?"

Sausalito joined the conversation with a nod. "They just tell us which piece they want to move where, and we do it."

"Yeah," said Seth. "Which means we have to trust them to get it right. Of course, if I lose, I can blame Sausalito for messing up somewhere, just like he messed up when he was sending that e-mail to Mom and Dad for me."

"No, no, no, Mr. Seth." Sausalito shook his head. "I know what I'm doing. I won't mess up. We're going to win."

"That's what you think, cousin," Hoboken said. "Mr. Jonny is a clever man. I think you have met your match."

"Listen, Hoboken," Seth said, "who's playing this game—Saus or me?"

"You are, of course, Mr. Seth."

"And I happen to have been the chess champ of Troy High, so I'd say I can give Jon-Paul here a run for his money."

"Hmm," Jon-Paul said, rubbing his chin thoughtfully. "Maybe we *should* be playing for money."

Seth shook his head. "I'd hate to see you go into debt."

"Go into debt, nothing!" Jon-Paul laughed. "I could use the extra change in my pocket."

"No one's going to win anything," Sausalito interjected, "unless somebody makes the next move."

"Whose turn is it?" Jon-Paul asked.

Hoboken laughed loudly. "Have you forgotten, Mr. Jonny? It's your turn. I've been waiting a very long time for you to tell me your next move. If you don't tell me soon, I'll have to make it for you."

"You can't do that," Seth said. "If you do, Jon-Paul forfeits the game."

"Not so fast, Mr. Seth," Sausalito said. "I've played chess with my cousin there many times. Believe me, you should go ahead and let him make the moves for Mr. Jonny. You are sure to win, then."

"No one's going to make any moves for me," Jon-Paul interjected, pointing an index finger into the air. "I'm almost ready. Just give me another minute to think."

When he turned back toward the window, Jane moved to Hoboken and studied the laptop over his shoulder. Diana had taught her to play chess when they were both teenagers. Jane wasn't particularly fond of the game, but at least she knew which piece was which and how each could move. "So—" she said, intending to ask a question, but Jon-Paul shushed her.

"Genius at work here." He rose up on his toes and back down. "I need quiet. All right, Hoboken. Here's my move. Knight to queen's bishop 3. Got it?"

Hoboken tapped at the keyboard. "Got it."

"Your move, Mr. Seth," Sausalito said.

"So," Jane tried again, "you guys have to remember all the moves? You have to remember where all the pieces are on the chess board?"

"That's right," Seth said. "It adds a whole new layer of challenge to the game."

"Except," Sausalito added, "if they need a reminder, we can tell them what is where."

"You weren't supposed to tell her that, Saus," Seth complained. "Now she won't be nearly so impressed."

Jane laughed. "Don't worry about that. I'm impressed enough as it is. How long has this game been going on?"

Hoboken looked at his watch. "About thirty minutes."

"Won't it take you all day to finish?"

"At the rate we're going," Seth said, "it's going to take a couple of months."

"Hardly!" Jon-Paul cried. "A couple of weeks, max."

Jane looked from Hoboken to Sausalito and back again. "What if you guys get caught doing this?"

"Get caught?" Hoboken shrugged. "We're not doing anything wrong."

"What about, you know, your jobs . . . taking care of the patients?"

"Oh!" Hoboken laughed. "This is our day off. We're not working. We just came in for the fun. Don't you see we are not in uniform?"

Jane hadn't noticed the jeans and T-shirts they were wearing instead of the aide uniforms. "So you've come in on your day off?"

"Of course," Sausalito said. "We couldn't miss this. But we are here only an hour since we have classes this afternoon."

"Yeah," Seth said, "and I've got a busy schedule too, you know. Physical therapy. Occupational therapy. The afternoon soaps."

Jane smiled at Seth. He returned it. How different his mood was today from yesterday.

"So, Mr. Seth," Sausalito said. "Time's wasting. It's your move, you know."

Seth shut his eyes, opened them again. "All right, I'm thinking. I can see it all perfectly in my mind's eye."

"So can I, Seth," Jon-Paul said, "and if I'm not mistaken, you're going to be in trouble soon."

"That's what you think," Seth countered. "I'm full of surprises. Now, quiet please while I concentrate."

Jane moved back to the vinyl chair and sat quietly, taking in the scene being played out in the room. Seth occupied with the game, rising to the challenge, even animated by it. The cousins from Uganda, casting the occasional competitive glance at each other. Jon-Paul, standing calmly by the window, a tiny smile at the corner of his lips. *He knows what he's doing,* Jane thought. And she was grateful.

Before Seth could call out his move, a man Jane didn't recognize wheeled himself up to Seth's door. "What's going on, comrades?" he asked.

Sausalito looked up from his laptop. "Hello, Mr. George. We're in the middle of a chess game here. Seth Ballantine versus Jon-Paul Pearcy. It's a fierce competition."

"Oh yeah?" George asked. "Well, how about if I take on the winner?"

Seth turned his head toward the door. "The game probably won't be over for some time yet, but I'll be glad to take you on as soon as I'm finished with Jon-Paul here."

"Hold on there, Seth," Jon-Paul said. "Not so fast. We're only just getting started. I've barely had the chance yet to show my stuff."

"Well, listen," George said, "whoever wins goes up against me next. Or . . ." He paused a moment as he backed up his wheelchair and looked up and down the corridor. "Hey, Glen!" he hollered. "Come down here a minute."

In another moment George and Glen were side

by side at the door in their wheelchairs. "What's up?" Glen said.

"You play chess?" George asked.

Glen shrugged. "Yeah, but I'm not very good."

"Perfect," George said. "I'll play you while these two clowns are playing, and then the winners will play each other."

Glen looked hesitant but Sausalito perked up. "That's a great idea, Mr. George! But listen, why don't we have a real tournament? Open it up to all the guys on the floor who want to play."

His suggestion was met with an enthusiastic murmur of agreement until Hoboken said, "But you know, in the day room there are only two chess sets, and one of them is missing several pieces."

"Some of the guys have laptops like mine and Jon-Paul's," Seth said. "They can play online."

"A few have computers, yes," Hoboken said, "but not many."

"So we'd need to get a bunch of chess sets if we want to have a tournament," Seth said.

"No worries," Jon-Paul assured everyone. "Consider it done."

"What?" Seth asked. "You're going to go clear the shelves at Walmart?"

"Maybe he owns stock in Parker Brothers," George said.

"Let's just say I have my connections," Jon-Paul said. "If you guys can find out how many chess sets we need, I'll get them here."

"I'll find out for you, Mr. Jonny," Hoboken said.

"Great. Seth, what do you think? Should we turn this thing into a full-fledged tournament?"

"Only if there's a cash prize involved."

"I'll pass the hat," George offered. "Ten-dollar entry fee."

"Don't be stingy, George," Seth said. "Make it twenty."

"Now you're talking," George shot back.

Glen shrugged. "My wife's going to kill me for losing the twenty, but count me in."

"Way to be confident, Glen," Seth said. "You haven't even set up your pieces and you're apologizing to the wife for losing."

"You don't know Glen's wife," George said. "He'd have to apologize to her even if he won. This poor henpecked guy has to apologize just for living."

Glen took off his baseball cap and swatted George. Seth and Jon-Paul laughed loudly. Hoboken closed up his computer and said, "I'm going to find out right now how many want to play. Then, cousin, you and I have to get to school."

Sausalito's face shone. "So when will the tournament begin?"

"Give me a couple of days," Jon-Paul said. "Soon as I can get the chess sets here, we'll begin."

"Terrific!" Hoboken said. "It's . . . what do you say? Game on!"

"Yeah, and I can feel the prize money burning a hole in my pocket even now," Seth announced.

"Well, I have just one question," Jane said, "and that's for Jon-Paul."

"And what's that?" Jon-Paul asked.

"You're always here playing the piano, and now you're playing games. Don't you ever work?"

Jon-Paul raised his brows. "Not when there are more important things to do."

Jane smiled up at him. He somehow must have known, because he smiled back.

— 27 —

Sent: Thursday, June 23, 2005 10:07 PM
From: Jane Morrow <jane1980@morrow.com>
To: Diana Penland <monkeytrial@unc.edu>
Subject: Some kind of wonderful

Diana,

Something wonderful is going on here, and I can't go to bed tonight until I tell you about it. Seth and another guy named Jon-Paul have started up a chess tournament, and over the last couple of days it's been going full steam ahead. Fourteen games are being played right now, and everyone involved has thrown $20 into the kitty, so at the end the winner will claim the prize of $560, which is nice but not nearly the best thing about all this. What's really wonderful is that since the tournament started, there's been a change in the atmosphere up on the fifth floor. That's where Seth is, and of course it's the spinal cord unit, so everyone involved in the tournament is paralyzed to some extent. Except for Jon-Paul, who isn't a vet and isn't paralyzed, although he's blind (more about that in another e-mail). Oh, and Truman, the older man I mentioned who's a doctor and who lives in the Community Living Center. Anyway, when I went to visit today, I could sense this air of excitement and expectation that wasn't there before, as though this little bit of friendly competition has lifted everybody's spirits. Including Seth's!

When I arrived, Seth and Jon-Paul were playing out on the big screened-in porch, along with a bunch of other people (five or six games were under way, I guess). Seth and Jon-Paul are playing the game on computers. Two of the aides are actually making the moves for them. A few others are playing on computers too, though Jon-Paul managed to bring in some half dozen or more chess boards for people without laptops. Anyway, as I was walking down the hall to join them, I heard this huge explosion of laughter coming from the porch. I stopped to listen.

Quiet, and then more laughter. It sounded more like they were having a party than playing chess. So when I got there I asked what was going on, and the aide who was making the moves for Seth (his nickname is Hoboken—I can't remember his real name) said in that sweet Ugandan voice of his, "Mr. Seth is . . . how do you say it? . . . he's cracking us all up with his stories." I was stunned. Seth telling stories? Making people laugh?

Jon-Paul said (in a wink-wink kind of way) that Seth was just trying to distract him so he'd make a bad move, to which Seth assured him that all's fair in love and war.

He was the Seth I used to know, the one who loved an audience, the one who loved to make people laugh. And the one who naturally drew people to himself because he was just so likable. Seth was enjoying himself, and I can't tell you how good it was to see that. It's a giant step forward!

But there's something else too. I was talking with Hoboken alone later, after Seth was taken down to PT. He said Seth had asked him to wheel him down to the new guy's room that morning. The new guy, Philip, just arrived from Walter Reed a few days ago. He's a C-6, which means his injury is nearly as bad as Seth's. From what Hoboken says, he's pretty depressed. Just like all the men and women who are trying to adjust to their paralysis. So somehow Seth heard about him and asked Hoboken to wheel him down so he could invite Philip to join the chess tournament. Philip said no because he doesn't know how to play chess, but instead of leaving right away Seth stayed and talked with him for a while because he could see the guy needed someone to talk to who was in the same boat. At least that's how it seemed to Hoboken.

I don't know whether Seth's attempt at kindness made Philip feel any better, but I do know it makes me feel better, because when I first got here a couple of long weeks ago I never would have imagined Seth doing such a thing.

I know I should guard against being unreasonably optimistic, but I do think things are starting to turn around. I think Seth might be—as Jon-Paul puts it—beginning to take inventory of what he has left rather than thinking about what he's lost. He can't do what he once wanted to do with his life, but he can do *something,* and that's what matters.

I feel much lighter tonight, much more hopeful than I've felt in a long while. For the first time, I'm looking forward to going to the VA hospital tomorrow to see Seth and the gang. Seth and the gang! Doesn't that have a crazy good sound to it!

All for now, but more soon, I promise.

Love,

Jane

— 28 —

The next morning Jane stepped out of the elevator on Five and hurried down the hall. She saw numerous games in progress in various rooms, the opponents bent over the boards in concentration. But when she reached Seth's room, he was alone in a wheelchair. Someone had parked him close to the window so he could see the view.

He turned to her when she walked in. "Hey," he said.

"Where's Jon-Paul?"

"He couldn't get away from the office."

"Oh, so he actually does work."

"A little, maybe." He tried to smile.

"Will he be coming by tomorrow?"

"I'm not sure."

Jane dropped her pocketbook on the floor and dragged the vinyl chair close to Seth. She sat, settled her elbows on the arms of the chair and laced her fingers over her lap. She felt at a loss as to what to do now, since the plans had changed. She looked around the room, back at Seth. How could a person feel so awkward with her own fiancé?

"So—" she began.

"I've been sitting here thinking, Jane," he interrupted.

"Oh?"

"Yeah. I've been thinking about the irony of it all."

Jane frowned, pursed her lips. "What do you mean?"

He hesitated, as though reluctant to explain. Finally he said, "Well, I joined the National Guard to help me get through college, you know?"

Jane nodded.

"But I stayed in it for us. I thought it could help us financially." He laughed lightly, sadly. "I actually thought it would help us."

She took a deep breath, let it out. "Listen, Seth, you couldn't know what was going to happen. It's not like any of us knows the future."

"Yeah, but still, I can't get past the feelings of guilt."

"I don't understand."

"It's what I did to you, Jane."

"To me?"

"I went to Iraq a perfectly normal healthy person,

and I came back like this. It's ruined everything for you. *I've* ruined everything for you."

"No you haven't, Seth. Please don't say that."

"But it's true."

"It isn't."

He closed his eyes as a pained expression crossed his face. "The first day you came here, you asked me to tell you that I don't love you anymore. Do you remember that?"

"Yes."

He looked directly at her, into her eyes. "I couldn't say I don't love you because I do. I do love you, Jane."

She almost smiled. "I love you too, Seth."

"But . . ." He paused. A muscle in his jaw quivered.

"But what?"

"I'm not sure that's enough."

She waited quietly for him to go on.

After a moment he said, "I don't want your whole life to be devoted to taking care of me. You deserve more than that."

"But what if that's what I want?"

"You can say that now, but what about five years, ten years, twenty years down the line? You'd be a nurse, not a wife."

"Other people do it and anyway, for better or for worse, remember?"

"That's after you get married, not before. You don't have to stay with me, Jane. I'm afraid if you did, you'd only grow to resent me. I couldn't live with that. Neither of us could."

She wanted to respond, but she wasn't sure she could speak without breaking down. She needed a minute or two to compose herself, to put up the steel rods in her chest that made her at least appear strong, however untrue that was.

"Jane, listen," Seth went on, "I'm sorry I asked you to help me die. That was stupid. I was just so . . ." He shook his head.

"It's all right. I understand," she whispered. "I know you think I don't, but I do."

"I wish I'd died when the bullet hit me—"

"Please don't say that, Seth."

"But don't you see? It would have been so much easier." He drew in a deep breath and let it out slowly. "But for some reason I'm still here. So I've decided I've got to try to make the best of it. Playing chess with Jon-Paul makes me realize I still have my mind. Maybe that counts for something."

"Of course it does. It counts for a great deal."

"So . . ." Another sigh. "I've got to concentrate on getting better, whatever that means."

She nodded and leaned forward in the chair. "I'm glad, Seth. I'm really glad."

"But, Jane?"

"Yes?"

"It's going to take every ounce of strength I've got."

Jane nodded, though she was unsure of what he meant.

"I'm not sure I have any strength left over to be what you want me to be."

"I don't want you to be anything other than what you are."

"It's not enough."

"It *is* enough."

The muscles in his jaw twitched again. "Right now I can only concentrate on trying to get better. I can't shoulder the responsibility of being your fiancé on top of that."

Jane felt herself go weak. She sat back in the chair. "What are you saying?"

"It's just that . . . something tells me that if I love you, I should let you go. I know it will hurt for a time, but you'll get over it. And then you'll go on and make a real marriage."

"Please don't let me go."

"But, Jane—"

"I don't want you to let me go."

"But I want you to have a real marriage."

Jane thought a long while. Seth seemed content to wait. At length she seemed to understand. "It would be better for you if we weren't engaged."

He turned to her with apologetic eyes. "Yes."

She nodded stiffly. "I'm not very good at giving up, but if that's what you want, I'll do it for you."

"I'm doing it for you, Jane."

She lifted her hand to her head in confusion. *Don't cry. Not yet. Not until after you leave.*

"What should I do now?" she asked.

"You should do whatever you want. But it might be best if you go on back to Troy."

"I want to stay here. Besides, I'm house-sitting for Diana."

Silence. Then, "All right."

"I want to keep seeing you."

"If you do, we'll be going back to square one."

"What do you mean?"

"You will be getting to know Seth the quadriplegic. You need to know who I am now, not who I used to be. We'll be starting over at the ground floor. We'll be starting as friends."

"It's a little hard to go backward, Seth."

"We're not going backward. We're wiping off the slate and starting over. Different man, different relationship. No ties. You're free to go at any time. If you meet someone else, I'm not going to stand in your way." He stopped, rolled his eyes up to the ceiling, then back at her. He laughed lightly. "I'm not going to stand in your way. Get it? Since I couldn't stand, even if I wanted to."

"It's not funny, Seth."

The grin slid off his face. "Sorry."

"I'm not sure I can do this."

"There are no other options, Jane."

Jane looked down at her hands, at the engagement ring she had so joyfully worn. She held it up for Seth to see. "I guess I should take this off?"

He nodded. "It would be best."

Reluctantly, she slipped it off and put it in her jeans pocket. "I'm going to keep it, though," she said, "just in case the day comes when I can put it back on."

"Fair enough."

Her stomach turned and something began to pound right behind her eyes. "I think I'm going to go now."

"All right."

She picked up her pocketbook and stood. "Can I . . . is it all right if I come back sometime?"

"As long as you know where we stand."

She looked toward the window, lifted her chin. "I guess you've made that pretty clear."

She turned to go, had almost reached the door, when he called her name. "Jane?"

"Yes?"

"It's only because I love you."

Love? Was there not one place to lay your heart where it wouldn't be broken?

She turned and looked at him. And then she turned away and left the room.

She strode purposefully down the hall, her eyes downcast, her gaze intent. She wanted to see no one, and she wanted no one to see her. The elevator came, the doors opened—it was empty, thankfully—and she rode down. The lobby was busy with patients and their families. No one played a tune on the piano in the atrium.

She pushed open the front door and stepped out into the heat of the June day. Her chest heaved with tears as she walked toward the parking lot.

Is this the answer to my prayer, God?

She clenched her jaw, quickened her pace. She wanted to get home where she could give in to the tears.

She had reached her Honda and was about to unlock the door when her cell phone rang. Digging it out of her pocketbook, she looked at the lighted screen to see who was calling. A local area code. But the name of the caller was given as Unknown, and she didn't recognize the number. She didn't want to answer. But she did.

"Hello?"

"Jane? It's Ted Taggert."

"Oh?"

"Listen, a group of us from the U are going to the drumming circle tonight. Do you want to come down and join us?"

— 29 —

It was a night she would later remember in bits and pieces. The long hunt for a parking space on the streets surrounding the park, long enough that she briefly considered giving up and going home. The familiar rhythm of the drums, the slant of evening light between the buildings, the dull relentless sense that she should not have come even as she stood at the edge of the park, scanning the crowd.

You're a fraud and a liar. Go home.

There was Ted, standing on the sidewalk along Patton Avenue, directly across from where she stood on College Street. He raised a hand, beckoned her over.

I have no business here.

"Jane," he said when she reached him, "good to see you. Glad you could come." He took her hand, leaned over, kissed her cheek.

"Thanks for inviting me," she said. At least she thought she said it. She couldn't hear herself speak, couldn't hear herself think, above the incessant thumping of the drums.

He introduced her to his friends. She heard their names and promptly forgot. They smiled, said hello, eyed her warily. Or maybe she just imagined their guardedness. Maybe she just imagined they could see right through her, all the way to the VA hospital, all the way to Seth.

The blond girl turned her face away, said something to Ted that Jane couldn't hear. Warning him? *Be careful. She's on the rebound.*

You don't give up your fiancé one minute and go meet another man the next. That's not the way it's done. Jane knew that. Then why was she here?

"So how you been?" He smiled at her, put a hand on her elbow.

She looked at him, tried to conjure up an answer, settled for the cliché. "Fine. I'm fine. How about you?"

"Busy," he said. "I was called out of town this past week on some business, or I would have called you sooner."

A broken heart was weak, became disconnected from the brain, had no rudder to steer it. A broken heart was prone to foolishness.

You should have said no. You shouldn't have answered the phone.

"We thought we'd hang out here for a while," he went on, "and then go catch dinner somewhere. Will that be all right?"

"Sure. Sure, that sounds good."

And then what? Pretend there was no Seth? Pretend that all was well in her life?

She listened to their conversation as though from a distance, heard them laugh. She winced at the sound of it. She knew she ought to join in, she ought to say something. She tried, but every utterance sounded banal and insincere. *So what do you teach at the U? Have you always lived in Asheville? I love your necklace. Is that a sapphire?*

She scarcely heard what anyone said in response.

Maybe Ted knew she was floundering. Without asking, he tugged at her hand, led her out to the dance floor. She was a puppet, to be pulled by strings.

If she let herself be pulled into the dance she might find the pleasure in it, just like last time, when dancing to the drums had made her laugh. After all, it was supposed to make her one with the universe, with the cosmic consciousness, with the divine. There had to be some joy in that, didn't there? Or peace. Or nirvana. The blowing out . . . the extinction.

Nothingness. That would be nice. Could one commit emotional suicide? Pry the emotion chip out of your heart and go on living?

The drumming went on and on. Hadn't they been here for several years now?

"Want to sit down for a while?"

She felt herself nod.

As they moved through the crowd toward the concrete tiers, he motioned toward a street vendor selling hot dogs and sodas. "You thirsty? Want something to drink?"

"No thanks. I'm fine."

They sat. The sun was low, the shadows long. Summer nights had always been her favorite slice of life, back in Troy, back in time, back in all the days before today.

He was there, too close, leaning toward her, his face near her hair. "Do you mind if I kiss you?"

"Yes."

Yes, I mind.

But he didn't understand. How could he? When he kissed her, she drew back, broke down in tears.

"What's the matter?"

"Nothing."

"Nothing?"

"I have to go." She jumped up.

"Wait a minute! Jane!"

She felt his hand on her arm, turning her around.

"Did I do something wrong?"

"No, I—"

"What's wrong with you? Why are you crying?"

"I'm sorry, Ted. It's not you. It's me. I shouldn't have come."

"But what—"

"I'm sorry. Really, I'm sorry."

Later, she wouldn't remember driving home, though she must have somehow found her car and driven from downtown across I-240 to Montford Avenue. She didn't recall the moments between Pritchard Park and the Penlands' house, but she slowly became aware of herself standing in front of the liquor cabinet, staring at all the pretty bottles.

There was only one sure way not to feel anything anymore. One sure passage to the place of no pain.

Oh, Seth!

— 30 —

She stayed away from the hospital for five days. On the morning of the sixth, Truman called and asked her to come.

"What's the matter?"

"Seth has pneumonia."

"How bad is it?"

"I'm not sure. I think he'll be all right, but why don't you come on in. They've got him in ICU."

Jane snapped her cell phone shut and steadied herself against the kitchen counter. At the thought of pneumonia, she felt all the strength drop out of her and gather in a puddle at her feet. She shut her eyes and took a few deep breaths. After a moment she pushed herself away from the counter and looked around the kitchen. She felt disgusted by what she saw. Piles of dirty dishes in the sink. A stack of unread newspapers on the table. Splashes of spaghetti sauce across the parquet flooring. And empty bottles everywhere. One on the table, one on the counter, one in the sink. Were there more in the den? She didn't know, couldn't remember.

For the past five days she had secluded herself in the Penlands' home, slowly sipping away the sorrow while Seth was in the hospital succumbing to pneumonia. How could she have let this happen? She suddenly felt she was in the wrong place—no, in the wrong *person,* as though she had slipped into her mother's skin and was consorting with a bottle while the one who needed her most was left alone.

Truman met her outside the doors of the intensive care unit. His eyes spoke before his mouth did, telling her he was worried.

"Thanks for coming, Jane," he said when she reached him.

She shook her head. "Of course. How is he?"

"He's one sick fellow, but the doctors are doing everything they should be doing."

"Last time I saw him, he was fine." But that was six days ago. A lot can happen in the span of a week.

"I believe it was Sunday he started getting sick. Cold symptoms, at first. The typical sneezing, watery eyes, sinus drainage. For most of us, just an annoyance."

Jane nodded.

Truman went on, "By yesterday it was full-fledged pneumonia. He was moved into ICU where they started him on IV antibiotics. He seems to be responding well."

"But I don't understand, Truman," Jane said. "He had a pneumonia vaccine."

"Yes, but there are different kinds of pneumonia. And of course someone who's a quad is particularly susceptible. Since the muscles around his lungs don't work, it's next to impossible for him to cough up the congestion in his chest. That's the real danger."

Jane looked away, down the long empty corridor. "Pneumonia is the number-one killer of quads, isn't it?" She looked back at Truman.

"That doesn't mean Seth won't get over this, Jane," he said. But his eyes, at least for the moment, spoke otherwise. He was having his doubts. "Why don't you go on in and see him? You're allowed ten minutes at a time. There are gowns, gloves, and masks outside his room. You'll have to put them on before you go in."

"All right."

"Ten minutes. That's all. Any longer and the nurse will ask you to leave."

"Okay."

Truman put a hand on her shoulder. "I'll be in the waiting room when you come out. If you want to talk."

She gave a small uncertain smile before pushing her way through the doors of the ICU.

His eyes were closed in sleep, though his face was far from peaceful. His brow was heavy and his eyelids twitched. His breathing was labored in spite of the oxygen mask that covered his nose and mouth. He looked as though he was listening to the lopsided battle going on inside his body, that of his compromised immune system against an invading army of microbes. The battle must have reached a fevered pitch, as fresh beads of perspiration broke out along his forehead.

"Seth?" Jane said.

He didn't respond.

Jane gazed at the IV dripping antibiotics into a vein beneath his collarbone. A second IV sent hydrating fluids into a vein in his arm. They were the fresh troops, the reinforcements sent to the front in the hopes of winning this war. Monitors above the bed displayed their progress: pulse, respiration, blood pressure. And on a separate monitor, the slow and steady beating of his heart.

"Seth?" she said again.

She touched his arm, remembered he had no feeling there. She moved her hand to his forehead. Even through the glove she wore his skin felt warm.

His eyes fluttered open. They looked glassy and bright, like the eyes of a porcelain doll. It seemed a great effort for him to focus on her face. "Jane?"

"Hi, Seth."

He tried to wet his lips with his tongue. His voice was muffled by the oxygen mask. "You look like a nurse."

Jane laughed lightly behind the surgical mask. "Yeah. Truman said we have to wear all this stuff to come in and see you."

Seth nodded. Then he asked, "You mad at me?"

"No. Of course not. Why would I be mad at you?"

"What I said. Last time."

"No. No, I'm not mad, Seth."

"You haven't been here."

"I just needed a little time away. But I'm here now. Truman called to tell me you have pneumonia. I wanted to see how you are."

"Well," he said, raising his brows, "I've been better."

"Listen, you shouldn't talk. Reserve your strength. I just wanted to let you know I'm here."

He seemed to fall back to sleep then. But after a moment he opened his eyes and looked up at her. "You know . . ."

When he didn't go on, she leaned closer and said, "What, Seth?"

"I won the game. I beat Jon-Paul."

She smiled, surprised by the surge of pleasure and pride that coursed through her. "But of course," she said, "I knew you would." She leaned over and, through the mask, she kissed his moist brow. "I have to go now. You get some more sleep. I'll be back soon."

Truman was in the waiting room, along with several other people who had family members in the ICU. Before Jane could sit down beside him, Truman said, "Listen, there's a small chapel right down the hall. The pews are kind of hard, but at least it's someplace quiet to sit."

"All right."

She followed him slowly as he moved on stiff knees down the hall. He turned into a small windowless room and slipped into a pew. Jane slid in beside him. The door and the altar were separated by only half a dozen pews. The entire chapel was almost as small as Seth's room on the fifth floor.

"It looks like they don't exactly expect a crowd for services," Jane noted.

Truman smiled. "There's a larger chapel off the front lobby where they hold services. This one seems to be reserved for people who want to come and pray."

The room was largely unadorned, save for a brass cross and a couple of matching candlesticks on the altar. Jane waited a moment, expecting Truman to ask her where she'd been this past week. But he didn't ask. He seemed to be waiting for her to speak first.

"Truman?" she finally said.

"Uh-huh?"

"How did you let Maggie go?"

Truman frowned in thought. Then he said, "I didn't have any choice."

"But you said you tried to get her to go away with you."

"Oh yes. I begged her to come. But I had very little time to convince her. Once we knew Tommy Lee Coleman was still alive, I had to get out of Travelers Rest. I had to disappear quickly."

"I just can't believe she'd give you up so easily."

"Easily? She saw me refuse to help a man. She saw me leave him to die. That's no small thing."

"I suppose. But part of me thinks she should have understood. After all, Tommy Lee's father left your brother to die."

Truman chuckled quietly. "As Mamma always said, two wrongs don't make a right."

"But, Truman, even if what you did was wrong, Maggie should have forgiven you. She should have allowed you to be human."

Truman shrugged. "I wish she had."

"Why didn't she?"

"Everything happened so fast. There was just no time."

"Did you ever contact her again, once you left?"

"No, I never did. I know it must seem strange to you, but I couldn't let my whereabouts be known. In the '60s a white man didn't need much of an excuse to lynch a black man. Well, the Colemans had an excuse, all right. I had to disappear, start all over again somewhere else."

"And you've never been back to Travelers Rest since?"

"No, I never have. But then, I had no real reason to go back. My folks moved to Greenville and lived there till their deaths. My siblings scattered, most of them leaving the South. Only one of my sisters stayed there in Greenville." He shrugged again. "I never had any reason to go back."

"Well, then, how do you know about Maggie's death?"

"Cecily—that was my sister in Greenville. She saw it in the paper, since by then Maggie too had been living in Greenville for many years. Cecily cut out Maggie's obituary and sent it to me. Cecily herself died not long afterward. Sending me Maggie's obit was just about the last time she was in touch with me." He shook his head, then reached for his wallet and rummaged through it. "I used to carry it around with me . . . Now what'd I do with it?" He shrugged and tucked the wallet back in his pocket. "Oh yes, it was getting dog-eared so I put it in my dresser drawer for safekeeping. Anyway, that's how I found out."

Jane pressed her lips together. "That's kind of a sad ending to the story, you know."

Truman sniffed. "Kind of a sad story all the way around, I guess. But then again, nobody's got it easy in this life."

"I don't understand why you didn't marry someone else. Didn't you want to?"

"I thought about it, of course. Even dated now and again, but"—he shrugged again—"it just never happened. Wasn't meant to be, I guess."

"That's what I'm afraid of."

"What? Of not marrying at all if you don't marry Seth?"

Jane nodded.

"I think you will."

"*You* didn't."

"That doesn't mean you won't. I was just a stubborn old coot, is all. Couldn't find anyone who lived up to Maggie, and I wasn't going to settle."

Silence. Then Jane asked, "Did you ever get over it, Truman?"

"Yes and no. It finally stopped hurting quite so much. In fact, I finally came to the point where Maggie became a fond memory instead of a painful one. But at the same time, I spent a lifetime hoping to make amends somehow. I'd have given just about anything to hear her say she forgave me. But, as I said before, it's too late for that now."

"The one unanswered prayer."

"The one unanswerable prayer, I suppose. There's no way I can hear her say she forgives me now. But listen, Jane, I'm wondering about you. Are you all right? Did something happen?"

Jane shut her eyes, took a deep breath. She opened her eyes and looked at the cross. "Last Friday Seth told me it'd be better for him if we weren't engaged."

"Ah. I see." Truman shifted on the pew, leaned forward with his arms resting on the pew in front of them. "I'm sorry, Jane."

"I'm trying to understand how he feels, what he's going through."

"He's got a long, tough fight ahead of him just to regain some sense of normalcy. That may be all he can handle right now."

Jane nodded. "That's kind of what he said. That he's only got the strength for so much, as though the engagement was an added burden."

"My guess is that he's afraid of being a burden to you."

"Yes. That too."

"So you're working on trying to let him go. At least for now."

"I guess, like you, I have no choice."

"You're going to be all right, you know. It may not feel that way at the moment, but later you'll see. You'll be all right."

Jane thought of the empty bottles at home. She was going to have to be stronger. She was going to have to do better than that if she was going to be all right.

"After all, you survived, didn't you, Truman?" she said.

Truman laughed lightly. "I guess I did."

"Proving that the human heart can be broken into a thousand pieces and still go on beating."

Truman nodded. He looked at his hands, at the cross, at Jane. He nodded again.

— 31 —

July first dawned hot and steamy. Jane spent the morning hours in the air-conditioned coolness of the Penlands' house, cleaning up from her days of mourning. She dumped the contents of half a bottle of bourbon down the kitchen drain and promised herself that was it. No more. It hadn't helped Meredith Morrow. It wasn't going to help her.

She made a mental note to replace everything she'd taken from the liquor cabinet. That way Diana would never know. Nor would she know what happened with Ted, how Jane had been foolish enough to meet him again, and how she had run. She cringed at the thought. That was the behavior of a schoolgirl, not a grown woman. And the drinking—that was college fare. In the last week she'd been slipping backward when she needed to go forward. *"Life's gearshift's got no reverse . . ."* Yes, but even as you moved forward in years, you could evidently fall backward in emotion and behavior.

After cleaning the house, Jane showered and dressed. Then she sat at Diana's computer to catch her up on the news about Seth's pneumonia. For her own sake, not Diana's, she tried to make it sound less serious than it was. She had always thought it bad practice to put her worst fears into words; to verbalize them was like giving them skin with which they could rise up and become real. *He's on powerful IV antibiotics,* she wrote, *and he should be fine, once he finishes this course.*

She paused before signing off. She wanted to ask Diana to pray. *Keep Seth in your prayers, will you?* Something simple like that. After all, people said that all the time, didn't they? Especially in times of tragedy or trial. *We ask that you keep them in your thoughts and prayers.*

But she knew Diana didn't pray. Diana didn't believe in God, at least not a god who could be persuaded by the pleas of mere mortals. *"If he's there he's completely hands off,"* Diana had once remarked. *"Honestly, I don't think he's there, but if he is, he set the clock ticking, and then he stepped back to watch all us little people get caught up in the cogs."*

Jane didn't agree with her. At least, she hoped Diana was wrong. She had spent enough years listening to Laney singing hymns in the kitchen to know that some people thought otherwise.

By noon Jane was at the hospital. She found Seth sleeping. For her allotted ten minutes she stood beside his bed, wanting both to wake him and not to wake him. She stood quietly, watching him breathe. Watching him struggle to breathe, for each breath was a battle.

"Keep fighting," she whispered.

The waiting room was empty when she sat down. Like the chapel, it was another small windowless room, furnished only with a dozen vinyl chairs, a couple of lamps, a coffee table littered with torn magazines. One framed print hung on the wall, a patriotic picture of men and women in military uniform, gazing at the American flag.

What should I do now? Jane wondered, and just as quickly she realized there was nothing for her to do but wait. Wait for the time to pass until she could spend another ten minutes with Seth. Wait until Sid and Jewel showed up later in the day. Wait for a change in Seth's condition, a turn in the course of his illness, hopefully a turn for the better.

Jane clasped her hands together and looked around the sterile room. She wasn't sure she could bear it. Maybe she should get up and walk. Maybe she should seek out Truman. Maybe she should leave the hospital altogether and come back later.

No matter what she did or where she went, though, it would be there, the nagging fear that Seth would not get better. It would be right there with her, rattling the cage of her heart, demanding her attention. She wouldn't be able to get away from it.

But she had to do something, *something*. She

couldn't just sit here and do nothing. Not, and keep her sanity too.

She put her hands on the armrests to push herself up, but before she could rise she heard movement in the hall. The rapping of footsteps and the fainter pendulum-like tapping of a cane against the polished linoleum floor, precise as clockwork.

And then Jon-Paul was in the doorway to the waiting room, his white cane poised in front of him. "Jane?" he called.

"I'm here."

He turned toward her voice. He made his way to where she sat and took the seat beside her, laying the cane to rest against his left leg. He had a book tucked up under one arm, which he settled on his lap. "Truman said I might find you here. How's Seth?"

"I'm not sure," Jane said. "When I saw him a few minutes ago, he was asleep."

Jon-Paul nodded, as though Jane's answer satisfied him. "I've been by every day since he went into ICU, just to check on him."

"That's nice of you, Jon-Paul. Thank you."

Jon-Paul waved a hand. "I'm concerned. I want to see him get better."

"Thanks," Jane said again. "I do too." She hesitated to ask, but at length she said, "Listen, you have to tell me, did you let Seth beat you at chess?"

He shook his head firmly, even as he smiled. "I'm guilty of many things, but of letting someone beat me at chess? Not a chance. Seth played a good game and won."

Jane smiled in return, then remembered Jon-Paul couldn't see her. "No offense," she said, "but I'm glad he won."

"No offense taken." Jon-Paul laughed lightly. "But you have to know that when he won, I challenged him to two out of three, and he accepted. If I win the next game, I'll be the one going on in the tournament."

"Will Hoboken let you do that?"

"Hoboken? What's he got to do with it?"

"He's keeping the flow chart, right? Maybe the others in the tournament won't think that's fair. By the rules, you should be out."

Jon-Paul laughed again and shrugged. "Our rules are pretty loose. So far no one's complained."

"And I guess you and Seth started the whole thing anyway. So you can do whatever you want."

"Yeah. There wouldn't be a kitty of prize money without us. So listen, soon as Seth's out of ICU, we'll start the next game."

Jane liked the way that sounded. *Soon as Seth's out of ICU.* As though it were a given that he would be.

"You'll be there, won't you?" he went on. "To watch the game?"

"Of course," she said. She couldn't keep the surprise out of her voice. "Why would you think I wouldn't be there?"

"It's just that you were gone a few days. You didn't witness Seth's victory."

"No." Jane shook her head. "I wish I had. I should have been there. But I needed a few days away."

"I understand." His hands moved to the book in his lap, as though he suddenly remembered it was there. "Since your visiting time with Seth is limited while he's in ICU, I figured you'd need something to do. I brought you a book."

He held it up to her. She took it and read the title: *The Spiritual Lives of the Great Composers.*

"I thought you might like it," he said, "since you seem to know something about music."

She opened the book and fanned through the pages. "Thank you, Jon-Paul. I was just sitting here wondering how to pass the time. How did you know?"

"I didn't. I just . . . I figured you might need something, and I wanted to help."

"Thank you," she said again. "That was nice of you."

Retrieving his cane, he stood to go. As he rose, Jane felt something spiral downward inside of her. The feeling was familiar, but it took her a moment to recognize what it was. The heaviness of disappointment.

She wished he wouldn't leave her here alone.

"Are you having lunch with your sister?" she asked.

"Yes. But just Carolyn, thank heavens. No more blind dates." He gave a small laugh and a nod. "Well, enjoy the book."

"I'm sure I will."

"And if Seth's awake next time you go in, tell him if he's not out of here by, oh, let's say next Wednesday, he forfeits the game."

Jane smiled. "All right. I'll tell him."

Jon-Paul stepped away. When his feet left the sullied carpet of the waiting room and touched the linoleum in the hall, he hesitated. Then he turned back. "Jane?"

"Yes?"

"Would you mind if I stopped by here tomorrow?"

The weight lifted. She took a deep refreshing breath. "I'd be disappointed if you didn't."

She saw the smallest hint of a smile form at the corners of his mouth. He tipped an imaginary hat. "Till then," he said.

"Bye, Jon-Paul." She listened as he tapped his way back down the hall, finding something oddly comforting in the measured rhythm of his cane.

— 32 —

She didn't see Seth again that day. Jewel and Sid arrived from Troy in the late afternoon and spent some time with him. Only two visitors at a time in the ICU, the nurse reminded them, and after Jewel and Sid saw him, the nurse decided that was it for the day. Seth was too tired for any more visitors. Everyone would have to come back tomorrow.

When they returned to the waiting room after seeing Seth, Sid was uncommonly silent, even for him, and Jewel pale and tense. Jane put a hand on Jewel's arm. "He's going to be all right," she said. "You'll see. He's going to get through this."

Jewel nodded but said nothing. Her eyes glistened.

Sid put an arm around his wife. "We're going to the hotel to get some rest, Jane. But we'll see you tomorrow."

"All right."

I should go too. But she didn't. After the Ballantines left, Jane sat and turned again to the book Jon-Paul had given her. An hour passed, visitors to the ICU came and went, some lingering in the waiting room, others stopping only momentarily to talk among themselves in quiet tones. Jane scarcely looked up. After a time she realized she was hungry. She should go home and feed the dogs and eat supper herself.

She was about to bookmark her page when a familiar figure approached.

Jane smiled. "Hello, Truman."

"You still here, Jane?"

"I was just thinking about going home and making supper. Seth can't have any more visitors today."

Truman eased himself down in the chair next to Jane's. "How is he?"

"Tired. Otherwise about the same, I guess."

Truman nodded. "His folks make it into town?"

"Yes. They were here a little bit ago. They've gone back to their hotel for the night, though."

"Have you been here all afternoon?"

Jane glanced at her watch. "I guess I have. I've been reading. Listen to this, Truman."

He leaned closer, expectantly.

"It's something Beethoven said." She smoothed the page of the book with an open palm and began to read. " 'It was not a fortuitous meeting of chordal atoms that made the world; if order and beauty are reflected in the constitution of the universe, then there is a God.' "

Truman lifted his eyes to her, cocked his head. "Yes. It seems so simple, doesn't it? If only everyone could see it that way."

"But . . . it's the beauty. It's . . ."

Truman nodded, waited for her to go on.

"It's not enough," she said.

"What do you mean?"

"I've always wanted it to be enough, but it isn't. It just isn't."

Truman frowned, fidgeted in the chair. "I want to follow you, Jane, but I'm not sure I do."

She shook her head, closed the book in her lap. "I don't think I can explain. I'm not even sure what I'm trying to say." She looked up at Truman, smiling shyly. "Maybe I'd better just call it a day and go on home."

Truman reached over and patted her hand. "You go on. I'll stand watch for a little while. I'll call you if anything changes."

"Thank you, Truman. I really don't know what I'd do without you."

"Oh, you'd get by," he said, patting her hand again.

When she got home, she went to the den and put on a CD, a collection of Beethoven. "Für Elise." "Violin Sonata in C Minor." "Symphony no. 9." Surely Beethoven had loved beauty too, but he knew it wasn't enough, knew it wasn't the final thing. It was only a witness. Beauty sang of the One who created it, the One who pulled splendor out of His own breast and sowed it with open palms across the earth.

By the time "Ode to Joy" began to play, Jane thought perhaps she was beginning to understand.

243

— 33 —

"Jane?"

"You don't have to try to talk, Seth. I just wanted to let you know I'm here."

He turned his head ever so slightly toward her voice while trying to focus weary eyes on her face. "Mom and Dad?" he whispered.

"They're here. They'll be in to see you in a little while."

"What day is it?"

"Monday. July fourth."

"It's the Fourth of July?"

"Yeah. I guess it is. I didn't even think about that. But now that you mention it, there's supposed to be a big fireworks display downtown tonight."

"Wish I could take you."

Jane smiled. "I wish you could too. Now, I mean it, Seth. You don't have to talk. You need to save your strength. Jon-Paul says if you don't get out of ICU by Wednesday, you forfeit the game."

Seth tried to chuckle but ended up coughing. Jane lifted his oxygen mask and gave him a sip of water through a straw. When he could speak, he said, "Tell Jon-Paul I'll be there. And tell him he's a glutton for punishment."

Jane smiled behind her mask. "All right. I'll tell him. Are you going to stop talking now, or am I going to have to leave?"

"Don't leave. But I want to tell you something."

Because he spoke so softly, Jane leaned closer. "What is it?"

"I was dreaming. . . ."

"Yeah?"

"It seemed so real."

"What was it?"

"Remember when we went to Folly Beach with Mom and Dad and we rented that place right on the water?"

Jane nodded. "Sure, I remember."

"I was dreaming about being there. You and I were walking along the shore, just the way we did when we were there. And it seemed so real. I mean, I could feel the sand and the water whenever a wave came in. It was so cold. I felt the wind. Remember how sometimes the gusts were so strong they just about knocked us over?"

"Yes." She laughed a little, though her throat felt tight. "But that was all right. You held me up."

He shut his eyes slowly, opened them again. "I was holding your hand. In my dream, I could feel your hand, Jane. And I was happy."

"That's not just a dream, Seth. It's a memory."

"I guess it is. I guess I wanted to live it again. I'm glad it seemed so real."

Jane lifted a hand to his face, stroked his cheek. "Me too."

A nurse appeared in the doorway and looked at Jane. "Time for you to go," she said.

Jane nodded toward the nurse. "All right." The nurse slipped away. "I'd better go," Jane said to Seth, "but I'll be back later."

"Jane?"

"Yes?"

A quieter whisper than before: "A part of me will always be holding you up, you know."

Their eyes met. She stroked his cheek again. "I believe that, Seth. Now get some rest."

When she reached the waiting room, Jon-Paul was there, dressed casually in a pair of jeans and a blue T-shirt. His attire reminded Jane that it was a holiday; his office would be closed.

She sat down in the chair beside him. "Seth says to tell you that you're a glutton for punishment," she said.

He arched his brows while smiling quizzically. "Oh? How so?"

"You're coming back for a second game."

He laughed. "I consider it a second chance, and I don't intend to lose this time." He took a deep breath and the smile faded. "So how is he?"

"He seems to be doing a little better."

"Really? That's great. I've been praying for him."

Jane cocked her head. "Really?"

"Of course."

She didn't know how to respond. Finally she said, "Thank you. I appreciate that."

He nodded. "I've decided he doesn't have to forfeit the game if he's not out of here by Wednesday. But don't tell him I said that. We'll let him sweat it out."

"All right. It'll be our little secret. Is the tournament still going on?"

"Oh yes. The guys on the floor are really into it. Truman's clobbered a couple and is moving up on the chart."

"Good for him. Maybe he'll even win the kitty."

"Maybe."

"I wonder what he'd do with the money," Jane said dreamily. "I think he ought to go on a cruise."

"A cruise? With five hundred dollars? That would hardly get you a row boat out on Lake Lure."

Jane laughed loudly. It felt good to laugh. Jon-Paul chuckled along with her. "Thanks, Jon-Paul," she said.

He looked puzzled. "Thanks? For what?"

"For coming. For making me laugh."

He smiled at that. "You're welcome, Jane."

They fell quiet as Jane looked away shyly. She didn't want to have a lull in their conversation because he might make an excuse to leave, feeling that he'd been there long enough. She didn't want him to leave. She blurted the first thing that came to mind. "Are you going to the fireworks tonight?"

"Well, no," he said awkwardly. "I mean, I would, except I can't see them."

"Oh! I'm so sorry. I didn't mean . . . it's just that, most of the time, I forget."

He sat up straighter at that. "Really? I'm glad. It's nice to be more than just the blind guy."

"To me, you're not a blind guy at all. You're, well . . . you're just a really special person. I'm sure a lot of people think so."

He sat back again, his face aglow. "I remember fireworks. I remember what they look like." He drew circles in the air with his hands. "All those bright lights in the dark sky. It's been a long time, though."

"Actually, I can't remember the last time I saw fireworks. We came to Asheville sometimes when I was a kid, but otherwise, we stopped having fireworks displays in Troy. It got to be too expensive for a small town."

"Well, I wish we could go tonight. Maybe we can. Maybe you could tell me what it all looks like." He stopped, looking suddenly pained. "I'm sorry, I don't mean that to sound like I'm asking you to . . ."

"Don't worry, it's all right. I'd like to go."

"Maybe Truman would like to go too. I bet he hasn't gotten out of this place in ages."

"That's a great idea! We should ask him."

Jon-Paul unclipped his cell phone from his belt buckle. "I've got him on speed dial now." He pushed a number, put the phone to his ear. "Truman? Jon-Paul here. Jane and I are in the ICU . . . yeah, in the waiting room. Can you come down for a minute? No, nothing's wrong. Just stop by if you can." He closed the phone, put it back in its clip. "He's on the way."

In another few minutes, he was there. "What's up?" Truman said.

"Jane and I are going downtown tonight to see the fireworks," Jon-Paul explained. "You want to come?"

A wide smile spread across Truman's face. "Sure," he said. "I can't remember the last time I saw fireworks."

"So they'll let you out of your cage long enough to go?" Jon-Paul said.

Truman laughed. "No problem there. I'm free to come and go as I please. I just haven't been doing any going lately. It'll be nice to get out. Thanks for asking."

"Sure, Truman," Jane said. She patted the chair next to her. "Why don't you sit down for a while?"

"All right." He eased himself into the chair. "How's our man Seth doing?"

"I think he's actually doing a little better," Jane said.

Truman nodded. "Good, good. It's a battle, but I thought once they got that IV going, he'd be all right."

"He's a fighter," Jon-Paul commented.

"Yes, he is," Jane said quietly. "I've been really worried, wondering whether . . . whether maybe he wouldn't make it. I have to remind myself that even if he does make it—"

"Of course he will, Jane," Jon-Paul interrupted.

"But even if he does . . ." She tried to go on, tried to say that even if he lived, she had lost him. They were no longer engaged. Everything had changed. She couldn't bring herself to say the words.

Somehow, though, Truman knew. He understood. "It will be all right, Jane," he said. "Everything will be all right. You'll see."

She nodded slowly. "I know, Truman. I just have to keep moving forward."

Truman smiled. "That reminds me of something. Did I ever tell you what Maggie used to say?"

"I don't think so."

Truman leaned forward, rubbed his chin thoughtfully at the memory. "She'd say, 'Life's gearshift's got no reverse, so you've got to just keep moving forward.' " He chuckled lightly, shook his head. "If she said it once, she said it a thousand times. 'Life's gearshift's . . . ' What's the matter, Jane? You don't look well. Did I say something wrong?"

— 34 —

Jane laid a hand on Truman's forearm and squeezed tightly. "Are you telling me that's what *Maggie* used to say?"

"Yes. But why? What's wrong?" Truman frowned, shook his head.

"Yeah? What's the matter with that?" Jon-Paul echoed.

"She said 'life's gearshift's got no reverse'?" Jane asked again.

"Yes. Is that so strange?"

"No, it's just that . . . it's just that . . . Truman, you said you have Maggie's obituary. Do you know where it is?"

"I believe it's in the top drawer of my dresser. In my room."

"Can we go get it?"

"Yes, but why?"

"I'll explain after I see it."

She jumped up, grabbed Truman's hand eagerly, and pulled him up out of the chair.

"Can I come?" Jon-Paul asked.

"Come on," Jane said. "Take my arm."

Jon-Paul folded up his white cane and slipped his hand into the crook of Jane's arm. As Truman led the way through the hospital to the clinic, Jane was mindful of Jon-Paul. Though he was sure-footed she wanted to guide him safely through the maze of corridors and past the ever-moving traffic of patients and visitors. At the same time, she wanted to hurry, wanted to know whether her suspicions were correct. *Could it be? Could Laney be . . . ?* But then, maybe it was a common saying in the Upcountry. Maybe everyone in the Greenville area said the same thing a thousand times over.

Jane tried to squelch the rising impatience in her chest as Truman moved forward on arthritic knees. If he knew what she was hoping to find in the obituary, surely for once he would move a little faster.

"I wish you'd tell us what this is about," Jon-Paul said quietly, giving Jane's arm a squeeze.

"I'm not sure yet. Maybe nothing."

"Well, if it's nothing, I'm going to be disappointed."

"Believe me, so am I."

Truman took them out a side door of the clinic and cut across the sidewalk to the Community Living Center. He gave Jane a perplexed look as he held open the door for her and Jon-Paul, but he said nothing. Once inside, they moved in tandem down the corridor to Truman's room.

"All right now," Truman mumbled as he opened the top drawer of his dresser. "I know I put it somewhere in here for safekeeping."

Jane stood by anxiously as he riffled through the contents of the drawer—pill bottles, old address books, a shaving kit, a jar of coins, several date books. "I know it's here," he said again.

"Are you sure you didn't put it somewhere else?"

"I'm sure. I . . ." He looked up from the drawer as his brows hung low over his eyes. "Oh yes, I remember." He turned away from the dresser and walked to the small bedside table. From the single drawer he pulled out a Bible. "I put it in here," he said. "Yes, here it is."

Truman lifted a small fragile newspaper clipping from the Bible's pages and held it out to Jane.

Jane took it and scanned it quickly, her lips moving as she read half-aloud. Her voice rose in volume when she came to the words, " 'Mrs. Dooley is preceded in death by her husband, Dr. Cyrus Dooley. She is survived by four children, a daughter, Magdalene and husband Roderick 'Clapper' Jackson of Greenville. . . .' " She looked up at Truman wide-eyed. "Magdalene? Laney?"

Truman took a step toward her. "What is it, Jane?"

Jane shook her head in disbelief even as she smiled. "Truman, you're not going to believe this, but my Laney is your Maggie's daughter."

Truman drew himself up and looked hard at Jane. For a long moment, silence hung over the room. Finally, Truman said, "Laney?"

Jane nodded vigorously. "Yes."

"She's Maggie's daughter?"

"Yes, Truman. She is."

"Are you sure?"

"According to this," Jane said, waving the obit in the air, "Maggie's daughter is married to Clapper Jackson. How many Clapper Jacksons do you know?"

Truman reached for the obituary with trembling fingers. "Do you think . . ." He paused, looked around the room as though lost. "Do you think we can find her?"

"I don't know. We can try. She's probably still living in Greenville. Listen, here's where we start." She pulled her cell phone out of her pocketbook and punched in the number for information.

She heard the ringing on the other end, then a weary voice asking, "What city, please?"

"Greenville, South Carolina."

"What listing?"

"Roderick Jackson."

"One moment please." A pause. Then, "We have a listing for twenty-two Roderick Jacksons. Do you have an address?"

"No, that's what I'm looking for. Do you have a listing for a Clapper Jackson?"

"Slapper Jackson?"

"No. Clapper. With a C-l."

"Clapper?"

"That's right."

"Who would name their kid Clapper?"

"It's just a nickname, but that's what he goes by."

"Well, we don't list nicknames here."

"Can you check anyway? Please. Just in case."

"One moment." Another pause. "No, we don't have any Clapper Jacksons listed. No Slappers either, for that matter."

Jane ignored her final comment. "Okay. What about a Magdalene Jackson?"

"Magdalene? Like Mary Magdalene in the Bible?"

"That's right."

"Holy Mother of . . . Listen, I'm busy here. I have a quota to make. If you're pulling my leg . . ."

"No, I'm serious. Do you have a listing for Magdalene Jackson?"

Jane heard a sigh. "One moment." Pause. Then, "No Magdalenes in Greenville. You might try the empty tomb, though."

"The what?"

Another long sigh. "Nothing. Never mind. Is there anyone else you want to try?"

"No. That's it."

"Judas Iscariot maybe? Pontius Pilate?"

Jane held the phone away from her ear and glared at it. Then she snapped it shut and rolled her eyes at Truman. "Somebody's not having a good day," she said. "I'd report her, if I weren't such a nice person."

Jon-Paul, leaning against the wall by the dresser, broke in. "Would somebody mind telling me what's going on?"

"You tell him, Truman," Jane said as she headed for the door. "I'll be back in a little while."

"But, Jane, where are you going?" Truman called after her.

"I'm going to go talk to someone who actually might be able to help."

She didn't want to call home on her cell from the hospital. Too much chance of static. Too many dropped calls. She'd rather talk on the landline in the Penlands' house. Roscoe and Juniper were delighted to see her home so early, but she didn't pay them much attention. She gave them both a dog biscuit and sent them out back to get them out of the way. Then she picked up the extension in the kitchen.

The phone at the other end rang four times, and Jane was afraid the answering machine would pick up. But just before the fifth ring, her father answered with the familiar formal Rayburn House greeting. Before he could finish saying, "This is Peter Morrow," Jane interrupted with "Hi, Dad!"

"Oh, hi, Janie. How are you?"

"Fine, Dad. Listen, I need to know . . . do you remember Laney Jackson?"

"Laney Jackson?"

"Yeah. She used to cook for us years ago."

"Um . . . oh yeah. Yeah, I remember her. Married to the guy with the funny name. What was it? Rapper?"

"Clapper, Dad. It was Clapper."

"Oh yeah. But that's been—what? Ten years?"

"More than that. But listen, do you know where she is?"

"Where she is?" He gave a small incredulous laugh. "I don't have a clue, Janie. Why? What's this about?"

"I want to find her."

"Okay."

"It's kind of important."

"Okay. But I'm not sure I can help. Maybe you can do an Internet search—"

"Is Gram there?"

"Uh-huh, she's here, but she's not in the best mood at the moment. It's the Fourth, and you know what that means. The Rayburn House has to throw the best party in Troy—"

"Dad, can I just talk to her for a minute?"

"I'll call her, but a minute is about all the time she'll give you."

"Maybe it's enough."

Jane heard her father holler at the other end, "Mother, can you come to the phone for a minute?"

Then, in the background, "Who is it, Peter?"

"It's Jane. She needs to talk to you for a minute."

"I'm just about to head out to the grocery store. Ask her if I can call her back tomorrow."

"No!" Jane said. "Dad, tell her I want to speak to her now."

"Mother, she wants to speak to you now."

Silence, then impatient footsteps tapped across the wire all the way from Troy. "Jane, I'm up to my eyebrows in preparations for the party tonight," Gram said. "Can you make it quick?"

"Do you know where Laney Jackson is?"

"What?"

"Laney Jackson. Do you know where she is?"

"The woman who used to cook for us?"

"Yes."

"Well . . . why?"

"Listen, Gram, I know you're in a hurry, and so am I," Jane said. "Do you know if she still lives in Greenville? The obit says she lived in Greenville—"

"The obit?"

"Yes. Oh, never mind that, Gram. I'll explain later. Can you just tell me if you know where Laney is now?"

"I'm sorry, Jane, I don't. Well now, wait a minute. We usually exchange Christmas cards. I think we did this past year too."

"Do you save them?"

"What?"

"The Christmas cards. Do you save them?"

"Jane, you know me better than to ask a

258

question like that. You know I save everything."

"Well, can you find the card and give me her return address?"

"I'll have to dig through some stuff. I can't do it today, Jane. I'm far too busy."

"Can you do it tomorrow, then?"

She heard her grandmother sigh. "I guess so."

"Thanks, Gram. It's really important."

"I can't imagine what—"

"I'll let you go now, but I'll talk to you tomorrow. Bye, Gram. Love you."

Jane, Jon-Paul, and Truman sat in folding chairs on the grounds of the courthouse, along with several hundred other people waiting for the fireworks to light up the sky over Asheville.

"So," Truman said, "your grandmother thinks she can find Laney's address?"

He had already asked the question a dozen times, but Jane just smiled and answered patiently, "She said she would try."

"And you'll call her tomorrow?"

"Yes, I'll call her tomorrow."

Jon-Paul cocked an ear toward them. "And what is it exactly you want to find out from Laney, Truman?"

The old man smiled as he shook his head. "I don't know, exactly. I guess I'd just like to talk with her, if I can."

"You know what I just remembered, Truman?" Jane said, sitting up a little straighter.

"What, Jane?"

"I saw Maggie once."

"You did?" Truman's eyes widened.

"Yeah. When I was a kid, about thirteen. She was sitting in the back of the car when Clapper came to pick Laney up at our house." She looked at Truman and smiled. "Just imagine. It kind of makes you want to say it's a small world, doesn't it?"

Truman shut his eyes, nodded, opened them. "How did she look?"

Jane thought a moment. "Dignified. Happy."

Truman nodded again. "Was Dr. Dooley in the car?"

"Yes, he was there."

"He was my partner once, you may remember."

Jane nodded. "He looked like a nice guy."

"He was. He was a good man. For a long time I was angry, you know. The two of them marrying and all. But"—he shrugged—"it all worked out for the best. I could know Maggie was well taken care of." He was quiet a moment before adding, "I'm glad you saw her, Jane."

"Me too, Truman."

The milling crowd settled into place as dusk deepened into night. Everywhere, faces turned upward in anticipation of the fireworks display. Finally, in the distance, a whistling split the air, followed by a brief explosion, a scattering of fire, flashy gemstones rolling through the sky, then slowly sinking earthward and giving out. But then another, and another, and another. Boom, boom, boom! The crowd gave up sighs of approval.

Jon-Paul leaned closer to Jane. "You're supposed to tell me what it looks like, remember?"

Jane smiled as she watched each burst of shimmering color move in waves across the sky. "It looks like . . . well. . . ." And then she knew. "It looks like hope."

Jon-Paul nodded and sat back in his chair, satisfied.

— 35 —

"Did you find the card, Gram?"

"Jane, it's nine o'clock in the morning. The party kept us up late last night, and I had to get up early to help with breakfast. I've hardly had time to breathe since we spoke yesterday."

"Okay, sorry to call so early. But can you please try to find it today?"

"I wish I knew what all the fuss was about—"

"It's a long story, Gram. I'll tell you all about it soon. Right now, I just want to get Laney's address."

"Well, you know it means climbing up into the attic where I keep all the Christmas stuff. I bet

I've got fifty shoe boxes filled with old cards. Why on earth I'm such a pack rat . . ."

As her grandmother rattled on, Jane felt her heart sink. How would Gram find the one card Jane needed when there was a lifetime's worth of junk up in the attic?

"Gram, maybe I should come home and help you."

"Don't be foolish. You don't need to come all that way just to help me find a Christmas card. I may have lots of junk, but at least it's organized."

"You won't get sidetracked, will you? I know how you are when you start digging around in the attic."

"I won't get sidetracked, Jane. I don't have time to be sentimental today. We have full occupancy, and I want our guests to be more than satisfied. That's what brings them back, you know."

"I know, I know, Gram. But listen, call me when you find the card, will you?"

She heard her grandmother sigh. "Yes, I'll call you if I find it. I can't say for sure when I last got a card from her."

"Well, just call me when you know anything at all, will you? I'll let you go now. I know you're busy."

"All right, Jane."

"And thanks, Gram."

"Don't thank me yet. Wait till I find the Christmas card, if there is one."

●●●

Jane hated putting on the gown, the gloves, the mask. She cringed at the antiseptic smells of the ICU, the various whooshing and beeping sounds, the lighted numbers above the bed counting out the heartbeats, the number of breaths. She had grown to dislike white linens and cheap woven blankets, metal beds, bare floors, and narrow windows that showed a world outside she hardly felt a part of anymore.

The world inside—that was Seth's world. And hers. Not a pretty place. Not a place she would have asked for nor wanted. But here she was.

Seth was asleep. Unlike a few days before, he now slept peacefully. His head was turned slightly to one side, as though today he was listening to something pleasant. And maybe he was. As long as he was sleeping, he could dream. And in his dreams he was whole again and life was good and pleasurable and full of promise, just as it had been before Iraq. She wondered what he was doing in his dream right now. She wondered where he was and what he saw and what he heard. Wherever he was, it was a place far better than this bleak room. Anyplace would be better than this.

She wouldn't wake him.

In the hall she stripped off the gloves and mask, stepped on the pedal of a stainless steel can to pop the lid, and tossed them in. She slipped out of the gown and stuffed it in a linen hamper.

She found Truman in the waiting room. He had two pint cartons of chocolate milk, one in each hand. He held them up for her to see. "It's a beautiful day outside," he said. "Want to join me in the gazebo for a drink?"

The cold milk was refreshing. She was surprised at how good it tasted, surprised too at how—between the milk, the open air, and the roses blooming around the gazebo—she felt a little more hopeful. A few snatches of ordinary life and just a glimpse of beauty and already she felt stronger than she had only moments before.

"Seth looked better today," she said.

Truman nodded. He took a final swig of the chocolate milk, closed the carton, and set it on the bench beside him.

"But it seems like he's been in the ICU forever," she went on. "Is it normal for someone to have pneumonia for this long?"

"Oh yes." Truman dabbed at his mouth with the cuff of his shirt. "Pneumonia can be one tough nut to crack. But I think Seth's looking a little better too, like maybe he's about to turn the corner."

"Do you really think so, Truman?"

Truman started to respond but was interrupted by Jane's cell phone ringing. Jane reached for her pocketbook. "Maybe that's Gram!" she said. "Maybe she found Laney's address."

She pulled the phone out of its pouch and looked at the number. She shrugged and shook her head at Truman as she opened the phone. "Hello?"

A woman's voice said, "Jane?"

"Yes, this is Jane."

"Oh my goodness, child, you sound all grown up. Jane honey, this is Laney. Laney Jackson."

"Laney!" Jane felt herself carried back to the Rayburn House kitchen in a warm rush of memories. Laney was there in her white bibbed apron, making biscuits and singing hymns and offering smiles to the love-starved little girl that Jane had been. Now Jane smiled and pulled in a deep breath, as though drinking in those long-ago days. "Laney, how did you get my number?"

"Your grandmother called. She said you wanted to find me."

"But how did she find *you?* I mean, how'd she find your phone number?" She glanced at Truman, whose eyes were wide, his face expectant.

"Well, she said she found the Christmas card I sent last year, and she saw our return address is the Travelers Rest Inn. It's not hard to find the phone number of the Inn. Travelers Rest isn't a very big place, you know."

"You live at the Travelers Rest Inn?" Another glance at Truman, whose eyes grew even wider.

"Yes, but more than that, we own it. Clapper and I. We bought it a few years back and now we run it as a B&B, just like your grandmother runs the Rayburn House."

"Really, Laney? That's wonderful! It's . . ." She

paused a moment, surprised by the sting of tears behind her eyes. "It's so good to hear your voice," she finished.

"It's good to hear your voice too, honey. Makes me realize how much I've been missing you all these years."

"I've missed you too. I wish I'd been better about staying in touch. I'm sorry."

"Nothing to be sorry about, child, especially since you've found me now. Goodness, but hearing your voice, it seems like time's been all squeezed together and it was just yesterday since I last saw you. Hmm, yessir . . ." Laney paused and sighed contentedly. "Those were sweet days, working for Mrs. Morrow, spending time with you. But listen, honey, I know you had a reason for wanting to find me."

"Oh." Jane looked up at Truman again and smiled. He was fidgeting restlessly now. "I'm spending the summer in Asheville, and I've met someone here who knew your mother."

"Really? Now who is that?"

"Well, Laney, do you remember your mother ever talking about Truman Rockaway?"

Jane's question was met with momentary silence. Then, "You're talking about Dr. Rockaway?"

"Yes. Dr. Rockaway."

"He's there?"

"Yes." Jane nodded. "And he'd like to meet

you." Another pause, one that needled Jane and set her on edge. Hesitantly, she asked, "Would that be all right, Laney?"

"I don't know what to say, Jane," Laney finally replied. "You've caught me off-guard. I thought he was long dead."

"No. I can assure you he's not dead. He's sitting right here across from me."

"Well, now, isn't that something. I'm . . . I'm . . . and you say he wants to meet me?"

"Yes. Would that be all right?" she asked again. For the first time, Jane realized it may not be all right at all. To Laney, Truman Rockaway may be nothing more than the man who broke her mother's heart. "But, of course, if you'd rather not, I'm sure—"

"No, no. I'd be happy to meet Dr. Rockaway. It's just that, I'm going out of town on Saturday, and I'll be gone a month. Do you remember my son Eugene?"

"Sure, I remember him."

"Well, he's in graduate school, and he's got an internship out in California."

"He does? Little Eugene?"

"Not so little anymore. All grown up like you, Jane honey. Time's gone by."

"Yes." Jane laughed lightly. "I guess it has."

"So Sarah and I, we're going to California with him just for the adventure. Poor Clapper's going to stay here and man the store."

"What about Frankie?"

"He's staying home with Clapper, helping out around here while he's taking some summer classes at Furman University. By the way, he's Frank now. Won't answer to Frankie."

Jane sighed at the thought of time passing, things changing. "So you say you're leaving Saturday?"

"That's right."

"And today's Tuesday."

"Uh-huh."

"Listen, Laney, how about if we drive down tomorrow?" Jane looked at Truman, who nodded.

"Sure, honey. Come on down. Stay a couple of days. This is a big place, and we got plenty of room. We'll keep a couple rooms available for you and Dr. Rockaway. No charge."

"Really, Laney? You want us to stay a couple of days?"

"Of course. Honey, I haven't seen you in a dozen years. As long as you're coming down, you might as well stay awhile."

"Well, that'd be great. I'll let Truman know." Jane glanced up as Truman rose from the bench. Flustered, she watched him begin to leave. "Thanks, Laney. Really, I can't wait to see you."

"Oh, honey, I can't wait to see you either."

"Good. Tomorrow then, all right?"

By the time Jane said good-bye and snapped the phone shut, Truman was halfway across the commons. "Truman! Where are you going?"

He hollered over his shoulder as he continued toward the door, "I've got packing to do!"

Jane smiled as she watched him lope away on his old arthritic knees, the shoelace of one battered leather shoe trailing behind him.

She was glad Seth was awake when she went to see him later that afternoon. She wished she didn't have to wear the mask so that he could see her smile.

"How are you feeling?" she asked.

"A little better, I think."

"You look better."

He nodded weakly.

"Listen, I have to go away for a few days, but I'll be back soon."

"Where you going?"

"I'm taking Truman to Travelers Rest to meet Laney."

He offered a puzzled frown. "What?"

"It's a long story."

"So tell me."

"I don't have time. The nurse will kick me out before I can finish."

He appeared to shrug. He closed his eyes a moment, opened them again.

"Is it a long drive from Troy?" he asked.

"From Troy? We're not in Troy, Seth. We're in Asheville. Remember?"

His eyes wandered off as he thought about that. When he didn't respond, she said, "You're in the VA hospital, and I'm staying at Diana's house." At the mention of Diana's house, Jane realized she'd have to ask her friend whether a neighbor could look after the dogs for a couple of days. She'd take care of that as soon as she got home.

Seth focused his eyes on Jane's face again. "Oh yeah," he said. "How could I forget?"

"Blame it on the drugs. They've got you pumped full of them."

"Drugs, or wishful thinking, maybe."

"Yeah, well, another couple of months and we'll both be back in Troy. Your folks are getting the house ready for your homecoming, you know."

Seth sighed heavily as two lines formed between his brows. "So you and Truman are going somewhere?"

"Yes. Travelers Rest."

"And when will you be back?"

"Friday. Today's Tuesday, so like I said, it's just a few days."

"All right."

A nurse appeared in the doorway. "Time's up," she said.

Jane looked at her, back at Seth. "I have to go."

"Okay."

"By the time I get back, I expect you to be out of the ICU."

"I'll do my best."

She wanted to tell him that she loved him, but she stopped herself. She glanced over her shoulder at the doorway. It was empty. Defiantly, she pulled the mask down, tucking it under her chin. She leaned over the bed rail and pressed her lips gently against Seth's forehead. His skin was cool and moist. "Good-bye, Seth," she said. "See you soon."

By the time she straightened up, his eyes were closed and he'd already drifted off. She settled the mask back in place and left the room.

— 36 —

The highway sloped downward as the Honda traveled from the mountains of western North Carolina to the foothills just across the South Carolina line. Jane felt every mile of I-26 rolling beneath her, separating her from Seth. A particularly sharp pain shot through her as they passed the sign for Chimney Rock and Lake Lure at Exit 49A. Jane averted her eyes and tried to tamp down the memory of the day she became engaged to Seth. She glanced at her left hand on the steering wheel; she didn't wear the ring anymore, and they were no longer officially engaged, yet leaving him behind was hard. It was the timing that was bad. She wanted to see Laney, and she wanted to take Truman to Travelers Rest, but she wished she hadn't had to leave Seth while he was still in the ICU. If he were over the pneumonia and back in his old room, she wouldn't feel quite so anxious about being gone a couple of days. But that was the thing, Jane told herself. It was only a couple of days. She'd be back in Asheville the day after tomorrow, and by then he really might be over the crisis and back in his old room.

Jane glanced at Truman in the passenger seat beside her. He wore freshly pressed gray slacks, a long-sleeved shirt, and a tie. The shirt was pale blue; the tie a paisley pattern of blue and brown. The expression on his face was an odd mix of anticipation and apprehension. He had brought his walking cane along. The rubber tip poked at a point between his feet, while his hands, one on top of the other, rested on the curved handle. His fingers flexed and twitched. His eyes darted from the road ahead to the blur of trees off to his right and back again. He cleared his throat, inched himself up in the seat, wiggled his fingers again.

"You all right, Truman?" Jane finally asked.

He looked straight ahead as he nodded. "I haven't been home in forty-four years, you know."

"You still think of Travelers Rest as home?"

He smiled faintly. "Oh yes. It'll always be that. I just didn't realize how much I've missed it."

"Then I'm glad we're going back."

"I am too."

"By the way, what's the story behind the name of the town?"

Truman rubbed his brow before saying, "There's no story, really. The town was just named for what it was—a place for travelers to rest. Back a couple hundred years, drovers from Tennessee and Kentucky used to herd horses, sheep, pigs, all kinds of livestock down the mountain trails toward the marketplaces in the South Carolina low country. It was a long journey and a hard one. Along the way they needed a place to stop and rest for the night. So inns sprang up and stores and taverns. The smartest innkeepers had livestock pens available, so the drovers could know their livestock was safe during the night while they slept. That's how the town got its name."

Jane nodded thoughtfully. "It seems nice to have a place to rest."

"Yes, it does, Jane. It sure does. Seems like I could have used such a place many times in my life, especially early on, when I always seemed to be running."

"I feel like I could use a resting place right now," Jane said.

"No doubt you do." Truman looked at her, gave a nod of understanding. "No doubt you do," he said again.

Several miles rolled by in silence. Just beyond Hendersonville, Jane picked up I-25, the road that would take them to Travelers Rest.

Once she had regained a comfortable speed, she asked, "Do you remember the inn, the one Laney owns now?"

"Oh yes, I remember it well. It's the largest inn, and the oldest, in Travelers Rest. I believe it was built somewhere around 1850. Of course, it was built by a white man and owned by a succession of white men. But just imagine, Maggie's daughter owns it now." He smiled. "Things really have changed some, haven't they?"

"For the better, thank heavens."

"Oh yes. That's not to say there's not a long way to go, but at least things are moving in the right direction."

"Do you suppose anyone in Dr. Coleman's family still lives in Travelers Rest?"

Truman thought a moment before lifting his shoulders in a shrug. "I would think so. Probably even old Tommy Lee himself still lives there . . . if he lives anywhere. He'd be pretty old by now."

"I bet he'd only be about your age, wouldn't he?"

"Hmm. I guess he's not so old, then." One corner of his mouth drew back in an amused grin.

"You wouldn't be in any danger, would you? I mean, if he found out you were in town?"

"No, I don't think so. But if he still wants to string me up, so be it. All I want now is just to see Maggie's daughter. Then I'll be ready to go."

Jane gave him an exaggerated frown and shook

her head. "Well, listen, Truman, you're not going anywhere except back to Asheville with me at the end of the week."

"All right." A small grin. "I'll hold you to it."

Jane lifted a hand from the wheel and pointed to a sign by the roadside. "Look, Truman, we're crossing into South Carolina now."

"Well, I'll be . . ." He kept his eyes on the sign until they'd passed it.

"So we'll be there in another twenty minutes or so."

Truman flexed his fingers and took a deep breath.

"It won't make you sad, will it?" Jane asked. "To go back, I mean?"

"Probably."

"Then . . ."

"But I want to go. Maybe by meeting Laney, I can finally put Maggie to rest."

"I hope so, Truman."

"I hope so too."

With that, Jane left Truman to his thoughts while her own wandered—from Seth, to Laney, to her mother, father, grandmother, and back to Seth again. Just knowing she was about to see Laney brought back a tangle of memories and emotions . . . some sweet, some laughable, some bitter. Maybe, like Truman, she too could put some of them to rest.

As they moved along the two-lane highway, they passed numerous roadside stands offering strawberries, fresh tomatoes, hot boiled peanuts. They passed scattered cabins and single-wide trailers, small antique shops and barbeque restaurants, a mobile home park called the Foothill Estates, and a novelty shop flying several Confederate flags. Jane glanced over at Truman. He must have seen the flags, those reminders of a slave-owning South, but he pretended not to notice. Then, on the right, two large estates, gated and set back from the road, as though their aloofness said they were not really a part of the town that Jane and Truman had just entered. There was no sign to welcome them, not from this direction anyway. Just the sudden appearance of motels, gas stations, a Dunkin' Donuts shop, and finally, as though to remove all doubt, the Travelers Rest Bank, the Travelers Rest Community Services building, the Travelers Rest Fire Department.

"We're here," Jane said.

Truman nodded as he looked from side to side. "If I didn't know this was Travelers Rest, I wouldn't recognize it. Everything's different. So much is new."

"You don't recognize anything?"

"Some of the buildings." Truman squinted. "Some were here. My, how the place has grown."

"It has? If this is big, what was here before?"

Truman laughed loudly. "Not much. It was always just a little bit of a town. Never had many people here. Most people who say they come from Travelers Rest live between here and Greenville somewhere, like my family did. Still, we claimed this little town as home rather than the larger city of Greenville."

"Well, do you think you recognize enough to tell me how to get to the inn?"

Truman looked around. Then he pointed straight ahead. "Sure. Just follow this road and turn left. We can't miss it."

Jane did as she was told. In another moment, she saw what had to be the inn. It was a large two-story clapboard structure with a wide front porch and gingerbread trim. A pebbled circular drive cut through a lush green lawn dotted with dogwood and evergreen trees. The inn itself looked well kept and as though it had recently been wrapped up in a new coat of white paint. Black shutters accentuated the cream-colored drapes in the windows. Six hanging baskets of red, white, and pink begonias hung in neat precision above the porch railing, while the same number of wicker rocking chairs waited for takers there in the shade. "I'm assuming that's it," Jane said.

"That's it, all right," Truman acknowledged, not taking his eyes off the inn.

Jane pulled the Honda into the circular drive, put the car in park, and cut the engine. "Well, Truman, you ready?"

Truman nodded once and reached for the door.

They met in front of the car and headed up a flagstone walkway toward the porch. Even before they reached the steps, the front door of the inn opened and a woman stepped out.

"Janie Morrow," she said, holding out her arms. "Come here and let me look at you."

Jane climbed the steps and moved into the warm embrace of Laney Jackson. After a moment Laney pulled back and cupped Jane's face in both her hands. "Uh-huh," she said, "I can see you in there, Janie. But you're all grown up and more beautiful than ever."

Jane laughed and brushed aside the compliment. "And you haven't changed at all, Laney. It's so good to see you."

"It's good to see you too, honey. I've thought about you so much over the years, wondering what had become of you. Your grandmother never included much news about you in her Christmas cards."

"It's my fault, Laney. I should have written once in a while instead of falling out of touch."

"Well, never mind. You're here now. That's what matters."

They shared a smile as Jane studied Laney's

face. It wasn't true that she hadn't changed. She had, but only slightly. A few wrinkles, some streaks of gray in the dark hair that she wore twisted into a bun at the back of her head. But the eyes were the same—sweet, gentle, twinkling with an unmistakable joy.

Only after a moment did Jane remember Truman, who stood waiting at the bottom of the steps. He leaned on his cane with stacked palms, and Jane realized he'd probably brought it with him so he always had something to do with his hands. "Laney," Jane said, waving an arm toward Truman, "I want you to meet my friend, Truman Rockaway. Truman, this is Laney Jackson."

For a moment, neither spoke. Truman stood immobile on the walkway, looking up at the woman on the porch. The noonday sun caught the glint of tears in his eyes, and his jaw worked, as though he was trying hard not to let them spill over.

Finally Laney held out a hand and said, "Welcome, Dr. Rockaway. I'm very happy to meet you."

Slowly, Truman climbed the steps and clasped her hand. "Please forgive a sentimental old man," he said quietly. "It's just that you're the spitting image of your mother. For a moment there I almost thought I was looking at Maggie again."

"I take that as a compliment, Doctor," she said, smiling kindly. "Mamma was a beautiful woman."

"That she was. I'm pleased to meet you, Mrs. Jackson."

"Please call me Laney."

Truman bowed slightly as he withdrew his hand. "And please call me Truman."

"Well, then." Still smiling, Laney looked from one to the other. "Won't you come in? Lunch is almost ready."

Laney led them past a wide, polished staircase and down the hall to an expansive dining room, situated between a large front room and the kitchen at the back of the inn. The room was arrayed with six round tables, all covered in white cloths and set with painted china and linen napkins. At the far end was an antique corner cupboard filled with serving plates of all kinds and a serving buffet on which sat glass pitchers of ice water, sweet tea, and an eclectic collection of glasses, cups, and saucers. Overhead, three ceiling fans turned lazily, augmenting the air-conditioning by giving off the slightest hint of a breeze. Several guests of the inn were already seated at the tables, sipping iced tea from tall glasses. They glanced at the newcomers as Laney and her guests entered the room. Some nodded and exchanged polite greetings.

Laney waved Jane and Truman to a table set for five. "Clapper and Bess will be joining us in a minute," she said. "Go ahead and have a seat. I'll let them know you're here."

Jane watched Laney disappear into the kitchen

before she pulled out a chair and sat down. "I don't remember anyone named Bess," she said. Absently, she unrolled her napkin and laid it across her lap.

Truman shook his head, two lines forming between his brows. "I don't know who she is either, unless . . ."

His words trailed off, but Jane didn't seem to notice. She gazed about the room, taking it all in. "It's a lovely place, isn't it? Have you ever seen the inside before?"

"Oh no. Back when I lived here . . . well, folks like me didn't come to places like this. Unless, of course, we were employed here."

Jane nodded her understanding. The other guests chattered and laughed casually. As Jane listened, she became aware of music coming from another room, something classical, matching the quiet dignity of the inn. Like the name of the town, the Travelers Rest Inn had an air of restfulness. "Are you glad we're here, Truman?" she asked.

"Oh yes." Truman drew in a deep breath and smiled contentedly. "I'm very glad. I have the sense that . . . how to explain? I'm finally in the right place at the right time. I guess that's the only way to describe it."

"I think I know what you mean. It's almost as though this place drew us to itself, as though we're supposed to be here."

"Yes, it's—"

Jane waited for him to go on, but his sentence hung in the air, unfinished, as his attention turned toward something across the room. In another moment he pushed himself away from the table, wincing slightly as he eased himself up to his full height. Jane followed his gaze and saw that Laney was returning to their table accompanied by an older woman. Dark and slender like Laney but much smaller, the woman wore a blue cotton dress and white shoes with buckled straps, the heels of which added a couple of inches to her diminutive height. A string of imitation pearls hung around her neck, their gleaming whiteness mirroring her large-toothed smile. Her red lipstick was color coordinated with the fiery nail polish that accentuated her tapered fingers. She had a pleasant face rimmed by a bob of wavy gray hair, though her flashing black eyes told Jane this woman had a feisty streak beneath her unruffled exterior.

"Jane, Truman, this is my Aunt Bess," Laney said when she reached the table. "She'll be having lunch with us."

"Bess," Truman said quietly, holding out a hand. "Of course. Maggie's baby sister."

Bess laughed amusedly as she took Truman's hand in both of hers. "I wasn't a baby when you knew me, Truman, and I'm certainly not one now. I'm a grandmother six times over, and the great-grandmother of one."

"Impossible," Truman said.

"Not at all," Bess said. "It's true. I have the photos to prove it, if you'd like to see them."

"I certainly would."

"Well, not right now," Laney said, "or you'll get lunch all over them. You can do the picture show later, Aunt Bess, after we eat."

Truman pulled out the chair to his right and motioned toward it. Bess nodded her thanks and sat down.

Laney chose a seat too, saying, "Clapper will be joining us in a minute. He's just wrapping up a few details in the office."

"You don't do the cooking here in addition to everything else, do you, Laney?" Jane asked.

"I do some. But I also have two cooks on staff. One is Geraldine Crowley, who's been with us from the start. The other is a young man who's just here for the summer, in between college semesters. His name is Richard Coleman."

Truman looked up, startled. "Coleman?" he asked.

"That's right." Laney gave Truman a knowing smile. "Tommy Lee's grandson. He helped prepare our lunch today."

"You don't say," Truman said incredulously.

"I believe I just did." Laney laughed.

"Is Tommy Lee still alive?"

Laney shook her head. "He died some years ago. Heart attack, I believe."

"Aneurysm," Bess interjected. "I wasn't there, of course, seeing as how it happened at a white church. But as the story goes, it was a Sunday morning and he was helping take up the collection during the service. He'd just taken the plate from Mr. Abernathy when he fell over dead right there in the aisle. What a commotion! Women screaming, money flying everywhere, and old Tommy Lee laid out on the floor dead as a doornail. Serves him right."

"Aunt Bess!"

"Well, Laney, the man was a hypocrite. A member of Buncombe Street Baptist and a member of the Klan too."

"He wasn't a member of the Klan."

"Laney, girl, there are some things you don't know—"

"But, Aunt Bess—"

"Truman," Bess said, turning stern eyes in his direction. "You were right, you know. Tommy Lee should have gone on and died down there by the river. It'd have saved a lot of people miles of heartache if he had."

"Aunt Bess!" Laney hissed. Jane noticed her anxiety as Laney scanned the room to see if anyone was listening.

Bess waved a hand. "Hush, Laney, I'm just speaking the plain gospel truth. About time somebody did."

The table fell silent. Jane looked at Truman; his

freckles stood out against his now pale skin. His mouth hung open slightly, and his eyes were round and gleaming.

"I'm sorry, Truman," Laney said. "Aunt Bess has no right to bring that up." She shot a reprimanding glance at the older woman.

Truman shook his head as though to loosen the words on his tongue. "It's all right, Laney. It's—"

"Truman, I never understood Maggie's decision," Bess interrupted. "She did you wrong by not going north with you."

"Oh no, Bess," Truman said quickly. "No. She . . . she was right. I was a doctor and it was my duty to help. My sworn duty. Even if I wasn't a doctor, it's not right simply to leave a man to die, no matter who he is. Maggie knew that—"

"Even so, I'd have gone with Charlie, should the same thing have happened to us, and heaven knows Charlie wasn't even near worth it."

"Charlie?"

"My late husband."

"Aunt Bess! How can you say such a thing about Uncle Charlie? He was a wonderful man."

"He had his good points," Bess agreed, "but bear in mind, Laney, you're not the one who had to live with him day in and day out for thirty-seven years. I know a little bit more than—"

"Clapper!" Laney called as a man approached the table. She sounded relieved. "Clapper, I want you to meet our guests. This is Truman Rockaway—"

"Now, don't get up, Dr. Rockaway," Clapper interrupted. He came to the table with a huge smile and a hand extended. "I can shake your hand just as well with you sitting down."

"All right, then." Truman took his hand and the two men shook. "Happy to meet you, Mr. Jackson."

"Everybody calls me Clapper."

"And you may remember Jane," Laney went on, "though I don't suppose you'd recognize her."

"Well, I'll be!" Clapper exclaimed. "Are you really the little girl that used to live at the Rayburn House?"

"One and the same," Jane said with a laugh.

"Well, I'd never have known. My, oh my. You've grown up real nice, Miss Jane."

"All right, Clapper," Bess snapped. "Get your tongue back in your mouth and take a seat already. I'm hungry and I want some lunch."

"My tongue wasn't hanging out, Aunt Bess. I was just paying our guest a compliment."

"Yeah, yeah. And I'm Martha Washington with a suntan. Now, where's the appetizer?"

Truman chuckled. "I don't believe you've lost any of your spunk, Bess."

"You got that right," Clapper volunteered. "She's only gotten spunkier with age—"

"Clapper!"

"That's a compliment, Laney. A compliment. Nothing wrong with having a good dose of spunk."

As Clapper spoke, an angular young man with a narrow face and sandy hair came out of the kitchen with a pitcher of water in one hand and a pitcher of tea in the other. He approached the table, politely asked who wanted what to drink, and began to pour. Jane noticed Truman watching him intently, the grandson of the man who had knocked his life off course. Richard Coleman must have felt Truman's gaze, because he cast a quizzical glance at him. But Truman disarmed the boy with a smile and a nod, and Richard Coleman, pouring sweet tea into Truman's glass, smiled in return.

He'll probably never know, Jane thought. He would never know who Truman was, or how his own great-grandfather refused to care for a little Negro child, or how his grandfather had caused Truman Rockaway to run from everything he knew and everyone he loved.

When the drinks were poured, the unapprised Richard Coleman began his spiel. "For our main meal today," he said, smiling courteously as he moved his gaze around the table, "we're having grilled salmon with cream sauce, boiled red potatoes, and asparagus tips. Dessert will be strawberry shortcake, with fresh strawberries, of course, as well as homemade whipped cream. If you'll excuse me a minute, I'll be right back with your salads."

With a slight bow, he left abruptly for the kitchen.

"That sounds wonderful," Truman said.

"What does?" Bess asked. "The meal? Or hearing a Coleman treat you with respect?"

Truman nodded thoughtfully. "They both sound pretty good, now that you mention it, Bess."

Bess sniffed and lifted her chin. " 'Bout time things got straightened out around here."

Jane regarded the two of them with a kind of wonder and curiosity for what they had seen and experienced, things she herself would never know, things that had happened before she was born. History, she saw, was simply people's lives, the large events the sum total of individual stories, and much of it rode on a man's or a woman's response to heartache. Racism wasn't the nation's story, it was Truman's and Bess's and Laney's and Clapper's. Just like the war in Iraq wasn't a world story. It was Seth's and hers and even Truman's too, because it had brought them here, back to the place Truman had had to flee but that he could now return to, since a page had turned and the story had changed. Truman had survived it all. For the first time Jane thought perhaps she could too.

She turned to Clapper and smiled. "So tell

me, Clapper, how did you happen to buy this wonderful inn?"

"You can thank my father-in-law for that," said Clapper, who glanced at Laney with a smile. "Yes sir, Cyrus was not only a fine doctor but a shrewd businessman. He started dealing in real estate back in the '70s, and then he got me involved and . . ."

As Clapper went on talking, Jane noticed Bess leaning toward Truman. Bess's entire face was a smile as she patted the old man's weathered hand. Softly, almost in a whisper, she said, "Welcome home, Truman."

Truman nodded, said quietly in return, "Thank you, Bess. It's good to be home."

— 38 —

They were finishing their dessert when Jane's cell phone rang. She pulled it from her pocketbook and checked the number of the incoming call. "It's Jewel." She looked at Truman first before glancing around the table. "Will you excuse me?" Flipping open the phone, she rose from the table and headed for the front porch.

Twenty minutes later, Laney joined her there, carrying two fresh glasses of sweet tea. She handed one to Jane, who took it gladly, then settled herself in the rocking chair beside her. "Everything all right, honey?"

Jane took a sip of tea before answering. She looked at Laney and tried to smile. "It's Seth," she said. "He's . . . well, he was my fiancé."

Laney nodded. "Your grandmother told me about him."

"So you know what happened?"

"Some. I know he was wounded in the war."

Jane took a deep breath and stared down at the tea in her hands. "Yes, he's paralyzed from a gunshot wound. He's a quad, Laney. He can't move much from the neck down."

"I'm so sorry, Jane." She reached out and patted Jane's arm. "It seems to me you've had more than your share of heartache in your lifetime. I wish there was something I could do to change things."

"Thanks, Laney. I do too. Most of all, I wish I could change things for Seth. He was a carpenter, you know, and now . . ." She finished by lifting her shoulders in a small shrug.

"What was the call about, honey?"

Jane took another deep breath to steady herself. "Seth's not doing well. Like I said, that was Jewel, his mother, calling from the hospital. He has pneumonia, you know, but now it looks like he's developed MRSA."

"MRSA?"

"Yes, that awful infection people pick up mostly in hospitals, of all places."

"Well, what does this mean?"

Jane looked out over the front lawn, as though searching for the answer there. Finally she said, "Jewel says they're doing all they can to treat it, of course. She just thought I ought to know."

For a few moments, Laney rocked quietly. Then she asked, "Do you think you should go back?"

"That's what I've been sitting here asking myself. Maybe I should, but Truman needs to be here."

"He can stay, even if you go back. He can stay as long as he wants. Bess will make sure he's well taken care of."

Jane couldn't help but smile at that. "Were you playing matchmaker for Bess and Truman?"

Laney chuckled and shook her head firmly. "When Bess found out Truman Rockaway was coming, she ran out and got her hair done, got her nails colored, and bought the dress she's wearing today. It's all her doing, not mine."

"It sounds like she remembers Truman pretty well after all these years."

"Honey, it seems to me she was probably sweet on him even back when he was dating my mother."

"You think so?"

"She'd never admit it, but yes, I think so. She was only a few years younger than Mamma; old enough to be interested in Mamma's beaus."

"Hmm. Well, Truman will be flattered, even if he isn't exactly in the market."

"What? You think he's too old for romance?"

"No." Jane thought a moment. "I don't think a person is ever too old for romance. But . . . I don't know, Laney. Somehow I think Truman never quite got over your mother."

Laney looked quizzically at Jane. "Men aren't much for hanging on to broken hearts, honey. I can't imagine that he never got over her. What happened between him and Mamma happened a lifetime ago."

"It's not so much that he still has a broken heart."

"No? Then what is it?"

"He told me he always wished for the chance to hear Maggie say she forgave him for what happened by the river, but he never had that chance. I think he regrets it."

"Oh?" Laney frowned and sat up straighter. She turned toward Jane. "He never tried to contact Mamma."

"No. From what I understand he was waiting for her to contact him, if she ever forgave him and decided to join him up north. But she never did."

"Oh." Laney sipped her tea slowly and thoughtfully.

"Did she tell you much about what happened?" Jane asked.

"Some, yes. I mean, I knew the story. It wasn't a secret or anything. Even my kids know about it, like it's just part of our family lore now."

"Well, why do you think she was never able to forgive him?"

"Oh, honey, I know she—"

"Laney," Clapper called as he opened the front door. "I'm getting Truman's and Jane's suitcases from the car. Remind me which rooms you've put them in."

Laney named the rooms, and then asked, "Do you need help?"

Clapper waved a hand. "Naw. Truman tells me they've got only one suitcase each. I think I can handle it."

He went off to dig the luggage out of the Honda as Truman stepped out onto the porch. He looked at Jane expectantly.

Jane knew what he was asking. "Seth has MRSA," she said.

Truman's face remained placid, but Jane recognized the flash of fear in his eyes. "What does Mrs. Ballantine say they're doing for him?"

"Everything they can."

"When was he diagnosed?"

"The report came back from the lab a couple hours ago."

Truman nodded, rubbed at the side of his face. "Do you want to go back?"

Jane looked out over the lawn again. Before she could respond, Laney said, "Listen, honey, if you feel you need to go, then go. Like I said,

Truman is welcome to stay as long as he wants."

"I'm not sure what to do, Laney. Jewel didn't ask me to come. She didn't say I *should* come, as though she thought . . ." She couldn't finish. She looked up at Truman again. She wanted to hear him say that Seth would be all right.

Instead, he asked, "What's in your heart, Jane?"

It seemed an odd question, and yet she understood. "I feel like I'm supposed to be here. I think I need to stay."

"Then that's what you should do."

Clapper came back with a suitcase in each hand and bounded up the porch steps. "All right, Dr. Rockaway, if you'll just follow me, I'll show you to your room. We've got you on the ground floor so you don't have to bother with any stairs."

"My arthritic knees and I appreciate that, Clapper. And now listen, it's Truman. None of this Dr. Rockaway stuff, all right?"

Truman followed Clapper inside, and when the porch was quiet again Laney turned to Jane and asked, "Are you tired after the drive down, honey?"

Jane sighed deeply. "Laney," she said, "I think I've been tired for a very long time."

"Anybody would be, after going through what you're going through with Seth. Maybe that's why you're here. You can get some rest over the next couple of days, see if you can't get to feeling refreshed."

"That sounds more wonderful than you can know."

"Come on, then. I'll show you to your room."

It was called the Rose Room, for the rose-colored wallpaper and the rose-patterned bedspread and drapes. The bed was an antique sleigh bed, with a night table on either side. The room was also furnished with a mirrored dresser, two wing chairs, and a writing desk beneath the window that overlooked the front lawn. As with all the rooms in the inn, the Rose Room had its own bath.

"It's beautiful," Jane said.

"I was hoping you'd like it," Laney replied with a satisfied smile.

"Oh, I do."

"And here's the bellhop with your luggage," Clapper announced as he entered the room. He settled the suitcase beside the bed and smiled at Jane. "Truman's taking a rest downstairs, and if you'll excuse me, I'm afraid I've got to get back to the front desk."

"Of course, Clapper. Listen, thank you so much for everything."

"Well, we're just glad to have you and the good doctor here. Make yourself at home. Supper's at six o'clock."

When Clapper left, Jane turned her attention back to the room. The afternoon sunlight slanted in through the window and draped itself across the bed. Jane noticed the light's reflection in the mirror, and as she turned toward the dresser her eyes were drawn to something familiar, a wallet-sized photograph in a tarnished metal frame. She stepped to the dresser and picked it up. "Laney, how on earth did you get this old school photo of me?"

"Your mother gave it to me."

Jane turned back to look at Laney. "She did?"

Laney nodded. "Yes. You were probably . . . what? Ten or so?"

"Nine, I think. I had that dreadful haircut when I was in fifth grade. Remember that? I never looked good with bangs."

"It wasn't a dreadful haircut. You looked as sweet as ever."

Jane laughed out loud. "Well, thanks for thinking so."

"I wasn't the only one who thought so, Janie."

"What do you mean?"

"Look at the back of the photo. It's all right. You can take it out of the frame."

Jane pulled the back off the frame and slid the picture out. Turning it over, she read aloud, "My beautiful daughter, Jane. Age nine."

For a moment she didn't speak. Finally she asked, "Mom wrote that?"

"Of course. You have to ask?"

"But why did she give it to you?"

"I believe it was tucked into a Christmas card one year."

"Mom gave you Christmas cards? I didn't know she even realized you were there in the house. For that matter, Laney, I think she hardly even realized *I* was there."

"She knew you were there, honey. She just didn't know how to be a mother to you."

Jane looked at the photo of her own nine-year-old face, the eyes distant, the mouth downturned. She had a vague memory of the photographer telling her to smile, but she wouldn't do it. "I certainly wasn't beautiful," she said softly.

"You were to your mamma," Laney countered.

"She never told me."

"She was a woman who could never find the right words. You had to listen to her speak through small gestures, like this." Laney lifted a hand to the words penned on the back of the photograph.

Jane gazed at her mother's handwriting another moment, then slid the photo back into the frame. Before she could settle it on the dresser, Laney said, "You keep that, honey. Take it home with you."

"But—"

"I've had it on my dresser all these years, but I want you to have it. The frame too. All I ask is that you send me a new one, a picture of yourself all grown up. And it'd be nice if you were smiling."

Jane smiled now, wistfully. "Thank you, Laney."

Laney put her arms around Jane and hugged her close. Drawing back she said, "Now, you get some of that rest you came here for, and then come on downstairs when you're ready."

Jane nodded. "What are you going to do?"

"I've got to track down Eugene, see if he can come over this evening with some of his work."

"His work?"

Laney moved to the door, turned around. "I think he might have something for Truman."

"You do? What is it?"

But Laney didn't stay to answer. She quietly shut the Rose Room's door. Jane listened to her footsteps moving hurriedly down the uncarpeted hall.

— 39 —

When Laney's footsteps receded and the inn was quiet, Jane looked at the photograph, still in her hand.

My beautiful daughter, Jane.

If only Meredith Morrow had said the words out loud. Even just once. But she never had. Jane would have remembered if she had.

And yet . . .

Jane moved to the dresser and settled the photo back in its place. She unpacked her suitcase, putting her change of clothing in the top dresser drawer and arranging toothpaste, toothbrush, lotions, and makeup on the bathroom counter. When that was done, she sat on the edge of the bed and kicked off her sandals. She thought briefly of calling the Penlands' neighbor, the one who was taking care of Roscoe and Juniper, but she decided to do that later. First, a little sleep. She lay down on top of the covers, sighing her way into the cradle of the bed.

"Mom," she said aloud. She hadn't said the word in years. In speaking of other people's mothers, yes, but not her own. "Mom, did you really think I was pretty?"

Did you love me?

That was the real question, after all. The one that had haunted Jane all her life.

Though it was always there, like white noise at the back of her mind, she'd never brought it out to examine it. She had always been afraid of the question. No, that wasn't quite right. She had been afraid of the answer.

When Meredith Morrow was Jane's age, when she was twenty-five years old, she'd been in Hollywood making movies, making people notice her, making a name for herself. In a few more years, it would all be gone. As Laney had said, after the roles dried up, no one worshiped her anymore.

Jane saw her mother in their apartment in the

Rayburn House, patting the couch where she sat, beckoning Jane to come. They'd sit there side by side, watching the old movies on videotape. Every time her mother sighed, which was often, Jane smelled the stench of alcohol on her breath.

"Your mother used to be somebody, Jane." She'd speak so quietly, Jane had to lean closer to hear. *"I used to be somebody, but not anymore."*

Jane never understood. Always there were the words, right on the tip of her tongue: *But you're somebody to me, Mom! I love you.*

Jane wondered now why she had never said the words aloud. Shyness? Fear of ridicule? A certain bitterness that had been a padlock on her heart?

Yet it would have been such a simple thing to do. It might even have mattered. Those few words might have made some difference.

If Jane had spoken, Meredith Morrow might have spoken back.

I love you, Mommy.

I love you too, Janie.

But the words were never said out loud.

"Well, I guess we're even, Mom," Jane murmured to the empty room. "But I'll forgive you, if you forgive me."

My beautiful daughter, Jane.

She shut her eyes and drifted off to sleep.

When she awoke, the afternoon had passed. It was almost five o'clock. Voices drifted up from below, from somewhere out in the front yard. Jane rose from the bed and looked out. Truman was walking up the flagstone path with Bess, small and sprightly, on his arm. With them was a young man, tall, dark-skinned, lanky, and handsome. He carried a laptop under his arm. He was leading the way. Jane hadn't seen him in years, but she knew he had to be Eugene Jackson.

She ran a comb through her hair, slipped her sandals back on, stuffed her cell phone into the pocket of her Capri pants, and hurried downstairs. She met the trio while they were still in the front hall.

"There you are, Jane," Truman greeted her. "We thought you were going to sleep right through supper."

"Jane honey," Bess said, "I want you to meet my nephew. This is Eugene Jackson, Laney's boy."

Eugene extended a long narrow hand. "How you doing?" he said.

Jane shook his hand. "I remember you from way back when. Your mom tells me you've got an internship in California."

"That's right," Eugene answered shyly. "We head out to L.A. on Saturday."

"That's just great," Jane continued. "Congratulations."

As Eugene nodded, Truman spoke up. "He's going to show us some of his work tonight. This

301

young man's been learning how to make documentaries."

"Oh! You're showing us one of your films?" Jane asked.

"Not exactly. Just one of the outtakes from something I worked on in college." Eugene glanced at Truman, back at Jane. "Mom thought you and Dr. Rockaway might be interested."

"In your bloopers?" Bess guffawed. "Now why would these fine folks be interested in your bloopers, Eugene?"

Eugene shrugged. "I'm not showing any bloopers, Aunt Bess. Just an outtake."

"Well, an outtake means it didn't get in the film, right?"

"That's right."

"And it didn't get in because someone made a mistake—"

"Not necessarily—"

"So maybe you should have sent it to *America's Funniest Home Videos*, won us some money—"

"But it's not funny, Aunt Bess, it's—"

"Well, whatever it is," Jane interrupted, "what time is it showing?"

"Right after supper, I guess. Mom just told me to set up everything in the front room where the television is."

"We'll be there," Truman said. "And we'd like front-row seats, please."

Eugene chuckled. "No problem, Dr. Rockaway."

Truman smiled at Eugene, and then held out an elbow to Bess. "You were going to show me those pictures of the grandkids, remember?"

Bess took his arm. "Let's go sit in the library where it's comfortable."

Together, they ambled down the hall as Eugene turned to Jane with a shrug. "Guess they've got a lot of catching up to do."

"Looks like it," Jane agreed.

"Well, I'm going to go get set up in the front room. See you later."

"All right. See you."

Jane took a last look at Truman and Bess and couldn't help smiling. The joyous feeling, though, was short-lived, interrupted by the ringing of her phone. Jane looked at the number of the incoming call. A shiver of dread ran through her when she recognized the number as Jewel's.

— 40 —

"Jewel?" Jane's heart pounded, leaving her light-headed.

"Hello, Jane. Yes, it's Jewel."

"Is everything all right? How's Seth?"

"He's holding his own. In fact, his temperature has dropped—just a little." Jewel sounded small and weary and faraway. "They're watching him like a hawk, of course."

"Okay." Jane's mind whirled, trying to process the meaning behind Jewel's words. "So he's getting better?"

A long sigh. "I don't know. At least he's not getting worse. Of course, we're praying he'll pull through all right."

Jane nodded. Yes, she must pray too. She must summon up some faith and pray for Seth. "If I could, I would pray him all the way back to the way he was before he was wounded," she said.

"Oh, Jane, so would I," Jewel said. "I hate to see him suffer. If only—" Her voice caught, and she couldn't finish.

"Are you going to be all right, Jewel?"

A short sob on the other end of the line, and then a deep breath. "Yes, I'll be fine. We have to trust God to do what's right."

"Yes." Jane wished she had the simple faith that Jewel had and that Jewel had passed on to Seth. If ever such faith was needed, now was the time. "Jewel?"

"Yes, Jane?"

"Do you want me to come back?"

After a long pause Jewel said, "No. Stay until Friday, just as you planned. Unless Seth gets worse."

"Are you sure?"

"Yes, I'm sure. I'm still hoping he'll turn the corner and be out of ICU before you get back."

"I hope so too."

All through dinner, Jane feigned attention to

the conversations going on around her. Truman was more animated than she had ever seen him, reminiscing with Bess about the past, talking with Clapper about the present, conjecturing with Eugene about the future. Jane got lost in the varied branches of dialogue as her mind went back again and again to her few minutes on the phone with Jewel. How to pray? Was it enough simply to ask? *Dear God, please make Seth whole.* Those were the only words she could think to say. But did they mean anything? And would God hear and respond?

Jane looked at Truman. As Truman Rockaway knew only too well, there were some prayers not even God could answer.

After dinner, the small group moved to the front room where Eugene had connected his laptop to the wide-screen television. Laney taped a handwritten note to the French doors that separated the room from the front hall: "Private party. Please do not disturb."

From the easy chair where she sat, Jane studied the faces of everyone assembled in a variety of chairs in front of the TV. Laney appeared to be trying hard to conceal her excitement, but she couldn't keep the corners of her mouth from turning up. Clapper looked amused, as though he shared Laney's anticipation. Truman, sitting in a wing chair, his cane at his side, appeared mildly expectant, ready to praise Laney's son for a job well done, whatever it was he'd done. Only Bess scowled slightly, a frown of puzzlement weighing down her brow.

"I don't know what all the secrecy is about," she complained. "Why doesn't somebody just tell us what we're watching?"

Eugene looked up from his laptop long enough to say, "I'm just about to do that, Aunt Bess, if you'll give me half a chance."

Clapper added, looking at Truman, "She was never a woman known for her patience, Doc."

"Hush, Clapper," Bess countered. "I've got more patience than you, Laney, and Eugene combined. I just don't always choose to use it."

Truman raised his brows and suppressed a smile.

Eugene snorted out a laugh. "Let us know if you ever choose to start using it, Aunt Bess," he said. "That'll be a red-letter day around here."

"All right, Eugene," Laney said. "Are you about ready there?"

"I'm ready now, Mamma, if Aunt Bess will just let me get started."

"Don't be blaming me for the holdup, young man—"

"Shh, Aunt Bess," Laney chided. "Let Eugene speak."

"Well!" Bess pressed her lips together, arresting any errant words that might be left on the tip of her tongue.

As the corner of Truman's mouth twitched, Jane chuckled softly under her breath. Clapper's cough barely concealed his laughter.

Eugene looked out at his audience and said, "All right, now. Mamma called me earlier today and asked me to show you this. Took me the better part of the afternoon to find it, but here it is." He looked down at his laptop then up again. "Oh, I'd better explain. This was filmed while I was doing a project on Jim Crow in the Upcountry. I interviewed a lot of the older folks around town here and some even down in Greenville, the ones who remembered the days before civil rights. It was for a filmmaking class I took a few years ago, back in college. What you're going to see wasn't in the final documentary. I left it out because . . . well, you'll see."

He pushed a button on his laptop, and an elderly woman appeared on the screen of the television set. She wore a lavender cotton dress and a colorful beaded necklace with matching earrings. Her gray hair was combed neatly away from her face and held back by some kind of clasp. Her dark cheeks displayed a hint of blush and her lips were a fiery red. She sat outdoors in a rocking chair, fanning herself with a funeral parlor fan. The sound must have been turned off, because her lips were moving but the screen was silent.

Truman leaned forward in his seat, squinting as though trying to make her out. Then quietly, almost under his breath, he whispered, "Maggie."

Eugene looked over at him and nodded. "That's right. I'm interviewing Grandma right here on the porch of the inn. I'm glad I did too, because she died less than a year later." He pushed another button on the keyboard. "Let me turn up the sound here."

". . . and there was danger in those days, real danger," Maggie was saying. "You didn't take a threat lightly back then. Wasn't anybody going to be arrested for hate crimes in those days. Killing a black man, that wasn't even considered a crime, not by the whites. Some of them, anyway. Not all of them were like that, but many of them were."

She rocked and fanned herself. She seemed to be waiting. From off camera, Eugene's voice: "So did you ever know any black folks who were killed by whites?"

Maggie's eyes shifted out toward the yard, back at the camera. "Sure I did. I remember several, killed for small things. Laughing at a white man. Talking back. A man named O'Neil Hopper, he was killed for lighting a white lady's cigarette when she asked him to."

Maggie paused and looked pensive.

Eugene's voice: "I find that hard to believe, Grandma."

A curt lifting of her chin and a flash in her eyes. "Whether you believe it or not, it's true. I knew O'Neil personally. That poor man was put in a no-win situation. He knew he might be killed if he lighted that white woman's cigarette, and he knew he might be killed if he didn't, seeing as how she asked him to. So he lit the cigarette, and that was it. No man deserves to die for something like that."

A third voice, off camera. Laney's voice: "Mamma, you know he didn't die for lighting a cigarette. He died because he was a black man, plain and simple."

Maggie looked beyond the camera and nodded. "You're right, of course, Laney. All the Jim Crow laws, they were just an excuse. They made it easy for whites to do to us whatever they wanted, even kill us and get away with it."

Eugene's voice: "Well, now, Grandma, you told me there were good white folks. Whites who helped blacks, defended blacks even."

"Well, sure there were. Plenty of good whites and plenty of bad ones. Just like the Negroes. Good ones and bad ones both. Evil isn't color-blind. Still and all, Jim Crow was a terrible time for us. A terrible time." She shook her head, rocked quietly a moment.

Eugene: "You told me before, Grandma, about how some black folks fled the South."

Maggie gave a small reluctant nod. "That's right. They had to go north just to try to stay alive."

Eugene: "And you told me about that one

309

man you were engaged to before you married Grandpa. What was his name?"

Maggie cast a stern look at the camera and fanned herself with brisk flicks of her wrist. "Truman," she said. "Dr. Truman Rockaway."

Eugene: "Yeah. Now, you said he had to go north. Tell me about that."

A surly frown on Maggie's face. "You already know the story, Eugene."

Eugene: "Well, tell me again, Grandma, so I can get it on tape."

A quick glance at Eugene, then away. "I'm not sure I want it on tape."

A sigh from behind the camera. "Come on, Grandma. You said you'd help me with the project."

"And I already have," Maggie snapped. "We've been at this for more than an hour."

Laney's voice: "If you don't want to tell Eugene the story, Mamma, I will. That way I can be in his movie."

"Fine. You can tell it. You want to sit here?"

Eugene: "No, Grandma, no. Just stay where you are. Listen, so you and Dr. Rockaway were having a picnic by the Saluda River, and you found the man who'd been shot, right? The white man."

Her eyes narrowed. She gave a resigned sigh. "That's right. Tommy Lee Coleman."

"Some other white guy shot him?"

"His own cousin." Maggie's eyes widened, and

she looked suddenly animated. "Can you believe it? His own first cousin shot him over a gambling debt."

"So what happened to the cousin?"

"He served time. Ten years for attempted murder, something like that. Eventually he got out and came back to Travelers Rest. By that time, he and Tommy Lee had gone and made up. They went into business together, just like the shooting never happened. Just like nothing ever happened."

"But something did happen, didn't it?"

Another glance at the camera. "You might say so."

"Truman Rockaway took off."

Quietly, almost imperceptibly, "That's right. He couldn't stay here after that. No, he surely couldn't stay here after that."

"Why didn't you go with him, Grandma?"

Her eyes lowered, she shook her head slowly for a long time. She didn't answer.

"Weren't you afraid to stay?" Eugene prodded. "I mean, Tommy Lee Coleman had seen you too. He could identify you."

Maggie looked up sharply. "I wasn't afraid. It wasn't me he wanted. I wasn't the one who refused to help him."

"But Dr. Rockaway did?"

"Yes."

"Refused to help him?"

"That's right."

"And why was that?"

Maggie looked out over the lawn. "You know that story too, Eugene."

"Come on, Grandma, it's for my assignment."

Maggie sighed heavily.

Laney's voice: "Maybe you could take a break for now, pick it up later."

"Later's not going to make any of it any easier, Laney."

"Well then, Mamma, you don't have to talk about it, if you don't want to."

"But you said you would, Grandma, to help me with this project."

"Let's let Grandma rest, Eugene, and finish this another time."

"Just one more question for now, Grandma."

"What is it, Eugene?" Maggie sighed again and turned reluctantly toward her grandson.

"Are you sorry you didn't go with him?"

Her jaw worked, and she opened her mouth a time or two before finally saying, "There's only one thing I'm sorry about, Eugene."

"What's that, Grandma?"

She fanned herself. Her eyes glistened. She gave another small lift of her chin. "I'm sorry I never asked him to forgive me."

"To forgive you? For what? For not going?"

"No. For not understanding why he did what he did. For loving my own virtue more than I loved him."

"So, Grandma, did you ever forgive him? I mean, for not helping that white guy?"

The glistening eyes looked directly at the camera. "Eugene, I forgave him before he even left town. I was just too proud to tell him. Now he'll never know."

A pained expression settled over Maggie Dooley's face like a shadow at dusk. With delicate hands she pushed herself up from the chair and exited the porch. The chair went on rocking without her. The screen faded to black.

— 41 —

For several minutes no one spoke. It was a poignant silence, sweetened with grace. Jane looked in wonder around the room. Laney wept quietly but openly. Eugene gazed at his laptop while Clapper pondered his hands. Bess, who sat close enough to Truman to reach him, covered one of his hands with her own. Truman sat motionless, his face without expression.

Finally Eugene said, "So Mamma thought you might like to see that, Dr. Rockaway."

Several more seconds passed before Truman leaned forward in the wing chair. "Son," he replied, "I've been waiting forty-four years to hear those words. I thought it was too late." His brow furrowed; he paused to wet his lips. "Eugene, thank you. And Laney, thank you." He patted Bess's hand, then eased himself up from the chair and took hold of his cane. "If you'll excuse me, I'd like to be alone for a little while."

He looked at Jane but only fleetingly, his eyes like sparrows unwilling to land. He turned and stepped slowly out of the room. Jane watched him go, her heart both full and weightless.

Clapper dug around in the pocket of his slacks and offered Laney his handkerchief. She took it gratefully, blew her nose, dabbed at her eyes. Eugene tapped at his keyboard with an index finger, then unhooked the laptop from the television set. Bess cleared her throat and straightened her back. Her mouth was a small tight line. "Well," she said, "I'm big enough to admit when I'm wrong. I don't think that was a blooper. Lord knows, I don't think that was any kind of mistake at all."

Clapper laughed softly. "Aunt Bess," he said, "I hate to admit it, but for once I've got to agree with you. What just happened here, that was surely no mistake."

An hour later, Jane found him alone in the library. The door was open, but she knocked anyway. "Truman?"

He looked up and smiled. "Hello, Jane. Come on in."

The library was a cozy room with built-in book-cases, a fireplace, several comfortable chairs, and small tables. Truman sat in one of the leather club chairs, his hands folded in his lap.

"I don't mean to disturb you," Jane said.

"Not at all." He waved toward a second club chair, separated from his own by a small table. "Join me."

She sat down, returned his smile. "I just wanted to make sure you're all right."

He shut his eyes, nodded, opened them. "I'm far better than all right. I'm . . . I'm . . ." He looked around the room, as though looking for the right word. He shrugged, unable to find it. "Now I know why we're here, why we had to come. Jane, if I hadn't met you—"

"But you did."

"Yes. That's what I've been sitting here think-ing about. If I hadn't met you, if you hadn't known Laney, if Maggie hadn't always said her two cents' worth about life's gearshift . . ." He paused and chuckled quietly. "But here we are. I've been thinking about how all the small steps finally fit together to bring me to the right place. I have no doubt that each one was orchestrated by a divine hand."

She gazed at him intently. "So that your unanswerable prayer could be answered," she said.

Truman nodded slowly as the small muscles in

his jaw worked. "That's the amazing thing. I heard Maggie say it herself, the words I've wanted to hear all these years. She forgave me."

Jane reached across the table and laid a hand on Truman's arm. "I'm happy for you, you know."

"Thank you, Jane." His dark eyes glistened as he covered her young hand with his old weathered one. "Thanks for your part in bringing me here."

"You're welcome. But listen, I wouldn't have missed this for the world." Giving his arm a squeeze, she rose and stretched. She glanced at the cherrywood clock on the mantel and saw that the hour was getting late. "What are you going to do now, Truman?" she asked.

With that, he sank a little lower into the worn leather of the chair and smiled contentedly. "I'm going to bask in Maggie's forgiveness. I'm going to breathe without pain. If I could dance on these old arthritic knees, I'd get up and dance." He laughed out loud, his eyes raised toward the ceiling. "I'm going to enjoy this feeling of happiness for as long as it lasts."

Jane nodded happily. "Then I will leave you to it," she said. Strolling to the nearest row of books, she tilted her head to read the spines. She pulled a paperback from the shelf and opened to the first page. "This looks like a good one," she mused.

"What is it?"

"Just a love story of some kind. I'm sure it has a happy ending. Maybe kind of like yours." She turned back to Truman and gave him another smile. "I guess I'll go read awhile, then call it a night."

"All right. Sleep well, then. I'll see you in the morning."

"Good night, Truman."

She headed for the door, but he called her back. "Jane?"

"Yes?"

"You'll find out too. Before we leave."

"Find out what?"

"Why Travelers Rest called you."

Jane thought a moment. "Do you think so? Maybe I'm just the chauffeur, the one who was supposed to bring you here."

Truman shook his head. "No, I think there's something for you here, something real."

"Well . . ." Jane lifted her shoulders in a small shrug. "I guess we'll find out tomorrow. Good night, Truman."

"Good night, Jane."

She held the book close to her heart and ascended the stairs to the Rose Room.

— 42 —

At breakfast the next morning, Jane flipped open her cell phone to see if there were any messages. The screen came up empty. She frowned at Truman, who was sipping coffee beside her. "My phone's dead."

Truman settled the cup back in the saucer. "What happened?"

"I don't know. It was working last night when I talked with Jewel."

"Did you plug it in overnight?"

"Yes, it was charging all night."

"Here, let me take a look." Truman held out a hand for the phone. He looked at it a moment, snapped it shut. "Your battery must have given out completely."

"I wonder why."

Truman shrugged. "Happens sometimes."

Jane sighed. "And you didn't bring your cell phone with you, right?"

"In my rush to get here, I forgot. Sorry, Jane."

"That's all right. But I need to let Jewel know. I'll ask Laney if I can make a quick call on their phone in the office. I'll pay her back for the long-distance charges."

"I'm sure that'll be fine. Though knowing Laney, she probably won't let you pay her back."

Jane stirred cream into her coffee. Accustomed to drinking coffee from a mug, she liked the way the spoon clinked against the delicate china. The dining room was empty except for her and Truman, who were sharing a late breakfast of bacon, fried eggs, and toast. "What would you like to do today, Truman?" she asked.

"I've been thinking about that." He stabbed at his eggs with the prongs of his fork so that a slow lava of yolk flowed out. "First, I'd like to take a little drive, see some of the old haunts. There's one place I'd like to visit for sure before we leave tomorrow."

When he didn't go on, Jane paused with a piece of toast halfway to her mouth. "Do you want to visit Maggie's grave?"

Truman shook his head. "No. I'll let her and Cyrus rest in peace. But I'd like to go back to the river, Jane, if you don't mind taking me."

"You mean where you found Tommy Lee Coleman?"

"Yes. I don't know why exactly. Except that I used to love that river. Maybe a person sometimes has to make peace with a place."

Jane nodded. "I'll be glad to take you there, and anywhere else you want to go. The day is yours, Truman."

The sky was cloudless, an open expanse of blue. If Jane's car had been a convertible, she and

Truman would have ridden with the top down. As it was, they elected to roll up the windows and turn on the AC against the hot and muggy air outside. Truman, in a short-sleeved shirt and slacks, hunkered down in the passenger seat with his cane at hand, ready for the nostalgic ride. His eyes were bright and he seemed on the verge of laughter. It made Jane happy simply to be with him.

"Where do we go first?" she said.

"Anywhere," Truman answered with a wave of a hand. "Just drive around the town. Believe me, that won't take long. Then we'll head out toward the river. I can't exactly remember how to get there, and I'm sure things have changed a bit over the years, but don't worry, we'll get there eventually."

"I'm not worried. We have all day. I'll top off the tank at the nearest gas station, and we'll be set."

"All right. And you got hold of Jewel, right?"

Jane nodded. "Yup, called her from the phone in the office. I told her my cell is dead but she can call me at the inn. I gave her the number."

"How did she say Seth is doing?"

"That's the best part, Truman. She said he's doing better. He's talking and eating a little. He says he's hungry. Jewel's hoping they can move him out of ICU in the next few days."

Truman smiled broadly, his white teeth a flash of enthusiasm. "That's great, Jane. I'm glad to hear it. It'll be good to get him back up on five. He's got a tournament to win, you know."

Jane nodded and laughed. "Yeah, being up on five is the new normal. I can't wait to get him back to normal. Winning the tournament would just be an added bonus at this point. But a nice one, of course." She glanced at Truman and smiled before looking back to the road.

"So how are Jewel and Sid?"

"They're holding their own, I think, though I know the whole thing's wearing on them."

"Of course it is."

"Jewel said she'd call if there was a change and otherwise she'd see us Friday."

When Truman didn't respond, Jane glanced at him and said, "You *are* coming back with me tomorrow, aren't you?"

"Oh yes," he replied. "Yes, I'm going back with you. Hey look, there's a gas station up there on the left. Why don't we stop and fill up." He dug his wallet out of his back pocket and pulled out his credit card. "Then after that, turn right at the light up there, and I'll show you where we lived when I was growing up. We can go on to the river from there."

Jane pulled into the station and allowed Truman to gas up the car. After they rolled back onto the street, she turned right at the light. "Do you think you'll ever live in Travelers Rest again, Truman?" she asked.

Truman squinted slightly as the corner of his mouth turned up. "Stranger things have happened, I suppose."

The house Truman grew up in was gone, razed to make room for a strip mall on the far outskirts of town. Truman took the change in stride, saying it wasn't much of a house to begin with, and who knew but maybe it had even fallen down on its own.

From there they traveled south of Travelers Rest to find the Saluda River. It took them awhile of driving and backtracking, but Truman eventually recognized the slight bend in the river where he and Maggie had set down their picnic basket on that long-ago day.

Jane parked by the side of the road, and the two of them got out of the car. She followed Truman a short distance until he stopped several yards from the water's edge. He poked at the ground with his cane. He looked up the river and down until he was satisfied and then said, "This is it. This is the spot."

The riverbank was shaded by a variety of leafy and pine trees. The river itself was narrow and rocky; bubbly in spots, quiet in others. The place was one of benign beauty, not particularly memorable, yet worthy of an afternoon for a young couple in love.

"This is where your whole life changed," Jane said.

Truman nodded. "Yes."

She tried to imagine the day: a young Truman and Maggie and a picnic basket on a blanket, the anticipation of a quiet afternoon together, and then the abrupt intrusion of gunfire, a car door slamming, an engine revving, and a man left bleeding in the grass. If only Truman had chosen another place, another time. If only.

"If you could do it all over again," Jane asked, "do you think you would help Tommy Lee?"

Deep in thought, Truman's eyes narrowed and his brow sagged. Finally he said, "I don't have an answer to that. If I say I wished I'd done it differently, then I'd be living with regrets, and I don't want that. My life turned on a dime and headed in a different direction, but who's to say it was the wrong direction? In fact, the more I think about it, the more I'm satisfied everything turned out the way it was supposed to. It's been a good life and I can't complain. Anyhow, you know what Maggie always said." His eyes rolled toward Jane. " 'Life's gearshift's got no reverse—' "

" 'So you have to just keep moving forward,' " Jane finished. With that, they shared a smile.

Truman looked back out over the water and sighed deeply. It was a sigh, Jane knew, of contentment and not of longing. After a moment, Truman said, "You know, I think I could use a drink."

Jane nodded. "We passed a Dairy Queen a few

miles back. I bet they could mix you up a tall glass of chocolate milk."

"Well, then"—Truman turned and headed toward the car—"what are we waiting for? Let's go."

— 43 —

They sat in the brown leather club chairs in the library, the small empty table between them. The clock on the mantel showed the hour to be near midnight. They'd put 154 miles on the Honda in their tour of the Upcountry. After the stop at Dairy Queen they'd driven well into the afternoon, catching lunch in a small café in Pelham, a postage stamp of a town somewhere between the larger cities of Greenville and Spartanburg, which they also visited. Now they were tired.

"What time do you want to head home tomorrow, Truman?" Jane asked, leaning her head against the cushioned chair.

"Not too early," Truman replied. "These old bones are rather fond of sleeping in."

"My bones feel the same way," Jane said. "But listen, you don't have to go back tomorrow, you know. Laney said you can stay as long as you want."

"Hmm-huh," Truman said. "Why do I get the feeling you're trying to get rid of me?"

Jane lifted her head and looked at Truman. "I'm not trying to get rid of you. I'm just trying to . . . well, to give you some time, is all."

"Time for what?"

"Oh, I don't know. To be home again. To get a little better acquainted with Bess—"

"Uh-huh."

"Come on, Truman, you know she'd like you to stay awhile. Or stay for good. I saw the way she was watching you at supper tonight. She's broken-hearted because you're leaving tomorrow."

Truman looked down at his hands and shrugged. "My home's in Asheville now. I've got to go back."

"And what about Bess?"

"What *about* Bess?"

Jane feigned an exasperated sigh. "She's attractive. She's funny. She's available. She's Maggie's little sister."

"She's not Maggie."

"She doesn't have to be, does she?"

Truman thought a moment. "No, she doesn't have to be. But, Jane, I'm too old for all that now."

"Don't be silly, Truman. You're never too old for love."

Truman laughed lightly. "Well, young lady, just wait till you're my age and see if you still believe that. Love's not so easy when you're falling apart."

Jane leaned her head against the chair again.

"You know something, Truman," she said. "I don't think love's ever easy."

Truman nodded, stuck out his lower lip. "I think you're probably right about that."

"I thought I was going to have a lifetime of it with Seth. Now I know there are no guarantees."

"Nope. No guarantees. You can't place a warranty on something so fragile."

"And yet the crazy thing is, Truman, we're always . . ."

"Always what, Jane?"

She thought of the words of the poet. "We're always crying after it, you know? We're always crying after love. It's such a fundamental desire, but there's nothing to satisfy it, is there?"

"Well." Truman looked up at the ceiling, offered a sigh. "Humanly speaking, probably not. Momentarily, maybe. Sometimes maybe for years. But not for a lifetime, no."

"What then, Truman? Why are we always looking for something that isn't there?"

While waiting for Truman to respond, Jane shut her eyes. That was the irony, she thought. Like everyone else, she was looking for fairy tales in a story of heartache, a dime-store-novel ending to what was one huge Shakespearean tragedy. Everything was doomed to fail. And yet, for Truman, there had been a sort of redemption, hadn't there? Hadn't the answer to his prayer meant something?

Truman was speaking, saying something . . . she wasn't quite sure what. She should listen, would listen if her own thoughts weren't weighing her down, lulling her toward sleep. She wanted to know his answer but . . .

Footsteps approached, moving down the long uncarpeted hall. Someone was coming. Jane opened her eyes, sat up straighter in the chair. Who was coming to the library at this hour? Laney, maybe, with tall glasses of sweet tea on a tray? Clapper, making the rounds, checking on doors and windows before bed?

The footsteps stopped in the doorway. Jane gasped at the figure captured in the hallway light.

"Seth!" Her heart thumped as her breath quickened. She wanted to jump from the chair and run to him, but her body wouldn't respond. "Seth, I don't understand. How . . . what are you . . . ?" She stopped, unable to find the words.

Seth made no move toward her. He lifted his hands, palms up, as though to show her he could do it. "I'm all right now," he said. "I just wanted you to know that."

"But how, Seth? How?"

"Look," he said, "I can't stay long, but I have something for you."

"What?"

Seth nodded toward the table between Jane's chair and Truman's. On it was an open bottle of

wine that Jane hadn't noticed before. "Wine?"
Jane asked.

Seth smiled. Jane thought of the Penlands'
cabinet, all the bottles lined up inside. "But I
don't want it, Seth. I'm sorry, but—"

"It isn't wine, Jane."

"It isn't?"

"No. It's what you've been looking for. It's
love."

"Love?"

"Show her, Truman."

Truman seemed at ease with what was
happening, as though he were used to paralyzed
men walking and wine appearing where there
had been none. Serenely, he picked up the bottle
and poured a small amount of wine into two
miniature glasses. Setting the bottle back on the
table, his hands moved to an uncut loaf of bread
that lay beside it. Jane hadn't noticed the loaf
before either.

Truman tore off a piece and gripped it for a
moment, his lips moving as though in prayer.
Then he extended his hand to Jane, offering her
the bread as he said, "This is His body . . ."

Before she could take it, a phone rang somewhere, knocking Jane into a dazed wakefulness.
She stretched her cramped muscles, felt her skin
rub against the cool leather of the club chair. She
slowly became aware of birdsong and of dawn

struggling to come in through the gauzy curtains covering the windows. She saw she was alone in the room, though in the next moment Laney was there, standing in the doorway in a white cotton robe, holding the cordless phone in both hands like it was a wounded bird. Before Jane was even fully awake, she knew that Seth was dead.

— 44 —

Two Weeks Later

Jane moved down the familiar hallway of the Community Living Center, made no less bland by the occasional cheap painting and other attempts at hominess. She thought for the hundredth time that Truman deserved to live out the rest of his life in a better place, a real home, maybe even a house in Travelers Rest.

She took a deep breath when she reached his room, paused at the door, knocked on the doorframe.

He greeted her with a smile and a wave. "Jane, come on in."

"Hi, Truman."

He was sitting in his chair, eating his lunch from a tray on the overbed table. He paused as Jane approached, his fork poised over the remains of a fish stick, a small mound of potatoes, and a few scattered peas. Beside the plate sat an untouched dinner roll and a pat of butter cradled in paper.

"Sorry to interrupt your lunch," Jane said as she sat in the opposite chair.

"On the contrary," Truman said, glancing down at the food. "Thank you for interrupting." He settled the fork on the tray and leaned back, clasping his hands at his waist. For a moment he seemed to be studying her. Then he asked, "How was it?"

Jane nodded, one small lift of her chin. "It was a beautiful service. Exactly what Seth would have wanted, I think."

The two weeks since their return from Travelers Rest had been a storm of activity for Jane. She had gone back to Troy to help Jewel and Sid plan the funeral and afterward had helped write thank-you notes for the deluge of flowers, meals, and condolence cards that had poured in.

"I wish I could have been there," Truman said.

"Me too. You picked a bad time to have the flu. How are you now?"

"Better," he said simply. "More importantly, how are *you?*"

She offered a small, brave smile. "I'm all right, Truman. I really am."

He looked skeptical and waited for her to say more. When she didn't go on, he asked, "And Sid and Jewel? How are they?"

"Heartbroken, of course. But at the same time, strong. They're such strong people, really. Whenever I saw Sid, he was comforting someone else instead of the other way around. And Jewel . . . well, she just kept saying they hadn't really lost him because they know where he is."

Truman pressed an index finger to his lips in thought. "She has a good point."

"And their other son, David, came back from Alaska for the funeral, of course. He's decided to stay put in Troy for a while, which is a good thing for Sid and Jewel. Having David there will be a comfort for them."

"I'm glad, Jane."

"I am too."

A brief silence before Truman pressed, "And you're sure you're all right?"

Their eyes met as Jane nodded. "Yes, I'm sure. I miss Seth. I miss him a lot. But by the time he died I had already been grieving the loss of him for a long time. I think I'm ready to begin moving forward."

"And what will you do now?"

"I'm going to finish out the summer here, taking care of the Penlands' house and their dogs. When Diana and Carl come home at the end of the summer, I'll go back to Troy, back to my teaching job there."

"While you're here, will you continue to visit me?"

"Of course I will. How could I not?"

Truman nodded, glanced toward the window, back at Jane. "Something tells me, even after you return to Troy, this friendship of ours is a keeper."

Jane smiled. "No question about it. I think we're bound together for life. So don't worry. After I go back to Troy, I'll come up to visit as often as I can."

"And what if I'm not here? What if I'm in Travelers Rest?"

"Travelers Rest?" Jane's eyes widened. "Do you think you'll move back there?"

"Lord willing, I just might. Eventually, that is."

"Is it Bess?"

Truman chuckled. "As the young folks say today, we're talking."

"Burning up the airwaves, are you?"

"Let's just say it's a good thing I have unlimited long distance."

Jane laughed out loud. "I thought you said you were too old for any of that, Truman. You know, it's hard to fall in love when you're falling apart."

Truman chuckled quietly. "It seems I've discovered a little spunk of my own, a little bit of spunk I didn't know I had until I met Bess again."

Jane looked at him a long moment before saying, "I'm really glad for you, Truman. You deserve some happiness."

"No." A shake of the head. "That's the thing. I

don't deserve it. It's a gift, plain and simple. A gift I never thought I'd have."

They were quiet then, though the silence didn't seem awkward to Jane. It just seemed peaceful. Finally Truman said, "Did you hear about the kitty?"

"The kitty?"

"The kitty from the chess tournament."

"Oh? Did someone win?"

"No, not yet. The tournament's still going on."

"What about the kitty, then?"

"Everyone involved in the tournament decided to donate the money to Children's Hospital as a memorial to Seth. It's been earmarked for the spinal cord unit."

Jane drew in her breath. "Really, Truman?"

He nodded. "Really."

"That's wonderful. I'll have to thank everyone. If Seth knew, I'm sure he'd be thrilled about it."

Truman nodded. "I like to think he knows. Somehow."

"Speaking of Seth," Jane said, "I'm supposed to let you know about the concert."

"The concert?"

"Yeah, it just kind of happened. Some of the guys on five wanted to do something for Seth, so they asked Jon-Paul to come and play as a tribute to him. There'll just be a few of us in the atrium, but do you want to come?"

"Of course. When?"

"Just a few minutes, I think. Jon-Paul and the other guys are spreading the word in case anyone else wants to join us."

"I'm supposed to play a game of chess with Stan Griffin right after lunch, but we can postpone. He'll probably want to be at the concert anyway."

"Great. Jon-Paul said he'd call me when they're ready to start."

Jane laced her fingers together and rested them in her lap. She gazed out the window at the gazebo surrounded by the midsummer gardens of roses, day lilies, delphinium, and forget-me-nots. "You know," she said at length, "right before we left for Travelers Rest, Seth had a dream he said was very real, so real it was almost like he was there. He dreamed he and I were walking on the beach, and he could feel the sand and the wind and the water, and he could feel his hand in mine. Well, at the inn, I had a dream like that. It was so incredibly real." She looked at Truman and gave him a bittersweet smile. "You were there too."

"Oh?" Truman said, leaning forward slightly in the chair. "What was the dream about?"

"I dreamed that Seth was healed. He could walk again. He was just like he was before Iraq only—I don't know—better somehow. I can't explain it. But anyway, you and I were at the inn, and we were sitting in the library talking when we heard footsteps in the hall, and suddenly there he was. Just standing there in the doorway like he'd never been hurt. And he said he was all right now."

Truman looked at her a long moment. "Anything else?" he asked.

She thought about the wine and the bread, and though she didn't fully understand it, she wanted that to be her gift alone. She wanted to keep it to herself, like a love letter meant for no one else. She looked at Truman and shrugged. "I like to think Seth really is all right now. I mean, that he's with God and he's all right."

Truman nodded. Before he could respond, the tapping of Jon-Paul's cane in the hall announced his arrival. In another moment, he was at the door. "Jane?"

Jane looked toward Jon-Paul and smiled. "I'm here."

"And, Truman?"

"Here. How are you, friend?"

"I'm doing well, thanks. Did Jane tell you about the happenings in the atrium?"

"Yes, she did."

"We're ready to start."

"Wonderful. I'll be there. You two go on ahead. I've got to call Stan and tell him we're postponing our game."

"All right. We won't start till you get there, though." Jon-Paul turned slightly and held out an elbow. "Jane?"

Jane stood to go.

"Oh, before you go, Jane," Truman said. "Just one more thing."

"Yes, Truman?"

He beckoned her closer with a lift of his chin. She took a step toward him and watched as he picked up the dinner roll beside his plate. Carefully, almost ceremoniously, he tore off one corner, placed the bread in Jane's palm, and curled her fingers around it.

When he looked up, Jane found herself gazing into the kindest eyes she had ever seen.

Truman gave a small nod and squeezed her hand. "Broken for you," he said.

— 45 —

Jane walked in silence through the corridors with Jon-Paul, the bit of dinner roll still clenched in the palm of her hand. What had it meant? she wondered. Had she and Truman shared the same dream, or had they somehow been given a glimpse of heaven?

When he gave her the bread, she had wanted to ask him: *Truman, were you there? Was it real?*

But she didn't ask. Because she knew instinctively that it didn't matter. What mattered was that here in this huge VA complex, among all the broken bodies from all the senseless wars, there was a reminder in her hand of one more broken body from one more senseless war, and the brokenness of that body, the brokenness that Laney called a sacrifice, was the only thing that made any sense at all.

"It's love," Seth had said. *"It's what you've been looking for."*

She knew now what she hadn't quite been sure of, that it was true. There was only one sure place to lay a heart where it could rest securely and never be broken.

As she and Jon-Paul entered the atrium, Jane gasped. She signaled him to stop with a tug on his arm.

"What is it, Jane?" Jon-Paul asked.

"I had no idea . . ."

"What?"

"I had no idea this many people would be here."

"How many?"

"It's . . . it's . . ."

Before Jane could continue, they were approached by Hoboken and Sausalito. Hoboken waved a hand toward the crowd. "It's . . . what do you say? It's standing room only!"

"Yes." Jane nodded.

The atrium was filled from wall to wall, and overhead in the lobby a solid line of people leaned on the banister looking down, waiting for the concert to begin.

"Did all these people know Seth?" Jane asked.

"Everyone knew Mr. Seth," Hoboken answered.

"Not only that," Sausalito added, "but they loved him. We are all here to pay our respects."

"We have a chair for you, Miss Jane," Hoboken said. "Please follow us."

Jane and Jon-Paul followed the cousins through a crooked path in the crowd. Two padded chairs waited by the piano. Hoboken waved Jane into one as Jon-Paul took a seat on the piano bench.

"Who's the other chair for, Hoboken?" Jane asked.

The young Ugandan gestured with a nod of his head. "Here he comes now."

Truman walked stiffly toward them through the shifting crowd. Sausalito went to him, laid a hand on his shoulder, and guided him to the second chair. Truman eased himself into it with a sigh. His eyes met Jane's, and they shared a smile, though neither spoke.

In another moment Jon-Paul raised a hand to silence the crowd. When a hush fell over the atrium, he said loudly, "Well, I want to thank you all for coming to this impromptu concert, which isn't really a concert so much as a tribute to our friend, Staff Sergeant Seth Ballantine of the North Carolina National Guard."

At the mention of his name, a cheer went up and the crowd applauded. Jane looked in wonder around the room until her gaze came to rest once more on Truman. He nodded at her as though to say, *Yes, he deserves the applause. He died a hero.*

When the cheers diminished, Jon-Paul went on, "Now, anyone who's heard me play before knows I'm not a concert pianist. I'm just someone who likes to bang out a song once in a while—"

"Don't sell yourself short, Jonny," someone shouted overhead. "You're terrific!"

Jon-Paul laughed as the crowd applauded again. "All right, thanks," he said. "But anyway, this isn't about me. It's about Seth. A great guy. A good friend. A terrific soldier. And a super chess player!"

Whistles. Cat calls. More applause.

"So this is for Seth," Jon-Paul finished as he raised his hands to the keys. "And because I know he'd want it this way, it's also for all the guys—all the men and women—who've given their lives to, well . . . as I've heard Hoboken put it, to defend the blessings."

With that, an expectant calm filled the moments before Jon-Paul's hands began to move. When the music started, Jane recognized the opening notes of Beethoven's "Ode to Joy." She thought it an odd choice as a tribute to a fallen soldier, but as she became aware once more of the moist, doughy bread in her fist, she realized it was right. Even in a world such as this, there was joy.

For thirty minutes Jon-Paul played, moving without pause from one song to another and another. The crowd stood motionless, shifting only to let the occasional passerby through. Jane listened as though enchanted, the music carrying her back to childhood when she sat in the window seat in the parlor, grasping at the beauty beyond the glass. Once more, there was Grandmother on her knees in the garden, weeding the rows of freshly sprung tulips and budding delphinium, the early evening sunlight resting tenderly on the grass. And in the kitchen, Laney, singing her sad songs of hope as she washed the dishes yet one more time at the end of another sweet day. Only now Jane saw what she hadn't seen before—God was there, master over all creation, scattering those seeds of beauty with open palms.

When at last Jon-Paul's hands came to rest, the crowd broke out again in thundering applause. Jon-Paul seemed not to notice. Neither did he acknowledge it. Instead, he leaned toward Jane and settled his eyes on her face as though he could see her. He was smiling. "And this last one," he said quietly to her alone, "this one's for you, Jane."

She knew what it was before he began to play. She listened as the familiar strains of "Clair de Lune" rose from the piano and twined themselves around the crowd. Jane felt herself wrapped up in moonlight, and as she watched Jon-Paul play for her, she was at peace.

— Epilogue —

Three Years Later

As Jane settled the vase of freshly cut gladiolus above the fireplace, she took a moment to run her hand along the mantelpiece. *Seth would have liked this,* she thought as she studied the hand-crafted scrollwork ornamenting the hearth. No doubt Seth would have fallen in love with every inch of the Travelers Rest Inn had he had the chance to visit. She could just imagine him walking through its rooms, observing with great diligence all the varied woodwork put in place a century and a half before. Certainly few visitors saw all that Seth would have seen had he been there.

But no time to think of that now. There was a celebration to prepare for, and the guests would be arriving in less than an hour. Laney was in the kitchen, frantically working up trays of hors d'oeuvres. She and Clapper had invited nearly a hundred guests to join them in marking their twenty-fifth wedding anniversary. Jane had come early, along with a few other volunteers and the three Jackson kids, to help cook and clean and set up and decorate. They'd been at it for hours, but they were almost ready. Jane glanced around the front room and decided the only thing miss-ing was the food and the guests.

Some were still on the road, coming from long distances. Her grandmother and father were on their way from Troy; they should be showing up any minute. Though they still owned and lived in the Rayburn Bed & Breakfast, Gram was no longer involved in the day-to-day running of it. She had finally decided to retire to her gardening and her books and her music, and so she had hired a young couple to work alongside Peter Morrow. From what Dad said, David and Olivia Ballantine were doing a great job publicizing the place, bringing in new guests, and making sure each and every visitor was happy and comfortable during their stay.

Jane smiled at the thought of Seth's brother running the old B&B. David wouldn't appre-ciate the woodwork the way Seth had, but he no doubt appreciated the job in the midst of the current economic downturn. He was, after all, a family man now, his wanderlust having been permanently excised by the former Olivia Springman. He had run into her, his old high school flame, when he came back from Alaska for Seth's funeral. Some months later, in a there's-no-place-like-home kind of moment, he married her and once again planted his roots in the same Carolina soil he had formerly shaken off his feet. David and Olivia were expecting their first child in the fall. Sid and Jewel Ballantine were ecstatic. Dad said Olivia wasn't even showing when David started handing out cigars.

Jane was just turning away from the fireplace when Bess walked into the room, holding a cheese tray in front of her with both hands. She was in her party dress of yellow eyelet, and even from a distance Jane could smell her perfume. Bess smiled at Jane with lips painted a deep shiny red. "Can you tell me where I ought to be putting this, Jane honey?" she said.

Jane pointed to one of the tables covered in white linen. "Cheese trays go right there next to the punch bowl."

Bess nodded and placed the tray on the table. "Call it a miracle, but it looks like everything's going to be ready on time."

"That's good," said Jane, "though I think we're all going to be exhausted by the time the party starts."

"Speak for yourself, young lady. I'm ready to cut a rug till the wee hours."

Jane laughed. "Does Truman know about this?"

"He knows he best keep up with me, or I'll leave him in the dust."

"So where is that husband of yours now?"

"In the kitchen begging scraps," Bess said, her voice feisty. "Where else would you expect Truman to be?"

"What? You don't feed him enough?"

"Honey," Bess said, drawing herself up to her full five-foot height and putting her hands on her hips, "you know I feed that man plenty. He claims he's still making up for the years of what he calls his old retired veterans food. You'd think they were feeding him C-rations instead of hot meals, but I know better. Maggie always said he had the appetite of a horse, and now I know it's true."

Jane shrugged nonchalantly. "The only thing I ever thought he liked was chocolate milk."

Bess threw her hands up. "He drinks that stuff like there's no tomorrow. He drinks it for breakfast, for lunch, for supper, and every hour in between. Sometimes he even brings a glass of it to bed. I have to tell him, 'Truman, baby, you be careful now. You spill that chocolate milk in this bed and you're on the couch tonight!' "

Bess's comment was followed by hearty laughter from Truman as he walked into the room carrying a tray of finger foods. "Now, Bess," he said, "we're two years married and you've never once put me in the doghouse."

"Yeah?" Bess shot back. "So far you haven't spilled any milk. Just wait and see what happens when you do."

"Hmm." Truman nodded. He set the finger foods down by the cheese tray. "That's settled, then," he said.

"What's settled, Truman?" Bess asked, frowning slightly. "What are you talking about?"

"No more chocolate milk in bed." Truman smiled and shrugged. "I don't want to spend a night away from you. Not a night and not a day. Not ever."

Bess clasped both hands over her heart and laughed merrily. "Truman Rockaway! You're a hopeless romantic. That's what you are!"

Truman winked, bent down, and kissed his wife. "That's right, Mrs. Rockaway. Nothing's going to come between me and my bride."

Jane watched as they kissed again, Truman leaning far down to reach the lips of his tiny wife. They'd been married in this very room, the front room of the Travelers Rest Inn, and had honey-mooned in Charleston before setting up housekeeping together in Bess's home just a few miles from the inn.

To Jane, the wedding seemed like yesterday. It had been one of the happiest days of her life. She smiled now as she watched Bess and Truman move arm in arm toward the door. Before they stepped into the hall, Bess stopped and said over her shoulder, "Speaking of hopeless romantics, Jane, where's that young man of *yours?*"

"I think he's still upstairs with Maggie."

"Well, you best tell him to get dressed and get on down here. Guests will start showing up soon."

Jane looked at her watch and nodded. "I'll tell him to get a move on."

While Truman and Bess disappeared down the hall, Jane headed up the broad staircase to the second floor. When she came to the guest room that was hers for the weekend, she paused in the doorway and looked inside. She could see just the back of her husband's head above the rim of the padded rocking chair by the window. He was humming quietly while he rocked.

Gram had been thrilled when she learned Jane was marrying a lawyer and moving to Asheville. Initially, the fact that the young man was blind gave her pause, but once she met him her concerns largely disappeared. "He seems quite capable of a normal life," she'd told Jane.

"Oh, Gram, of course he is. And I'm not marrying him because he's a lawyer. All that doesn't matter."

"Well, dear, at least I know he'll be able to give you a comfortable life."

Jane paused a moment, smiled. "It isn't comfort that I care about, Gram."

Gram had looked puzzled, but Jane didn't explain. There was really only one reason she was marrying Jon-Paul Pearcy. She couldn't help it. She loved him.

Jane felt a rush of that love now as she stood in the doorway to their room. He had been patient and understanding, allowing her time to finish grieving Seth before pursuing her. She'd gone back to Troy for that first year, and though they'd stayed in touch, he let that year go by before deciding he had waited long enough. Finally he'd called and asked her if she might consider going on a blind date. She'd laughed and said she'd be delighted. A few months later, shortly after Bess and Truman's wedding, Jane and Jon-Paul too were married in the front room of the Travelers Rest Inn.

Jane started when Jon-Paul spoke, interrupting her thoughts. "I know you're there, Mrs. Pearcy," he said quietly. "Why don't you come in? What are you doing?"

"Well, Mr. Pearcy," Jane answered, "I'm just standing here thinking how happy I am."

"Really? That's funny."

"What's funny about it?"

"I was sitting here thinking exactly the same thing."

Jane smiled. She walked to where her husband sat and gazed down at the baby in his lap. The baby's eyes were closed and her moist pink lips had stopped sucking at the bottle in Jon-Paul's hand.

"Maggie's asleep," Jane said in a low voice.

"I know."

"Why don't you put her in her crib?"

"Because there's nothing better than having her in my arms."

Jane gazed lovingly at Magdalene Meredith Pearcy, not quite six months old. "She'll steal the show tonight, of course," she said. "She'll take all the attention away from Laney and Clapper."

"And that's to be expected," Jon-Paul replied. "I'm sure Laney knows she'll have to play second fiddle to the most beautiful baby in the world."

Jane laughed lightly. Laney adored the baby, as did Truman and Bess, Maggie's honorary grandparents. Everyone adored her, it seemed. Gram was spoiling her first great-grandchild terribly, with the cooperation of Peter Morrow, the proud grandfather. Peter's whole countenance had changed when he first laid eyes on Maggie, then changed again when he learned the child's middle name was Meredith. "Are you sure, Jane?" he had asked. "Your mother wasn't much of a mother to you."

"I'm sure, Dad," Jane had told him. "I want Mom to have her name on something other than a bunch of old movies. She needs to be remembered for something more important than that."

Jane lifted the bottle from Jon-Paul's hand and set it on the dresser. "You'd better let me put her down for her nap," she said. "You need to get dressed. The guests are going to start showing up any minute now."

"All right. If you insist."

"I'm afraid I do."

Jon-Paul sighed even as he smiled. He lifted Maggie to his lips and kissed her cheek. Then he handed her over to Jane.

Just as when the baby was born, Jane wished momentarily that Jon-Paul could see Maggie clearly. She wished he could gaze unimpeded at her perfect round face and into her clear blue eyes, but the sight he had left wouldn't allow it. And yet, she was the one who ached, not Jon-Paul. He was decidedly content. He knew exactly how beautiful she was. Some things, he said, didn't have to be seen to be believed. Some things could be taken on faith.

Jane laid Maggie in her crib and turned on the baby monitor attached to the railing. Jon-Paul reached into the closet for a freshly ironed shirt. Outside, a car pulled up in front of the inn. The engine was cut and the driver's side door opened and closed. Jane stepped to the window in time to see her father helping Gram out of the passenger seat.

"Ah, Peter and Grandmother are here," Jon-Paul said.

Jane turned wide-eyed from the window. "How did you know it was Dad and Gram?"

"Easy," Jon-Paul replied as he worked his way down the buttons of his shirt. "I heard you smile."

Before Jane could respond, more cars rolled up the drive. Tires crunched on gravel. Doors opened and slammed shut. Chatter rose up and laughter rang out. Jane paused long enough to give her husband a kiss before hurrying off to welcome family and friends to the place called Travelers Rest.

— Acknowledgments —

A huge thank-you to each of the following who shared their lives and their expertise with me. This book wouldn't have been possible without their help.

Tom Mattox, PA-C, Spinal Cord Injury/Disease Clinic, Department of Veterans Affairs, Charles George VA Medical Center, Asheville, North Carolina

Dennis Mehring, Public Affairs Officer, Department of Veterans Affairs, Charles George VA Medical Center, Asheville, North Carolina

Judy L. Davis, Low Vision Technician, Low Vision Center, Mission Hospitals, Asheville, North Carolina

Preston R. Jones, Area Rehabilitation Supervisor, Department of Health and Human Services, Services for the Blind, N.C. Division, Asheville, North Carolina

Bobbie Sue Resh, RN, Spine Unit, Neuro Unit, Mission Hospital, Asheville, North Carolina

Jim and Claudia Blair Bulthuis, The Blair House Bed & Breakfast, Troy, North Carolina

Chris Donaldson, Owner, Chris' Custom Carpentry, Asheville, North Carolina

Carrie Wagner, author, photographer, and former missionary to Uganda with Habitat for Humanity, Asheville, North Carolina

Thanks also to the kind and helpful librarians at the Sargent Branch of the Greenville County Library in Travelers Rest, South Carolina.

— About the Author —

Ann Tatlock is the author of the Christy Award–winning novel *All the Way Home*. She has also won the Midwest Independent Publishers Association "Book of the Year" in fiction for both *All the Way Home* and *I'll Watch the Moon*. Ann lives with her husband, Bob, and their daughter, Laura, in Asheville, North Carolina.

Center Point Large Print
600 Brooks Road / PO Box 1
Thorndike ME 04986-0001 USA

(207) 568-3717

US & Canada:
1 800 929-9108
www.centerpointlargeprint.com

~~OCT~~ U ~~2012~~

ELKHART PUBLIC
LIBRARY
Elkhart, Indiana